mud girl

mud girl

ALISON ACHESON

COTEAU
BOOKS
FOR TEENS

Edited by Barbara Sapergia.
Cover image: "Teenage girl wearing woolen hat" by Jacques Copeau/ Taxi/ Getty Images.
Cover and book design by Duncan Campbell.
Printed and bound in Canada by Gauvin Press.

Library and Archives Canada Cataloguing in Publication

Acheson, Alison, 1964-
Mud girl / Alison Acheson.

ISBN 1-55050-354-5

1. Title.

PS8551.C32M84 2006   jC813'.54   C2006-904635-2

10   9   8   7   6   5   4   3   2

2517 Victoria Ave.
Regina, Saskatchewan
Canada   S4P 0T2

Available in Canada & the US from
Fitzhenry & Whiteside
195 Allstate Parkway
Markham, ON,   L3R 4T8

The publisher gratefully acknowledges the financial support of its publishing program by: the Saskatchewan Arts Board, the Canada Council for the Arts, the Government of Canada through the Book Publishing Industry Development Program (BPIDP), Association for the Export of Canadian Books and the City of Regina Arts Commission.

The Canada Council for the Arts
Le Conseil des Arts du Canada

SASKATCHEWAN
ARTS BOARD

Canadä

CITY OF REGINA

For Maia

One Good Thing

You can be friendly with someone for only so long before you start to know them, and they know you. Aba Zytka Jones and Horace Boyd have known each other through her three high school years, as long as she's been riding his bus home down River Road. "Time I really knew something about her," thinks Horace. "Time to put my hand out. There's something not right here." He's thought that for a long time now. Can't quite put a finger on what it is, though. "She's always alone. She's always on time — that's not right, not at her age, when just about anything can get in the way of your path: a giggly friend, a boy...especially a boy."

Come to think of it, he's never seen Abi with a friend, boy or girl. Horace wonders if Abi even notices the boy with the shaggy yellow hair who once in a while sits in the back. He

1

knows the boy sees her, and knows the boy has a worry knot on his forehead when he looks at Abi. Of course, such a worry knot doesn't necessarily mean anything romantic – if anyone even knows that word these days, he thinks. But it means *something*. "No, it's not right. And it's the last day before summer. Today, I'll say something. There's no time like Right Now. The summer is long when you're sixteen." He remembers that. These thoughts and more go through the head of Horace, the bus driver.

Abi, on the other hand, would prefer to keep the friendship – such as it is – as it is. Horace can be the bus driver. She can be the passenger. His is a face she can count on. The reason she's always on time for his bus is simply that she likes him. She's on time for other things because her mother – God Rest Her Feet – taught her to be on time. She likes to sit and talk with Horace. He is the one good thing about the bus ride home. Sometimes, he's the one good thing about her day.

Abi's not good at judging age. She does know that Horace has quite a lot of grey hair, and some amazing lines that spill out from his eyes and curve down his cheeks. She thought he'd be somebody's Grandpa, but he told her no, and he laughed. "I look that old, do I?" Apparently, he's never had kids. Seems a waste, Abi thinks. She always sits across from Horace on the seat near the door so they can talk – at least until a really old person comes along or somebody with a baby or a white cane or what-have-you. What-have-you is a Horace phrase for sure.

"Last day of school today," he says as she pulls aboard, knapsack heavy on her back. She meant to throw out most of the school junk before leaving, but the vice-principal stopped her, wanted to talk, and she would have missed the bus. He just had to tell her what a wonderful student she *could be*, and how much he looks forward to seeing her in the fall. "Only one more year," he reminded her. He must suspect she'd like to quit.

"Guess I won't be seeing you for a while." Horace pulls a bag of juice berries from his pocket and hands them to her. The familiar gift makes her feel almost old, and a lump that feels oddly of regret pushes its way into her throat. She wishes suddenly that it wasn't the last day of the school year, with the summer stretching ahead. For ten months she's been able to spend most of her days away from home, but now the days are going to be long, and they're going to be spent with a man who used to be her father, but is now a stranger.

The juice berries are stuck together from the warmth of Horace's body, but they taste good and Abi offers Horace one. He puts it in his mouth and pushes it into a cheek before speaking. "What have you got planned for the summer?"

Such a normal question; if he only knew.

Thought I'd fly down to Australia, or look for my mother along the Nile...or was that the Amazon...maybe do a bicycle trip down the coast...tell Pops he can take me to Disneyland now...

"I was thinking it's time to find a job." Abi watches the road. Heading east, they've left the town of Ladner, and rising on the south are concrete buildings: the "Industrial Park" they call that area, with an ice rink at one end, and a few small coffee shops for the employees who work in all those ugly, square buildings.

On the driver's side, to the north, is the Fraser River, a tidal river and salty. At this time the tide is down, and with the windows open she can smell the briny odour and the mud – the smell that says *home* for her; an ocean smell, out of place this far inland.

"You're going to find a job?" Horace turns to look at her for a quick moment, then his eyes go back to the road. He's a good driver, Horace, careful – not like some.

"I'll be seventeen later in the fall. I should have had a job last year." Sixteen is old enough for a few things: old enough to quit school; old enough to have a job; almost old enough to leave home. A job would be a start.

Horace has turned back to her, and he's been looking at her for so long he's making her nervous after all. But his hands begin to turn the wheel even before his eyes are back on the road. He does know every curve. Soon they'll pass the little convenience store, the cedar mill, the paint store.

Then it'll just be scrubby fields and the odd old house.

"Hmm," is all Horace says. Then: "You do have that look."

"What's that?"

"That look of wanting to be somewhere else."

She turns away, toward the river. *I didn't think anyone could see that.*

"It's okay," he goes on. "Now, speaking for myself, I take long journeys by train. That's how I travel."

"You don't travel!" Horace hasn't gone anywhere on holiday as long as she's known him.

He grins. More lines spread over his face. "All the time!" He laughs. "I have my own train – tunnels, bridges, stations to stop at, forests to go through, hills to climb. It's in my yard, front and back. My neighbour figures that's why I don't have a wife. Maybe you've seen it? Just up from the corner of Trunk and Fifth?" A thought comes to him: a way to hold out his hand. *Here – take it.*

"You should come and see!" he says, and he strikes the steering wheel in excitement. "Yes! Do that. Do come and see my train!" He pulls into a stop with something of a flourish, and the door swings open. "All ABOARD!" he calls out, exactly as a train conductor would.

"You bring back memories, you dear man," says a quavery voice, and a shrunken woman appears from the step well. "Next, you'll be punching my ticket!"

Abi hears his laugh as Horace rises from his seat to help her, and Abi stands and makes her way through the crowd to the back so the old woman can take her seat.

"Abi?"

She can hear Horace behind her, but she doesn't answer. He has to stretch to see to the back of the bus in his rear-view mirror, and he can see her slight form as she wraps her arm around the pole near the back door. Always so on-her-own. Oh, maybe he shouldn't have said what he did. These days, it's so tough just to be friendly to someone.

In the meantime, Abi's thinking, Now, why did he have to go and do that? They're just bus friends, nothing more. But he's going to ruin it. She doesn't want to know where he lives, but even more than that, she doesn't want him to know where she lives. She's managed to hold that secret for this long. Besides, she's never met an adult with a toy train. Every adult has some weirdness – her dad has his messages, her mum had her tomato plants...but a toy train?

Nobody rings the bell for her usual stop, not even Abi. But Horace brakes anyway, waits for her to climb off. "Bye, Abi!" he calls out. "Come visit over the summer!"

She's glad for the people between them, standing and chatting. She tells herself that Horace can't possibly hear, even if she did say something. She climbs down from the bottom step and stands, as always, until the bus is out of sight, and the diesel smell is replaced by the cedar of the mill.

She walks along the gravel edge. Cars pass, and long dragging trucks. Their tires growl and the air tries to pull her into the rubber molars. She holds her arms across her chest, head down, almost to the next bus stop. From there, Abi's house is across the street and four metres from the roadway. The front of the house sits on the bank of the river, and the bank is steep, so there is a narrow wooden bridge that reaches to the front porch for when it's muddy. Out back, the house rests on pilings, heavy and stained and standing in river mud when the tide's down, and in swirling water when it's up.

She crosses the bridge and the door slams shut behind her; that same pull of air from yet another truck. Her father, in his chair in the middle of the room, doesn't seem to hear or to feel the sway of the floor.

Bairn

Once Abi found a pamphlet – can't remember where exactly – *Expanding Your Vocabulary*. The pamphlet promised that if you expanded your vocabulary, you could go anywhere you wanted. Of course, she knows that's not true. When you're a teenager, in high school, you can't go anywhere. But still. Now and then she looks up words because she likes the thought. Usually she carries the falling-apart paperback dictionary on the twenty-minute morning bus trip – so different from Horace's afternoon bus – full of morning silence and perfume strong enough to last until five o'clock. Makes her wish there was a school bus on this road, instead of just the regular bus. Makes her wonder about the adult thing. Makes her think about being sixteen – and how close it is to being one of these soldiers in overcoats, armed with briefcase and cell phone. Lipstick smacked on. But with a school bus it would be a matter of time, a short time, before someone would say something, and they'd come poking around and take her away to some place. A foster home. Someplace where no one really cares about you, or worse, someone might hurt you. A place chosen for you by people who don't know you. A place that might be in the newspaper someday, with a big ugly headline over it. Or maybe it wouldn't be in the papers; maybe it would be a place where secrets happen.

Sometimes, Abi is convinced, the only reason she looks up new words is to distract her from the old.

Here's one, in the dictionary. *Bairn. A child.* Funny how when she thinks of it she can only hear the word *wee* in front of it. Wee bairn. The dictionary says the word is related to the verb *bear*, but all she can think of is the noun, and an angry she-bear protecting her...wee bairn. Abi likes that mental picture of a fighting mother-bear. She wishes it had more in common with the picture of her own mother, which is not bear-like at all.

Somebody gave Mum a New Age baby name book when she was pregnant. The first name in the girl section was Aba, which means born on Thursday. Abi was actually born at one in the morning on Friday, but by then her mother had spent twenty-four hours thinking she'd be born on Thursday for sure, and she said "close enough." Zytka was the last name in the girl section, so that's her second name. Abi suspects her mother never looked at the rest of the book.

Of course, she'd never asked her. She'd never thought of that until it was too late. There were many questions Abi hadn't asked. Some she'd thought of before, and some have popped into her mind over this past year. The biggest is: Why?

Why did you leave, Mum?

Abi tries to come up with the answer. "Because I had to." Could be like one of those games you play with a little kid. *Why did you have to...* It could go on forever. Abi suspects that her mother could even tell her why and Abi still wouldn't know the real answer. Not an answer that satisfies. But maybe she has pieces of answers – enough pieces to put together even. She knows a few things.

Just in Case

Abi knows that when Mum said *blue* she meant the pale blue of the early morning sky, or perhaps the blue of china plates people might hang on walls. Abi wondered – after Dad painted the back of the house – how it was that he didn't know that. How could he bring home that blinding colour? What had he called it – a mistint?

"That's someone else's colour gone bad," Mum had said, in that frighteningly calm voice she had sometimes.

Dad hadn't seemed to notice the voice.

"It's the luck of the thing," he said. "I walk in, I say I'm looking for the most beautiful blue for the most beautiful woman on the earth, and they show me this, and it's the only blue they have. I figure it's destiny."

11

"Not everything that falls across your path is destiny," Mum said. "Sometimes what falls across your path is just there to trip you."

Abi can remember what Dad's face looked like then. It was as if Mum had walked over and shaken him.

But all she shook was her head, looking sorrowfully at him, then at the back of the house. Abi can still remember her like that: clinging to the railing on the dock as it moved in the river, head shaking over the blue. "Next time you choose paint chips," she said, "you bring them home, we discuss together, we choose together, then back to the paint store where they make up the colour. If a mistake happens someone else can buy it. It can be *their* mistint."

Dad hadn't gone to the paint store, hadn't chosen paint chips. The front and the sides of the house remained white and the back blazed blue and that's how it was.

"Mary," he'd say on occasion, "where's your sense of adventure?"

"Brought me as far across the Atlantic as this side of Canada, then left me for someone else," would be her answer.

But Abi, listening, wasn't at all convinced that her mother had ever had a sense of adventure. A sense of something, yes, but it wasn't adventure. What had brought her to Canada from Britain? What had caused her to stay in Canada? Abi knew the answer to the second question: Dad.

Abi would hear these exchanges between them and feel dread. What bothered her most was that she couldn't take sides.

Now she could take a side; that was one of her first thoughts when they discovered Mum had left. But she couldn't. She didn't want a side; she wanted an answer.

Here is another piece about her mother: she loved this place, this narrow greenhouse, with its one bench, and three shelves, and glass. Most of the glass is broken. She even loved it like that, though she cried when the first piece broke, one of two times Abi ever saw her cry.

The greenhouse sits on one of two connected small docks that float at the end of the wharf. The wharf starts as a wooden walkway by the front door, goes down the side of the house, and runs all the way into the river water at the back of the house. The first dock is connected with enormous hinges, so that it can move with the tide, and the greenhouse dock is attached to that. Her mother asked her dad to attach extra chains to hold the greenhouse in place – "just in case," she said. She said that often. She grew those spindly tomato plants and fried up their green fruit in the fall. Abi doesn't remember any red ones ever. So many little seed containers, the size of a thumb. Her mother always planted too many seeds, and they'd come up all white stems, looking like grubs, until they collapsed in despair. Maybe if Mum had realized she loved this place and she could just sit here with her coffee – she didn't have to try to grow all those stupid things – maybe things would have been different. Sometimes Abi comes here and thinks about that: just why did her mother grow all those sad, stupid plants. Other times she sits here, pries pieces of broken glass from the window frames, drops them through the floorboards into the river, and makes a wish. The glass sinks; it's not like her dad's bottles, plastic and floating. The bottles with their messages in them are wishes themselves. No, Abi uses her mother's glass, and makes a wish. She always wishes the same thing, even when she tries to think of something new.

I wish…

"Knock, knock!"

Abi jumps at the spoken words. Wishes don't come true. And even if they did, it would never be this quick.

"Knock!" The voice is chirpy, bird-like. Abi stares out at the river for one more moment, and puts together a mental picture of this person: a woman; skinny (chicken legs, definitely); hair like feathers and close to her scalp; a sharp nose; eyes like burnt raisins in gingerbread.

"Knock, knock!" This time someone actually taps on the wooden door frame. You could think that's brave or you could think that's stupid. Of course a piece of glass falls and smashes on the slats of the floor.

"Oh! Oh! Oh!" Chirp. Chirp. Chirp.

Abi turns around, but can see only the top of the person's head. She's bent over trying to pick up the glass. Such a useless thing to do. Makes Abi feel sorry for her. But the thin hair on the top of her head makes Abi feel even more. Something very sorry about a balding woman. Then the woman looks up and Abi can see that she was so wrong about the eyes.

A word comes to Abi's mind, as her own eyes connect with this woman's: *steadfast.* Such an odd old word, and perfect for these eyes that are clear and do hold Abi fast. They're a bit unnerving, really. Abi feels grateful that the rest of this woman is soft and round. Otherwise those eyes would be too much.

The glass falls between the boards and spins to the water below.

"No one answered the door," says the woman. "So I thought I'd come around to the back."

She was going to say "yard," wasn't she?

"You knocked on the front door?" How brave after all.

She looks embarrassed. "I tried the window, too. A bit."

She means she had to pound. Heck, if she broke it, he'd never notice.

"The television was on," she says.

"Full blast."

"The traffic *is* very loud." So she did see him, there in his chair. Those eyes wouldn't miss a thing. She doesn't have to

15

defend him, though, does she? With her face all twisted, as if she has to feel badly for him?

But the traffic is loud, so loud that sometimes late at night, if a high-speed car comes chasing around the curve, Abi braces herself: this is it, this time it will come through the front wall.

The woman says nothing about Dad in his chair. Instead, she looks around. "Could be nice if it was fixed up a bit, no?"

Did she notice the decrepit car bench seat on the small front porch? The peeling paint on the windowsills? "I think it's beyond that." Uh-oh. The eyes are suddenly even more clear as she looks at Abi, and Abi has the feeling the woman doesn't like her Fix-It-Up ability to be challenged.

"I'm your big sister," she says then, and Abi almost falls between the floorboards. Her parents have given her enough surprises. It can't be. Her rational mind takes over: this woman is as old as her mother, maybe even a little older.

She liked that, Abi can see. She's had those words playing over in her mind. There's some little humour in her that wouldn't mind being let out now and then.

"Big sister." Abi laughs, awkward herself, but with something stirring in her mind. The school counsellor sent home some pamphlets. One from the Big Sister organization. She left them on the table for a week before throwing them out. Abi didn't think her father had even touched them.

"You were registered quite a while ago now. I'm sorry it took so long. It can take a long time to find a match." She doesn't say what takes long: the Big Sister part, or the little sister.

So. Dad does do something besides pour cereal in a bowl, sit in his chair, go for a pee.

The woman is waiting for Abi to speak.

"Well." Big Sister straightens and brings her round shoulders to attention. "Would you like to go for a walk?"

That's probably number three or four in the Suggestions for New Big Sisters list. Right after Friendly Approach and Say Something Nice About Surroundings.

"There's not really anywhere to walk around here," Abi says. Across the street is the old Halfyards' house, set far back and empty for years, boarded up, and their rusting car collection, with grass growing where seats used to be. And Abi hopes the woman doesn't say anything about the field that stretches for about fifty metres along the east side of the house, caught between the road and the river. A narrow strip of scrub bushes, blackberry, and the ancient willow. The field has nothing to do with the house or school or Mum or...anything. Except him. *My Boy*, is how Abi thinks of him.

Big Sister needs no more discouragement.

"Well, you know," she begins in a soap-opera-character voice, "I don't really like to walk all that much anyway."

Lower voiced and even more confiding. "I don't buy into all this women-should-be-fit-as-racehorses nonsense." She sits on the bench, and it gives Abi a jolt to see her there in her mother's place. Makes her remember her wish, and wish she hadn't. *What do they say? "Careful what you wish; it might come true."* Maybe people can get by with just one parent, even a sack-of-old-potatoes parent. After all, she has been getting by with Dad for ten months now.

Big Sister looks back toward the house. "That's quite the blue." She motions to the back wall.

"Yes," Abi agrees, "that's quite the blue."

"Isn't the front of the house white?" Big Sister looks perplexed.

"Dirty white," says Abi, and wishes she hadn't. She doesn't explain further.

"Well," Big Sister says, after a while. (Because Abi's so quiet?) "I guess I'll be going now."

Abi suspects she's not what the woman expected. By her age, she should know – nothing is.

"How about if I come back on Saturday? We'll go into town. Or something," Big Sister adds. "I'll think of something!"

Abi wants to say no. That's the word that comes first to her mind. But the summer days loom long and quiet ahead of her, and this woman won't last long; she'll probably show up the one time and that'll be it. Might even be interesting to see how long she *does* last. And there is that thinning hair and sad chirp. That's enough to make the "no" go away.

"After lunch," Abi says finally. She doesn't want Saturday ruined.

"Afternoon then." Now the Big Sister smile is slower. She turns to go, picking her way over the boards in her heels. She finally reaches the wharf that runs along the side of the house. "Can you sew?" Her chirp carries over the sound of the current, the constant of vehicle engines.

"Sew?"

She repeats. "Sew." Chirp. Smile.

"Of course," Abi says.

"Oh." Not quite so chirpy at that. She seems almost disappointed. "Well..." A pause. "That's good, really. Hardly anyone knows how to sew these days."

"My mother – God Rest Her Feet – taught me."

Big Sister's eyebrows have risen. "God Rest Her Feet?"

"She's not dead. She's on the run. Somewhere."

"God Rest Her Feet," the woman murmurs, "taught you to sew."

"Yes," says Abi, but she doesn't say anything about sewing being one of Life's Necessities. That's what Mum always called it. Along with knowing how to read a bus schedule and never have to ask the driver a question, and when to make eye

19

contact with someone, and when not to. Some of these bits of knowledge Abi will use always, others never. Her mother – GRHF – might have written her own book. *Island of One* it would be titled, with a subtitle of *The Book of Self-Sustainability*. The word "vocabulary" wouldn't even be in it.

"Buttons and hems – you have to be able to do that much for yourself," would be the title of one chapter. Another would be, "How to select vegetables and fruit in the grocery store to last a week," and another, "Always wear a black skirt to a job interview."

"But did she teach you how to knit?" asks Big Sister.

Knitting was not one of Life's Necessities, but Abi doesn't tell this woman that. It might crush her, she fears. So she says only, "No."

"Ah!" Triumph is there. "Well. I can teach you," she says, and her smile of very white teeth is surprising and even pretty, and then it's gone.

She must be too far away to read the expression on Abi's face.

She disappears around the side of the house, then reappears, her face a big mess of concern. "Oh my!"

"Well?"

"My name. I forgot to tell you my name."

"What is it?"

She hesitates. "Mary."

Okay, there are a lot of Marys in the world. Always have been. Mary the mother of Jesus. Mary, Mary, quite contrary. Mary, Abi's mother.

"Can I call you something else?"

She falters. "Well. My surname is Rhodes."

"I'll call you Rhodes then."

She hesitates, turns to leave, and back again, like she's in one of those old detective shows. *Just one more thing.*

"It must be tough..."

"What's that?" Abi says.

"Well, not having another woman in the house."

Who told her? Was it on the sign-up form? Or did someone say something?

"Yeah, sure." Superwoman, this. Abi can almost see her cape, the giant M on her shirt. At least when she's flying, she won't have to worry about tripping on those shoes; landing on them could be something else, though.

"You're smiling!" Rhodes says.

"Just at a picture in my head."

"Oh, I think this is going to be such fun!" Off she goes, on her heels, her hips swaying as if she's dancing. Abi didn't know it was possible to walk on heels like that. It's quite amazing, really. She's glad when the woman rounds the corner and there's no chance she'll turn back and catch Abi gawping after her.

Now what? Is Dad nuts? Last thing they need, someone poking around, finding out what they're about. Foster home, here comes Abi. Write the ticket now. Much as she hates this place, there could be worse. According to Mum, there could be worse. She tries not to think about what Mum told her – about when Mum was a kid – and she tries even harder not to think about what Mum never did tell her. What made it so bad. *What made it so bad, Mum?*

Murky Blue & Fuzzy Pink

Saturday mornings are different. Abi cleans the house. She doesn't know exactly why she does this, doesn't want to think about it that much, really. It's a feeling that comes over her when she does: as if, in some way *she* owns the house, instead of the other way around, which is how it usually feels. Or as if, just for a short time, she really does hold all the pieces of her life in her hand and they do fit together.

The front room is the kitchen and eating area, and the back of the house, looking out over the river, is the living area. The laundry is in a closet between. Dad's room is small, in the northeast corner, and Abi's is even smaller, just off the kitchen. The bathroom has a small and rusty tub, and camper-sized sink.

Abi always starts with the dishes in the sink. Then the sink itself, the faucets, the counters. Mugs on their pegs, and plates in a stack. The one cookbook and an old box of recipes in their place. Take out the garbage, to the trashcan on the narrow strip of porch out front. Then scrub the tabletop, the stove. Two burners dead this week. Maybe Dad'll fix it when all four are gone. The floor. Last, she shines the kitchen window that looks east, to the field. It's the only window that doesn't face the road or the river, the dust or the mud. On the other side of the house, where the river slows and sidles close to the road, there are no windows at all. The TV's by that wall. So are the letters sent to Uncle Bernard, and to Dad, by people who have found the bottles they sent out. (The one from off the coast of Oregon – the farthest away – is in the middle, framed, signed by T. Haliburton. It's always irritated Abi that there's no way of knowing if the T stands for Thomas or Tanya.) There used to be a photo of Uncle Bernard, but Mum always took it down, and Dad probably got tired of putting it back up. There was another photo, too, one of a sunset, taken by Mum. That's disappeared too.

But on this side of the house, out the kitchen window, there's the field, a patch of growing stuff that spreads wider as it moves away from the house. Mum tried to find out who owned it years ago, maybe with the thought to buy it, but it never worked out.

The rough-looking willow at the water's edge leans over as if the river's going to claim it, and beside the house and along the roadway there are the blackberry bushes that Abi's thankful for at the end of summer. The path between the blackberries grows narrower each year and there's a ragged patch of grass that dries in July.

But he's late today. *My Boy*. Almost half past noon. She opens the window a crack. Once she heard him whistling. The sound made everything inside her stand still. If she knew his name, she'd say it over and over in her head, and she'd die to say it aloud. So it's best she doesn't know. That way, when she thinks of him it's just a thought, a feeling that seeps into every nook of her mind – not loud echoing letters making her want to scream.

She can see him from the window on Saturdays, when he brings his lunch and sits on the old log washed up a million years ago, and she can wonder what he's thinking, watching the river. Once he almost caught her looking, but she moved quick enough. This house being what it is, he probably thinks no one lives here.

There he is, his hair brown and uncut, in waves falling across his face. She wonders what colour his eyes are: brown and warm; green, full of life; blue and bright. Her own: a dark murky blue-green, as if she's lived by the river so long it's become a part of her. Mud girl, living at the river's edge.

He sits with his back to her and she leaves the window. The sparkling kitchen mocks her, and she looks at the mouldy walls. The patches of soft grey are still there. Doesn't matter how much she cleans.

She hears a sound at the window, a tap, tap. And the chirp. "Aba! Oh, ABA!" that voice trills, and as Abi nears the window, she can see over Rhodes's hair, and see the boy's face looking in her direction with a grin. It's too late to duck.

Rhodes is decked out in black and brilliant yellow. Bumblebee bright, and heels of course. Another old-time word comes to Abi's mind: *fetching*. Yes, Rhodes looks fetching. She's not afraid to look as if she's not quite of her time and place. But just as Abi softens, again comes that voice.

"Aba!"

Abi suddenly doesn't want to be here, even though inside her something leaps: it's the first time she's seen *My Boy's* face directly.

"Yoo-hoo!"

Oh, no. Not "yoo-hoo." Don't call out that!

There's even a twitch from Dad's chair at the sound.

Now *My Boy* is laughing. Rhodes is close enough to the window for Abi to look down and see her scalp under her hair, hair carefully heaped and sprayed. Abi can even see globules of spray tacking it into place. She'd like to do something with that hair — wash out all that stuff for a start.

"Aba!"

Rhodesy's so...earnest. It's just not good to be earnest like that. She might as well be out there in her underwear. *My Boy* is still chuckling as he crushes his lunch things into a bag, lights a cigarette and leaves, back through the path in the blackberry bushes, back to the mill or wherever it is he works. Abi always imagines that smell of cedar when she thinks of him.

She waits until the bushes stop quivering, until it doesn't matter anymore, and then she goes out the back door and calls to Rhodes. Maybe she just has an urge to watch her trip down the wharf in those shoes. She starts toward Abi. "There you are!" Her entire body seems to chirp. "What ARE we going to do today?"

"I thought you were going to think up something," Abi says. She doesn't mean to be rude. It's just how it comes out.

Rhodes doesn't seem to notice. "Oh, I have, I have!" She glows. Abi thought only pregnant women were supposed to glow.

"In Betty – that's my car – " she says, panting somewhat, "I brought my flower pressing kit."

"Flower pressing?"

She gulps. "With the early summer flowers, I thought we could..."

Abi motions to the field. "There aren't too many flowers around here."

She falters. "The pale pink – the blackberry flowers." She points to them.

"I'm not picking those. They're full of thorns. Besides," and Abi heads back toward the house – suddenly she doesn't want to be anywhere near the greenhouse – "besides, I like to *eat* blackberries. If we pick the flowers, there'll be no berries."

Rhodes exhales. "Well..." She looks toward the field. "There must be some interesting grasses..." she begins.

"Yeah, sure," Abi says. She can hear Rhodes clicking behind her, then an abrupt snapping sound.

"Oh my!"

Abi turns around to realize Rhodes has lost a heel between two boards. "They're my favourites," the woman says, looking close to tears.

"Why would you wear them here then?"

She looks confused. "They're my favourites – I wear them everywhere."

Abi thinks of her mother's wedding shoes, worn once and still in their box in the back of the closet. Abi likes to think that she would have taken them if she'd remembered where they were. Good as new, they are.

Abi walks over to where Rhodes is, wraps her fingers around the heel and pulls hard. "Here." She hands it to her.

"Oh, thank you," she says gratefully. "Maybe we could sit and have a cup of tea."

Tea. Abi can't remember anyone having a cup of tea in this house. "We just ran out," Abi tells her, and realizes that Rhodes can't tell when she lies. So she embellishes: "My father usually drinks...Earl Bray, I think it is." *Wrong word*, her brain screams, but she tosses her head to let Rhodes know she doesn't care.

But Rhodes is puzzling. "Earl Bray?" she asks slowly. "Don't you mean Earl Grey?"

"Yeah, whatever."

A hurt look comes over her face. Really, you could knock this woman over with a down feather!

"We called it that when I was a little kid." Okay, this is absolute manufacture-on-the-spot. "Dad used to pretend he was a donkey, and I used to ride on his back."

Then Abi can't believe it: *this* is not made up. It's a memory with the top coming off. She'd forgotten. It's coming into full view now. "He used to throw his head back and bray like a donkey," she says. "He used to make me laugh." Rhodes probably can't even hear that last bit. But she seems to have, because she responds.

"Really?" she says. "He used to laugh..." she begins, but Abi doesn't wait to hear whatever it is that this woman wants to say about Dad in his chair. Now Abi's angry. Here she is feeling like she's going to cry or something. How dare Rhodes do that? Why would she cry for him? He doesn't cry for anyone.

"Let's go for that walk," Abi says. It would be good to move.

Rhodes looks down at her shoe.

"Maybe another day then," Abi says, and slams the screen door behind her as she goes into the house. *Just go away.*

Abi hears her uneven steps out to where her car is parked. Car door opens. Trip, trip to the front door. *Don't knock.* Then her footsteps back to the car and the engine roars off.

Abi opens the door to find a brown paper bag, crumpled. What's this? Inside are two metal pointed things…okay, she's not that stupid. She knows they're knitting needles, but she can't remember having held one of them in her hands. Yarn. Fuzzy pink. Rhodes isn't serious about knitting, is she? If she only knew how very un-pink Abi is. A *Knitting For Beginners* book. She can tell by the photos it's for right-handed people. Lotta good it'll do her.

Red & White

The first Sunday of summer holidays.

Dad's spent the night in his chair again. Abi wakes up to the drone of CBC television, off the air at this time of day and with bright stripes on the screen. Moments later, Dad wakes for his cue of "O Canada" and the morning animation of across-the-country, sea to sea: a seagull wheeling over the Atlantic; quaint buildings two hundred years older than she's ever seen; the CN tower; prairies; and last, the Rocky Mountains that keep her part of the country away from the rest. Finally to the West coast, just in time to catch the last bars of the anthem. Makes her feel funny somehow, being at the end like that, as if she's missed it all.

She steals a glance at Dad. His eyes have opened, but no other part of him has moved. Was he like this before? Before Mum left? Before his job came to an end? She wishes she could remember, wishes they had photographs – albums and scrapbooks of pictures, like normal people have. There aren't even wedding photos. There was some problem with the film, Mum told her once. There's just one photo that Abi has seen – a fuzzy unfocussed picture. No white dress, just Mum in a flowered dress, Dad in a white shirt, unbuttoned at the neck.

"That was on our honeymoon," Mum had said, looking over Abi's shoulder when she found the picture. That was all she said.

Yes, maybe photographs could remind Abi how it had been. Her memories are growing more and more hazy, and really she's not sure she trusts them. Some seem to have changed over time, but how can that be? And some fit too well into the puzzle-shaped holes deep in her spirit.

It's important to remember, she thinks, because she really needs to know, and because if Dad was like this before – this dead person – then she might have another piece of the answer to why Mum left.

There's a reminder from the TV: it's Canada Day. It's going to be a hot one. In the fridge, the milk is sour.

There used to be an insulated bag around, a lunch bag. It'll keep the milk cold as she walks home. She finds it stashed under the sink, throws it in her knapsack and heads off towards the Industrial Park. Away down River Road, and a bus hurtles past, almost pushes her off the gravel at the side. She looks after the bus, but knows Horace can't be on it: he's been a driver long enough not to work holidays. And he wouldn't have driven that close, not on this side with the river so near. She has a sudden image of him playing with his trains, and her steps quicken. In fifteen minutes, she reaches the convenience store: a small store that services the few scattered homes as well as the mill employees and others. There's always a small table with produce in rehearsal for its leftover stage.

Abi buys milk, more cereal, a big plastic bottle of ginger ale, and a small piece of cut watermelon. The clerk hands her a paper flag. "Happy Canada Day!" she says.

"You too," Abi says. She holds the bag close. "Are you looking for anyone to work here?"

The clerk doesn't take her eyes off the till. "I dunno. You'd have to talk with the manager."

Of course. I should have known. Abi feels a warmth spread over her face, and leaves.

The way home is dry and the dust rises with the traffic. The cedar being milled burns in her nose, and she imagines that that's where he works – *My Boy* – and he goes home with the smell. He's old enough to live on his own, young enough to live with a mum and dad, a brother or sister, someone who welcomes him with a cheery shout when he pushes the door open. Someone who asks how he is, and cares about the answer.

The stench of the river mud at low tide puts a stopper in her thoughts. Mud Girl and her Prince. *Bah. Humbug.*

A pickup truck kicks gravel over her knees, and she looks up to see a HELP WANTED sign in the window of the paint store – "Hood's Paint, Family-Owned Since 1954." So. She'll have to go and talk with the owner or the manager soon, and try not to ask a stupid or obvious question.

At home, she empties the ginger ale into a juice pitcher and puts it in the fridge. The green plastic bottle she rinses and dries. She sets it on a dented tray that must have belonged to Uncle Bernard, along with paper and a pen, and then she cuts the small piece of watermelon into halves – pyramids on rockers. She sticks a spoon and the paper flag into one, all red and white, and sets it on the tray too, then puts it on the TV table by Dad. She takes her own piece out to the greenhouse.

Cyan

A new word. *Cyan.* Never heard it, never seen it before. *A greenish-blue colour.* The word sounds pretty. Something Rhodesy might like. Abi wonders exactly what colour it is; there are no pictures in the dictionary. The colour of jade? Of a glacier lake? She's seen pictures of those.

She should go to Hood's Paints. She pulls on overalls and her cleanest sneaks.

There's a sound from Dad's chair as she opens the door.

"Pardon?"

"Where're you goin'?" he mumbles. He reaches for his glasses on the table beside him. She's noticed this past year that sometimes his glasses are still sitting in the same place they were when she left in the morning, and she's wondered how he's gone through entire days without them. He turns to look at her through them just for a moment before he turns back to the television.

Stops her cold; maybe he liked the watermelon or has a plan for the bottle. Maybe he's already begun to write one of his messages. It's been a long time. Not that she'd know, really. Her dad has felt like a stranger these few days since school finished. Will he begin to talk with her again now?

"I'm going to the paint store," she says, and waits for a response, but there's none. She shouldn't expect one.

She leaves for the dusty road to the paint store.

Cyan. The word pulls her through the door. *Got any...*

"Hi!" He's grinning at her. *My Boy.* His voice is everything she's imagined – even just with one word, she knows.

"You work here." She feels as if her lungs are collapsing. And there it is: a stupid thing to say.

"I work here." His chuckle is something to curl up in. He never seemed that tall sitting out in the field with his lunch.

"There's a HELP WANTED sign out front," she says, rescuing a bit of bravery.

"Yeah," he says. His eyes are almost black. "That's been filled." He goes to the window, takes down the sign. "You don't want to work here, do you?" That grin's back, behind his words. He's not taking her seriously.

"I do..." she begins.

"No," he says smoothly. "You don't. I know you don't. I've seen you," he says.

Abi feels embarrassed when he says this.

"You have better things to do," he goes on.

How can he say that?

"What was it you really came for today?"

For a half moment she can't think what.

"Cyan," she says then. "The colour. What is it?"

He studies her for a moment, then pulls a paintbrush – an artist's brush – from the side pocket of his cargo pants and brushes it lightly across her cheekbone. "You know the colour; it's in your eyes."

It's like one of those old movies that Dad leaves on early in the morning: she's the weak-kneed heroine and she has to reach out for the edge of the counter. Into her head flashes an image of Mary Rhodes. She'd appreciate this. She probably stays up late to see those old things, or maybe she has her own shelf-full to watch over and over, says the lines with the actors. But who's mush-kneed-Abi to laugh at her?

He studies the soft hair of the brush for a moment before putting it away. "Same eye colour as Dyl," he says, reaching into another pocket for his wallet. He flips it open, pulls out a photograph, soft at the edges and missing a corner. "This is Dyl," he says. Abi feels his eyes on her as she takes the picture: a very young child. "My son," he adds.

I still don't know your name.

"He lives with me and my mother." He plucks the photo from her fingers, slips it back into place, wallet away. "His mother left." He gazes out the window momentarily, then looks at her squarely.

I know how that feels. But she says nothing, just looks back at him and feels miserable. Is this what he knows about her? Is this what he's observed at her house? God-Rest-Her-Feet leaving, and her dad never leaving, and Abi wanting to?

"Maybe someday you'll come out of that house of yours and meet with me in the blackberry patch for lunch." The laughter has returned to his voice.

She nods dumbly.

A man – a Hood, no doubt – calls from a back room. "Jude! If you have a minute!"

"Coming!" *My Boy* answers. He whispers to Abi. "That's my boss. Thinks I'm going to take over here someday, and manage the place." He reaches for the artist's brush again, holds it in front of her. "But I've got dreams." He turns and disappears into the back room.

Abi leaves quickly and wishes there was somewhere she could go and shout the name JUDE. "Jude," she whispers as she waits between trucks to cross the road. "Jude." Deep inside her there's a feeling, fuzzier and pinker than she's ever felt.

And a son. A son he takes care of. She knew it somehow –
that he was capable of that.

Over the Line

"Would you like to go over the line? See the Fourth of July fireworks?" Rhodes stands at the door in a red-and-white striped western shirt with blue jeans, and heels with a narrow band of cut-out stars across the toes.

Abi tries not to smile at the shoes and shakes her head, mumbles something about the lineup there'll be at the border crossing. The few times she's been there, Blaine and Peace Arch were always busy. Besides, except for the flag and the watermelon, she doesn't usually do anything about Canada Day.

But Rhodesy is rattling on with her firecracker speech: "It's wonderful fun! The best. I never miss fireworks! Sure you don't want to come?"

Abi shakes her head. "No thanks." She resists saying that she doesn't have the right footwear.

"Well," says Rhodesy, "another time, then." Her car — Betty, is it? — is almost in the blackberry bushes, there's so little space by the road. She has to wait until there's a hole in the traffic before she can open her door. She gives a little wave of her round white hand before sinking into her seat, then she fiddles with the radio. Looking for someone to travel with, Abi thinks.

Mum always said, "You have yourself. That is enough. It's all in here." She'd tap her head. Abi can hear those words now. No, there was no looking for someone to travel with, with Abi's mother — God-Rest-Her-Feet. *Happy Independence Day, Mum*, Abi wishes. She wonders if Dad has ever sent Mum a message in a bottle. A bottle would have about as much luck at finding her. A thought comes to Abi now, though. *Mum is nowhere near water.* She turns the thought over in her mind. It looks the same upside down, and from any side. She knows it is true. So — one other piece about her mother.

Abi's head is in the kitchen sink. It's the easiest way to wash her hair, instead of in the rust-tub. The bathroom fixtures predate Uncle Bernard, who lived in the house before them.

The water flows at the nape of Abi's neck, round her ears, down her cheeks, and is cooling on a warm July day. Her eyes are closed, but she can feel the room change, and she reaches for a towel with one hand, the tap with the other, and gathers her hair into the towel and turns, and yes, he's here.

"I let myself in the screen door," he says.

She feels strangely unselfconscious. It should bother her that he's let himself in, and that she's standing here with wet hair in a terry cloth turban. But it doesn't bother her; quite the contrary – it feels right.

"In an hour it'll be twilight, and there'll be fireworks at the Point."

The Point: she'd forgotten Point Roberts, that little apple-pie-shaped piece of America that dangles from the Canadian border, just half an hour from here, population not much more than a thousand. Still has more trees than people, more vacation cottages than houses, though just the other side, the Canadian side, is a well-developed suburb.

"They have fireworks there?"

"Of course." He grins.

For Canada Day fireworks, you have to drive an hour into the city.

He holds out his hand.

"My hair," she says.

"You have no excuse," he says. "You've washed it, you're ready to go." He takes off her turban, makes a sort of dance step of it, turning her around under his arm. Then he combs his fingers through her hair.

"Perfect," he says.

Perfect. No makeup, wet hair, her mother's left-behind jeans. Okay, now she's self-conscious.

"Gotta get something else on," she mutters, and moves quickly toward her door. She wonders if he's noticed Dad yet. Doesn't seem to have, when she opens her door moments later, changed, hair slicked into a pony, a touch of Cinnamon lipstick. Mum's colour – went with everything, she said, sad days and happy. The woman at the drugstore warned Mum that the cosmetics company had discontinued it, and Mum bought every last stick. Went with everything, but not her; she left them all behind. Even so, Abi doesn't wear it that often.

They're at the door when Jude – JUDE, she shouts inside – says, "Are you just leaving the TV on?"

So he hasn't seen Dad yet.

"It's always on." They slip out.

"And I already know you don't lock the door," he says.

"Nothing to steal."

"You should lock it when you're home," he says.

She likes how he says that. Makes her warm. Could be early January instead of July and she still wouldn't need a coat, the way he says that. He opens the passenger door of the old blue pickup truck and closes it after her.

"Where's your son?" she asks suddenly, surprising herself. Didn't know the kid was bubbling near the top of her brain like that.

"He's with his grandma," he says easily as he pulls the pickup into the roadway.

Again she feels a stab of self-consciousness. She thinks of what it takes to make a baby. "Been there, done that," he could say. Evan kissed her once – a guy at school, the only guy who's ever offered her a ride home. She's wondered since if the ride and the kiss wasn't some sort of dare. Almost seventeen, and never really been kissed. She suspects that this is something she's supposed to worry about. That's probably what it says in those magazines that other girls read.

Jude is staring at her. "Hallo?!" he says, waving a hand in front of her face. "Earth to...whoever you are..." He laughs. "Who are you?"

"Aba."

"Like the old pop group?"

She shakes her head. "One B. Just Abi will do."

"What do you mean '*Just* Abi *will do*'?"

He stops the truck at a light and looks at her. The stop-light could turn green, but he's not going anywhere. She doesn't like this light-headed feeling: as if she might do something she would never do with her head clear and her feet on the ground. It suddenly seems to her that her head has always been very clear and that the ground has been *very* under her feet. "Know where you are, what you are doing, what you want," Mum always said. Clear and grounded. Until now.

The car behind them honks, and Jude – JUDE – moves forward. She breathes as he looks away. No, she doesn't like this at all.

For some reason she sees Dad in his chair. Is this how he felt about Mum? Is it possible Mum ever felt this about him? It's not possible, is it? If it was, they wouldn't be where they are now. You can't feel *this*, and become *that*.

The sun is setting as they reach the crest of the hill. The tall trees to the south of the border make it seem even darker, the lineup of tail lights shines warm colours.

"The fireworks are at Lighthouse Park," Jude says. "Do you come down here at all?"

She shakes her head. "Haven't been for a long time." *Don't go anywhere anymore.*

Then it's their turn; the guard stares at her. "ID?" he says.

Jude nudges her. "He's asking for your identification."

"Oh." She pulls the school card from her bag.

Even though there is a line of vehicles behind them, the guard scrutinizes the card, looking between Abi and her photo several times.

"Fireworks?" he asks.

"Yes sir," says Jude. "We'll be heading back when they're over."

"Drinking age is twenty-one down here. You know that." The guard looks so serious. Abi wonders if he has kids of his own. He makes eye contact, like a grade school teacher. She bets he's always warning his kids about everything.

"We drive in miles per hour, not kilometres."

"Yes sir," says Jude with not so much as a squeak of sarcasm.

The guard squints at Jude. "All right," he says sternly, and waves them on.

At the beach, Jude reaches into the back of the truck for a couple of blankets and two bottles of fancy juice in pretty, long-necked bottles that Abi has noticed at the store. "Can't be caught with anything else down here," he says. "Friend of mine was – Big Trouble he's in now."

How old is Jude anyhow?

He takes her hand as they walk down the beach. His is a big hand. Or perhaps hers is small. She never thinks about her hand in relation to anyone else's. It feels good. *In relation.* She can't remember when someone last touched her in any way, except maybe by accident in the school caf lineup. Or someone brushing by on the bus. She giggles and Jude squeezes her hand ever so slightly. She's afraid to look at him so she looks over the beach to where there's a group of children, voices loud in the summer evening. You can tell they're so happy to be up this late. But Jude pulls her in the other direction, toward a giant log lying on its side, to where the noise of the children seems far away.

He spreads one of the blankets on the sand, pulling the corners out just so, and readies the other blanket over the log. "Sit," he says, and they do, shoulder to shoulder. He reaches around and draws the blanket on the log down around them, and she's glad for the warmth. She hadn't realized how chilly the air had grown.

People are now spreading over the beach, people of all shapes, sizes, and ages. The sun is setting, warmth beginning to rise from the sand. Abi takes her sandals off and burrows her feet into the toasty grains. Jude looks at her, amused. "Just don't get sand on the blanket," he warns with a grin.

Out on the water, boats bob, their lights flickering, and between them and the boats are so many heads in silhouette.

BOOM! The first of the fireworks makes Abi jump. "Oh!" She's not even aware she's said anything until she sees a face, turned around and looking back at her. *Rhodesy!*

"Aba!" she says, and for just a second something passes over her face – not a look of anger; more of sadness, a grey sadness that causes her face to close down momentarily. Then her face opens again in a big smile. "I'm glad you won't miss them," she says, and motions to the sky.

Abi is glad for her pointing finger, and she looks quickly away to the green and pink against the dark.

"Wow!" breathes Jude.

"Dyl," Abi dares to say the name aloud, "would love this, wouldn't he?" *Wish I couldn't feel Rhodes right in front of me. Wish I didn't feel as if I've betrayed a friend. I hardly know her, really.*

Jude doesn't take his eyes from the exploding colour. "I suppose he would," he says, nothing more.

BOOM ! BOOM! BOOM! Will it ever stop? Abi is shivering now, and wonders how long it will go on. Ten minutes? Twenty minutes? Maybe someone will just drop a match and blow it all up at once and get it over with. *Please...* If only she didn't feel as if she'd made a promise, then broken it. She didn't promise Rhodesy anything. She just said "no" to her invitation. That's not the same, is it?

Beside her, she can feel Jude closer, can feel his weight. There's a warmth on her neck and she turns at the suddenness of it, and they're connected. Just like that.

Abi's not prepared for it. She always thought her first real kiss would be something she could recognize at the time. But before she can tell herself what's happening, it's over.

"What do you think?" he asks, his voice husky.

I don't want to think. She kisses him back because it's easier than talking.

She doesn't want to think about those magazines and what they say to do. She doesn't want to think about what other girls think. Mostly, she doesn't want to think about Rhodesy up ahead there. Something haunts Rhodesy, Abi can feel it. She doesn't want to know what, though, she really doesn't. She doesn't want to think that maybe she's added some bit of black to the blues in Mary Rhodes.

She kisses Jude again. No, no thinking.

Da Capo

Summer settles in. You might forget for a minute and think it's never going to rain again. Abi fixes the screen door with a few small nails to hold it in place, then leaves the front door open, the back door, the windows. She's glad for the noise of rushing water and engines, the roar of trucks to the mill. Time passes slowly, unmarked by bells and lunch announcements. She misses the school library and is glad she took out a few books before the end of the year.

Open the dictionary. Past B and C. Now it's D.

Da capo. A musical word. *Repeat from the beginning.* The dictionary shows the little sign that composers use for da capo. You look through the music for that sign – a swirly little thing, and you start from there. Where would Abi put a da capo in her life? Late last summer, just before Mum left? What would she do differently? Or would she put the da capo earlier?

She looks across the table to Dad. Where would she put the da capo for him?

Life Before the Chair.

"Look!" She remembers Mum saying. "Look what I found!" Mum had brought the chair home on the old wagon, from a garage sale over a mile away.

Dad took hold of it and together they brought it into the living room. Dad had laughed aloud. "I've been needing one of these." He'd flopped into the dark green plush and patted the wide armrests.

"I thought you'd like it!" She'd grinned, pleased with herself.

How could it have been like that? Mum doing and giving, and Dad laughing? And now, Dad not laughing and Mum gone. Even with all this trying to put pieces together, it doesn't make sense.

There'd been other good times, too. But there'd also been the times – maybe twice a year – when Mum would get a letter from "home" as she called it. During the cold months, she'd go into her bedroom to read these, and in the warm months, she'd sit on the car seat out front, with the thin piece of airmail paper in her hand, staring at it, and then staring out at the road. She never sat in the greenhouse to read those, and she never shared them. So just how did the pieces fit?

Always so back to back, Mum and Dad were: he looking to the river, and she to the road.

Home. It had always bothered Abi that Mum called another place home. Why wasn't this home? When would it be? How long did you need to stay in a place for it to become home? *What* exactly made a place home?

In the place Mum called home – Kent, Abi thought it was – there was no one there for her. Mum's parents had been dead since before Abi was born. So *home*? How could it be? When Abi asked who the letters came from, her mother would only say that they were from one of her cousins. There were a few, apparently, still living somewhere on the other side of the Atlantic. No one with enough money to travel to the far coast of Canada, it seemed. "Not a travelling people," Mum had said once.

Back to da capo. How about putting it before Dad lost his job? Or before they moved from the old house? Abi can hardly remember it. Might even have been an apartment. When was that? After old Uncle Bernard died, he left the place to them. Abi could barely swim then. Spent the first year in this house wearing a lifejacket "just in case."

All right – put the da capo before she was born... *No.* Abi's never thought like that before and she's not going to start now. *If I hadn't been born to these parents, I'd have come out somewhere, somehow. I've never not wanted to be. I'd just rather not be here.*

She closes the dictionary. On second thought, she opens it again, then SLAMS it shut. Dad's face does appear around the wing of his chair. He says nothing, but she's grateful for his look of annoyance. If he can still be annoyed, there's hope.

There's a mumble from him. "Why aren't you in school?"

So maybe there isn't hope. "Summer holidays."

He grunts.

She fights a sudden urge to throw the television out the window. Another D word: defenestration. *To throw something* (or someone?) *out the window.* And they think kids watch too much television. Try all the mind rot adults watch; takes their thoughts, like soda crackers, and grinds them into a soup of mindlessness. They don't even need teeth to eat it.

When was the last time she saw Dad outside the house? Really outside – not just on the dock? Can't imagine what it would take to get him out of that chair. He could put his glasses on for a start, and see where he was going.

Maybe she'll have to start a fire. No. Foster home for sure, and that would be after a while of wherever they stow Young Arsonists.

Ping! She turns to look at the east window. Again a pebble hits the glass. Dad starts, but doesn't move from his chair.

"Abi!" It's Jude, waving his lunch bag, a newspaper rolled up under his arm. She grabs a box of crackers and a chunk of cheddar, an apple with just a couple of bad spots, pulls the old car blanket from the chesterfield.

Outside, a wind has come up, and the river moves with caps of dirty white foam. The warm summer wind raises the downy hair on her arms. She sets out the blanket and sits in the middle.

"Hey!" Jude nudges her bum with the toe of his shoe. "You think you're alone here?"

She scoots over.

"You spend a lot of time alone?" he asks as he unwraps a sandwich. He checks between the slices of bread.

She doesn't answer.

"Your mum makes your lunch?" is her question.

He nods and bites into the sandwich. She can smell the heavy fragrance of a cheese Mum used to like. *Maybe still does.* She opens her box of crackers.

"Your mum doesn't mind taking care of your son?"

Jude looks surprised. "No, of course not."

"What's he like?"

"Who?"

"Your son," she says. "Dyl."

Jude looks at her. Just how she's not sure. As if he wants to read her mind?

"It's just a question," she says.

"Well," he begins, and finishes chewing his bite of sandwich. Then he grins. "He's two," he says, and promptly takes another bite.

She waits for more.

"Haven't you heard of the terrible twos?"

"I guess so, but I don't really know anything about it."

"You've never babysat kids?"

"Not too many kids in the neighbourhood," she says, pointing with her chin in the direction of the road. "Or anyone, for that matter."

"Hmm." His eyes become slits as he scrutinizes her. "Well, he says the word 'no' a lot, and he's kind of like a piece of Velcro: stuck on my pant leg all the time, you know?"

No, I don't know. But she says nothing, and begins to eat.

Jude's touch on her arm is light, and he draws from one freckle to the next. "Connect the dots," he says, "and what do you have?"

She hope he doesn't notice that her skin is suddenly goose-pimpled.

"You'll have dots with lines," she says. How can she feel so comfortable with Jude one minute, and the next so uncomfortable and with stupid words coming out of her mouth?

He pulls away slowly, sits back with his eyes on the house. "Can you hear the water under the house at night?"

His question comes from left field. Or at least, from some place she's not at all sure she wants to go with him.

"I used to like the sound," she begins. "When I was a little kid." *Before Mum left.* She doesn't want to add the other thoughts that push into her mind: how now the sound keeps her awake, and it's a sound that never stops, won't let her rest. On windy nights she can hear the greenhouse bumping up against the dock as if fighting to escape, and she lies awake listening for when the sound ends and for when that broken-down frame and bits of glass that Mum loved is gone too, away down the river.

When Mum first left, Abi had nightmares that pieces of the house would fall away, a section of floor, a bit of lower wall, and Dad and his chair would also fall away, moving with the current until out of sight, Dad never realizing where he was, remote control still in hand, head resting on one shoulder, sound asleep, feet bobbing in and out of the water, the chair turning, turning in the eddies of mud. But the dreams ended when she began to cover him at night. Now with warm evenings she doesn't have to remember to tuck a blanket around him.

Would Jude understand all this? The urge to say something is strong in her. Just for a moment.

A rattle of newspaper calls to her. Jude is holding the comics to her. He spreads out the front-page section for himself.

"I always read the Sports at breakfast," he says. "Whew!" He taps the paper. "Look at this!"

She leans over for a look. The headline's enough: FOSTER PARENTS CHARGED WITH... She doesn't want to know what. Jude is shaking his head in disbelief.

"How about this?" she says, and points to the Family Circus in the corner of her piece of news. She hasn't had a chance to look at the comic herself yet, but Jude gives a laugh and forgets to say more about the front-page piece.

"I'd better get going." He begins to pack up his lunch. He breaks a chocolate bar in two and gives her half. His lips brush the top of her head as he stands. "Gotta go."

She watches him leave. A blackberry stringer catches his overalls and he has to stop to loosen the barb. He turns back and smiles. "Soon," he says.

Not soon enough.

She stays on her side of the blanket and draws her knees to her chest. She huddles, looks at the house, and tells herself, "This is the house I live in, and this is my life," but she likes it here in the field. Maybe she'll move here and live in the open air.

She falls asleep.

When Abi wakens she can hardly move, she's so badly burned. The sun is low, the river louder than the traffic. Cooler air tries to tickle her, but her skin is hot and her head dizzy. That's how Rhodes finds her.

Underwear to Fill a Drawer

"Oh my," Rhodes says. Of course. She helps Abi to her feet. "Oh my," again, and then, "you haven't been...been..." She can't even say it.

"Drinking?" Abi asks. She motions around. "What do you think?" She takes the arm Rhodes offers. "I could've used a bottle though – a bottle of sunscreen."

"That's what I thought was your affliction!" There's relief in the woman's voice. So. This Little Sister business can still be pretty straightforward.

She helps Abi into the house. Abi has to keep her head down, looking at her feet. If she raises it at all, she feels as if she's going to keel over. The edges of her vision have a threatening darkness to them. "I feel as if I'm going to go blind." Abi's voice has a whine to it.

"Sit here," says Rhodes abruptly, and gently she pushes her down on the car seat. "Put your head between your knees. Breathe deeply." Rhodes wedges the screen door open with a rock, so it won't slam on her, and then goes into the house.

Abi can hear her holler. "William!"

Who calls Dad William? He's only ever been Bill or Will, or Billy. "William!" Rhodes shouts even louder. Dad must have written *William* on the form for Big Sisters.

"Try resuscitation!" Abi yells, and the effort is hardly worth it. She begins to feel as if she's going to throw up.

"Where are your aspirin?"

He finally does speak up, but only to say, "Ask Abi."

"Do you have GINGER ALE?" But now Rhodesy's question seems not to be directed at anyone, and she's opening the fridge as she speaks. She slams through a few cupboards, then her heeled steps are returning, faster and faster. "I'll have to take you with me. We need to go to the drugstore." She takes Abi's hand, pulls her up. Amazing: the gentleness of Rhodes's movement coupled with the heat in her voice.

"Lie down in the back seat. Don't worry about the seat belt."

She's in the drugstore for five minutes only, then she's back, bags rustling, the big old '70s car swaying with her bustle.

She hands a bottle to Abi – full of ginger ale, fizzing and spitting up her nose – and drops pills into her hand.

"Take two aspirin and go to bed," Abi murmurs.

"Exactly," Rhodes says briskly.

You can tell she enjoys this, taking care of somebody. It's a bit like a game to her – on the next go-round she'll pick up her two hundred dollars, take a ride on the Reading Railroad...

Back at the house, she tries to help Abi to the chesterfield.

"No, not that piece of crap," Abi tells her, still keeping her head down. She sinks to the floor, back to the wall. "There're springs coming out of the cushions. They coil right up your butt." She feels pleased when Rhodes chuckles – a girlish jinglebell sound. A sound Abi would like to hear more often.

"Can't have *that*," she says, and goes to get a cool cloth for Abi's forehead, then another to drape over the nape of her neck. Makes her feel a little less like passing out.

"What is this anyway?"

"Sunstroke," she says.

It feels good to have a name to attach to it.

Rhodes opens one of the bags she's brought with her. "Here's cream," she says, and she smooths the ointment over Abi's arms and upper back. Rhodes's fingers are light on her skin, and even that's too much. "The other things in the bag are for you, too," she says, an attempt to distract her, Abi suspects. She tries not to pull away from Rhodes's touch.

Other than Horace with his juice berries, Abi can't remember when someone last bought something for her.

Then she remembers how Mum took her shopping for clothes the week before she left. *Was she planning on leaving then? Is that why she insisted on two pairs of shoes – she only ever bought one at a time – and a trip to the lingerie department for two bras and enough underwear to fill a drawer?* Abi should have known then, right? Just thinking of that drawer of underwear makes her want to cry. Why has she never put this together before? Maybe it's got something to do with Rhodes's hands on her shoulders, gentle.

Abi opens the bag and pulls out a plastic bottle. TEEN MULTI-VITAMINS. "Worried about my nutrition?" she asks. Who wouldn't be; not a fresh anything in the fridge.

Next a bottle of Midol.

"I had terrible cramps when I was your age," Rhodes says in a low voice. As if Dad would bother to listen.

There's a box of Tampax.

"My mother left me a lifetime supply." It is, too. Takes up both shelves under the bathroom sink. *And what had I thought that meant? She was planning on having a period forever? Never shopping again? There was never enough money for bulk shopping.*

Abi feels foolish and sick, and she'd really like to be alone. She pulls herself up to stand. "I'm feeling a lot better now. Really. You don't have to be here."

Rhodes stares at her with those eyes, green and full of questions.

"Really," Abi says. "I'm fine. I'll just lie down, go to sleep." She ducks her head, put her hands out to the sides – *feel as if I need some balance* – and makes her way toward her room. She suspects that in the house plans, her room was actually a closet, but someone put a regular door on it. A door that opens into the kitchen. Otherwise you wouldn't get a thing inside.

"This is cozy." Rhodes has followed her.

"Yeah." Abi flops down on the narrow mattress. *Just go.*

But Rhodes has gone to get another cool cloth for her forehead. When she comes back, she kneels on the floor beside the bed, her hand resting on the cloth. Abi has to admit, it feels good, the coolness under her hand, the water running down her temples into her hair.

Rhodes spies the paper bag in the corner where she's thrown it. "Oh, have you had a chance to look at the knitting book?" Chirp.

"Pink's not my thing." Abi pulls the blanket up to her nose; she's shivering now.

"Oh, I have every colour there is," Rhodes burbles. "I'll bring something else next time."

Happy as a pig in shit, isn't that what they say? Abi wants to tell her to go, but it's too much effort to get the words out, so she turns toward the wall, and Rhodes is quiet, her hand on Abi's forehead. Abi closes her eyes and sees the fireworks – green and pink and Fourth of July.

"There's heat exploding on my eyelids," she says. "Looks a lot like fireworks."

There's a quiet and appreciative chuckle from Rhodes.

"So you never miss fireworks, eh?" Abi asks her.

Rhodes hasn't said a word about that night.

"When I watch fireworks I always feel the exact same wonder I felt as a kid. Exactly the same. Never changes." Maybe she guesses that Abi feels badly about turning down her invite, and then showing up with Jude, because next she says, "I'm glad you were able to see them."

She's glad? Abi manages to say, "You forgive too easily."

"You think?" is all Rhodes says, and her hand doesn't move from Abi's forehead.

Tucked into her Ribs

There's a knock on the door first thing in the morning. It wakens Abi. As she stumbles out of bed, something falls from her head: the cloth, crusty-dry and moulded to a rounded shape. The skin over her joints pulls and burns, and it takes longer than you'd imagine to get to the door.

There's an old man just walking away as she opens it. He turns back with a smile. "Food bank," he says with a wave, then moves on to the small red car half sitting in the roadway.

"Pardon?"

He comes over the wooden walkway with a box in his hands. Abi can see a box of Muffets, her favourite cereal, sticking out. She begins to salivate, realizes she's eaten nothing since yesterday noon.

He raises his knee under the box to support it, and frees a hand for her to shake. "You must be Aba," he says. "My name's Colm, and that there's my granddaughter, Fiona. Probably about your age."

Abi looks to the passenger window of the car and sees a girl. Or at least, the side of a girl's face. She's staring ahead as if the car is moving top speed down a highway. Her hair is pulled straight back and her brows are down over her eyes.

"Fiona!" her grandpa calls. He has to call her again before she turns.

Abi knows that face; she has seen her in English class at school. Fiona never speaks. She only whispers to other girls, and laughs, those *ha* sort of laughs. When she does raise her voice, it's to taunt poor Stu Stevenson. That rule about "ignore the bully – they'll go away..." Well, Stu Stevenson has had lots of practice at "ignore" and Fiona still doesn't go away. Abi's surprised he hasn't given up on bleaching his hair to that scruffy yellow. He just goes about his business, whatever it might be. *Doggedly* would be the word for how he does that.

"Come on out, girl!" says her grandpa. "It's all part of our deal! Move your bum!"

Colm heads back into the house through the open door, and his granddaughter stares after him. Abi wonders what he's done for that look. What is their "deal" about?

When the girl finally climbs out of the car, she slams the door shut.

Abi stands back as the girl makes her way over the wooden walkway, and she can't stop the grin that rises to her face. *I'm thinking the word "flounce"...does anyone even use that word anymore? Flouncing Fiona.*

"What're *you* grinning like an idiot about?" Fiona leans over Abi. She's a tall girl, the nasty granddaughter.

"Oh, Fiona – don't start," says Colm. And he just fits those words into the rest of his sentence, which is something about "this being Will, and this being Aba." There's a lilt to his voice that Abi likes. Something comforting to it.

"Yeah, I know. You told me all about them in the car," she says. "I know Aba Jones from school."

Abi would like to set her straight: just because Fiona has seen her at school doesn't mean she *knows* her. But there are a few things about Fiona that defy Abi to speak to her. Her tone, for one – low and angry; the sneer of her full lips; the bump in her nose that makes her look like an ancient statue that will withstand absolutely anything a plebeian like Abi might say.

Fiona is standing in the middle of the kitchen, and Abi realizes that she seems to be trying to hold her very long arms close to her body. Her elbows are tucked into her ribs, her hands hold each other, and there's a stiffness to her legs.

She doesn't want to touch anything in my house. Abi feels a glow of shame and turns away. Colm is right in front of her, and she blinks to hold back the swimming in her eyes.

"It's nice to meet you finally after coming here every week. Your Da has told me about you."

Da? Oh yeah, the guy who was going to take me to Disneyland.

"I'd forgotten he talks," she says.

"Aye!" Colm laughs. "He does forget he has a voice now and then, doesn't he?" He goes back out the door and reappears shortly. "One more box will do!"

Fiona looks at him; his cheerful tone must annoy her. "Are we done here?" she asks.

"You have something else to do on your holiday?" he asks with a grin. He should know better.

Her face says as much. She leads the way out the door. Colm rests his hand on Dad's arm. "Next week, Will, we'll have a game of checkers, we will." He turns once again to Abi. "You got something soothing for that burn?"

She nods.

"Good then," he says.

Dad follows them to the door and he and Colm share a quick, comradely hug that surprises Abi.

"Next week."

"Next week."

After the screen door closes, Dad lifts the boxes onto the counter and begins to unpack them.

"How long have you been getting groceries this way?" Abi asks.

Dad stops and thinks. "Before Christmas, I guess it was. Someone phoned about it. I went down to some church to pick it up a couple of times and met Colm. He said that because I don't have a car, he'd bring it over after he was done his shift. He said we could play checkers." Dad pauses for a long moment before a half-smile flickers over his face. "Last week he said he's going to find a chess set and teach me how to play something new."

"Do you always play a game when he comes?"

"Most of the time." Dad lines up a few cans of soup, a can of stew, a couple of beans.

Abi's mouth waters. She can't remember the last time she had brown beans. "Can I have those?"

Dad hands them to her.

"It doesn't bother you?" she asks, as she opens the can.

Dad looks at her. This also bothers her: how he has to concentrate on her question. She can see his eyes narrow to focus. She can hear his thoughts, like the water passing under the house, nearing, circling the words he wants to trap.

She asks again. "It doesn't bother you that we need the food bank?"

"It can't," he says then, simply. "The EI ran out, and welfare isn't enough."

She nods, trying to absorb that.

He reaches far into another cupboard. "I wondered when we'd use this." He hands her another tin, this one of pineapple pieces.

This used to be a favourite. Mum would make it for quick suppers on cold evenings, with pieces of sausage, and brown bread toasted on the side. She finds the can opener and splits open the edge of the tin, and the familiar smell fills her with a sadness and reminds her how hungry she is. She heats the beans and pineapple until they bubble and pop, and sets down two bowls. It isn't until she's filled the second, and puts it in front of Dad that he looks directly at her, surprised. "No," he says. "I don't want any. Thank you," he adds, looking down. She feels again the sense of him retreating into that place inside himself.

By herself, she sits at the table and empties her plate, then his. She wonders about what else she's missed, being at school all these months...and what's he going to do when she leaves.

Paper Boats

Abi's laid out her best. Well, not hers. Mum's. A long, narrow black skirt and white shirt. They don't have an iron, but she remembers how Mum used to steam clothes in the bathroom and after a night of hanging, it looks not bad. There are black shoes at the back of Mum's closet, and a belt hooked over a nail in the wall. The shoes fit perfectly, and the belt fits her waist three holes away from the one that Mum used. A bit of mascara, Cinnamon lipstick, hair in a perfectly smooth pony, and she's done.

I'd hire me!

Okay. She has her list of places to go, beginning with the one interview she managed to set up over the phone. *Mack's Coffee.* "Make sure you're here before eleven when we get busy," the manager had said. Abi hopes he doesn't always sound that grumpy. The only watch she has is an old one of Mum's. It reads twenty minutes after nine, and even though it's old, Abi knows it keeps perfect time. She slips it into the purse that was also Mum's, along with some bus fare from the jar on the counter, and gathers together the jobless résumés she made up the last week of school. One more trip to the toilet. She always has to pee when she's nervous.

She hears a cry. "No! No!" whimpers a voice. The screen door slams into place. There's a lower voice, murmuring, then the little voice again, crying. "No."

The murmuring voice rises. "Dyl. I have to. You have to."

Abi's out of the bathroom. "What is it?"

Jude is standing in the kitchen, and his son is wrapped around his legs. That must be the Velcro action Jude told her about. The boy's eyes are round and his mouth is in a matching "O." "Please," says Jude, "can I leave him with you? Mum's sick and I've got to work. There's nowhere else I can take him." As he speaks, his son's whimpering grows louder. Abi almost misses Jude's last words.

She starts to say something about Mack's Coffee, but Jude is bent over trying to un-Velcro his son. "I have a job interview," Abi says, not quite yelling, but now the boy is howling.

Jude looks at her. His eyes are round and dark, and he mouths words, but she doesn't know what he says. Then he's gone.

She feels a fury – a frustration so intense – she digs her nails into her hands. But now the boy is at the door reaching for the doorknob. It doesn't turn. *Jude must be outside, holding it.*

The boy tries again and again, then collapses in tears of defeat. His T-shirt is thin, and she can see his ribs heave with sobs. Outside, Jude's boots pass over the walkway, quick on the wood.

She hears movement behind her, and when she turns, she sees Dad looking on, his brow knotted.

"What do I do?" she whispers. *Don't expect an answer.*

"Sit with him," Dad says. His voice is gruff: first words of the day.

She lowers herself slowly to the floor and sits right next to the boy, but doesn't touch him. She has the feeling that if she does he'll howl even louder. After a couple of minutes, his sobs begin to subside. Still she doesn't touch him. She feels frozen, though she finds herself staring at the soft brown of his curly hair and something in her chest feels tight. He moves his head onto her knee and he's absolutely still, like a rabbit hiding in the brush. Then he shudders, and begins to breathe again.

Abi looks up to see if Dad is still watching. Imagine that: Dad coming up with how to do something. Who needs advice columnists? Just ask Dad. *Dear Bill Jones...*

He is watching and his hands are fumbling with his glasses. "They sure can wail."

"Enough to wake you," she says.

"Who is the little bugger?" Not unkindly.

"He's Jude's."

"Jude?" Dad looks puzzled, but doesn't seem to want an explanation. He turns back to the TV and changes the channel.

Abi doesn't know how long Jude's boy and she are like that, sitting on the floor, his head on her knee. Time passes — Dad watches an entire sitcom — and the boy sits up.

"Shuice!" he whispers. *What?* He goes to the fridge, pulls at the handle. "Shuice!" Now it's more of a whine.

"Why didn't you say so," and she pours some apple juice into a cup. He says something like "ang" — must mean "thanks" — and tries to pull himself up on a chair. Juice everywhere. That whine starts again. The sound makes her feel like covering her ears and hiding in her room.

"That's okay," she says. *Just stop whining. Please!* She mops up. "This house is very spillable." That's probably not something you're supposed to say to a kid.

Soon as she opens her mouth, his eyes are on her. She doesn't know how much he understands, but he listens. She pours a second cup.

"Danma sick," he says, then gulps his juice.

"D-a-n-m-a," she repeats. "Of course! GRANDMA!"

He frowns at her peevishly, as if to say, "That's what I said!"

Then, in one movement, he's down from the table, across the floor and looking out the window. The river.

"I have something for you." Somewhere around here there's that old life jacket. There's a bench by the door. She lifts the seat to look into the box. Gumboots. Was she ever a little kid who walked in the mud holding the hand of that man who spends his days in that chair?

She scoops out the fluorescent orange vest with its safety collar and loops and buckles. How she'd hated this vest. She always loved to swing her arms when she was little. And she paid for it too, with knuckles bruised on doorways, but she would have settled for those bruises over these straps.

She pulls open the zipper, and feeds the vest over one of the boy's arms, around the back, over the other. He doesn't fight her, but his narrow shoulders bunch, and one hand begins to pick at the strap. She takes it from his hand and draws it up between his legs to hold the vest in place; he's such a little guy, with such a nothing-there body, the vest could slip right off him. She remembers the buckle of this strap now: it wouldn't hold, and here, attached to the side of the vest edge, is the pin that Mum always used to keep it in place. With the memory comes an image of her mother's hands, tanned the colour of honey, and slim. There was always a sureness to them that never seemed quite to fit with the rest of her.

She hooks the strap into its buckle and tightens it just as her mother did, and that's when he begins to struggle. His struggle is silent though, as if by his saying nothing, she'll not notice what he's doing.

"You have to," she says and remembers those were Jude's words to him. How often does Dyl hear those words? She fastens the pin.

He frowns and looks at her as if trying to make sense of nonsense. Then he begins to pull at the vest, at the strap, the pin – the pin is old and gives way, and there's a ping of metal as it flies across the room. He yanks the strap until it's hanging like a tail behind him. Then he stands tall; he has scared himself a bit, she's sure of it, but there's triumph in him.

"Okay," she says, a little disarmed and even slightly in awe of his performance. "Let's go play in the field." *I might have to tie a rope around your waist, though.*

But no, he shakes his head. More shuice is what he wants. His request is another whisper. Does he ever speak up? The longer he's here in her house, the wider his eyes grow. He seems to be more apprehensive with time, not less. She fills the cup again, then sets about looking for a ball or something – anything – to play with.

There's an empty cereal box, a couple of tins, and in the corner is a heap of stiff, yellowed newspaper. "Paper boats," Abi says, pleased with this bit of inspiration. He has no idea what she's talking about, and stands there with his hands wrapped around the cup, that frown moulded to his face. So far, she can picture his face in distress, running over with tears, or like this – all creased and closed. Maybe a paper boat will bring a smile. She begins to fold.

Funny how it comes back, the folds, the turns. She and Dad used to make them all the time, lower them to the river, see how long it took until they disappeared into the white sun.

The boy holds his, while she makes one for herself.

"One for Dad," he says, and he looks at the door.

Should she tell him it might be a while? She doesn't even know how long Jude will be.

"All right." She continues folding.

"One more," he says when she's done. And "one more" again. He takes each as it's finished and puts it next to the last, nose to nose. His little fingers are precise. She didn't know little kids could move like that. He waits, moving with a little hop on first one foot, then the other, back and forth, while she folds the next.

"I'll fill the sink now," she says.

He looks panicked. "No! One more!"

"We might run out of paper," she says, but he looks at the thigh-high stack of classifieds — EMPLOYMENT (lots of red-pen circles) — and she starts to laugh. "Okay, maybe not!"

She plugs the sink, and turns the tap on.

"No, no!" He's followed her, cup of juice still in hand, and grabs hold of one of her legs. Even with just one arm, he has an amazingly tight hold. *Velcro-kid, right?*

"I can't fold boats all day!" She leans over to free herself, and up comes the juice — yellow pours down the front of her white shirt. *My white shirt. Job interview.* Her yell makes him drop his arm, step back, and his face is fearful. The shirt sticks to her skin as she struggles with the buttons. "Oh no," she says. "Oh no!" *I probably sound like Rhodes. But what am I gonna do?*

The boy is edging backwards, away from her, and she only begins to register the fear on his face, and then the phone rings. She's pulling off the shirt. The sink is filling. Might as well throw the shirt in. She rolls it in a loose ball, and it lands in the sink as she picks up the receiver.

"Miss Jones?" asks a voice on the other end. Grumpy.

"Speaking."

"It's after eleven," says the voice, then waits.

Who?

"You needn't bother coming for your interview." The voice is stiff.

"But..." she begins, but he's gone. The job, too.

A sound does break through the rush in her head: the sound of the back door clicking closed.

"Dyl!" she calls, her voice squawking as if she has a reed instrument stuck in her throat. "Dyl!" She hurries after him. *No. No. No. Can't be.*

She can't see him when she steps onto the deck. *No. No. No. Can't be. There's been no splash. Not that she's heard...*

She forces herself to go to the edge, to look into the water. She doesn't want to see what she expects to.

But there's no little body in the water. Maybe he's gone under, sucked down...or he's beneath the boards. She gets down, lies on the boards. She can feel the rough wood against her midriff. *Oh yeah, I'm in an orange-stained bra.* She looks through the cracks. Just dark water.

She hears a sound. A lilting sound. A sort of hummy-singsong in the field. She gathers herself up. There he is, in the midst of the grass, some of it high as his waist. As she nears him, he turns to her. In one little mitt of a hand he's got a clump of dandelion buttons. *Rhodes's flowers*, is all she can think, as she takes his offering. She kneels in front of him, and can hear her own breath. His eyes are on her, and are again filled with fear. Not his, but hers this time. He must see it in her.

"Don't ever do that again," Abi says, her voice like a rusty saw in wood, and then she's shaking. Couldn't stop if she tried. He frowns – how many times a day does this kid frown? There's just too damn many thoughts in his head – and he tentatively stretches his arms around her shoulders. Her sun-burned skin is still sore, but she doesn't pull away. Not until she hears the car horn honking, the catcall. Then she remembers what she's wearing. Or rather, what she's not, and she hurries him to the house.

Her shirt is like a great yellow-streaked balloon, bubbled and floating over the edge of the sink. The telephone receiver beeps from the counter where she dropped it as she ran for the back door. She can see the door to Dad's bedroom opened just a crack and her guess is that he's gone for a nap, probably with his pillow over his head as he sometimes does. Water is everywhere, and she splashes through to turn the tap off. She picks up the shirt, and wrings it out right over the floor. She thinks how you're probably not supposed to swear in front of a two-year-old, but Dyl stops her blast in his own way.

"Boats!" he cries, and before she can stop him, he's dived onto his front and is lying full-length in the water, two paper boats floating at the tip of his nose. "See! See!" he shouts out. He looks up at her. "See? See? Boats!"

She stretches out opposite him. The water is deliciously cool on this July day. "I see," she says, and nudges a boat into race position. She shows him how to blow the little crafts – he does, huffing and puffing, with his bum in the air – and it isn't until the boats are soggy and the water has mostly seeped into the floor, that the front door opens, and there's Jude.

"What the..."

"Daddy! Boats. See!"

But Jude is staring at Abi in her bra, and she feels awkward as she gets to her feet and goes to her room for a sweatshirt to pull over. When she comes out, Dyl is trying to convince Jude to be a wind for his soggy boat, but Jude is shaking his head.

"Got to go, Dyl. Daddy's tired. We were busy at work. We're still trying to find a – " He breaks off as he sees her. "Thanks, Abi. My boss really needed me for a few hours. I think he would have fired me if I hadn't come in!"

She nods numbly, and all at once they're gone, and the house is quiet. She's left with a soggy floor – nothing new in that, though – sad paper boats, and a question: What were they still trying to find at Hood's Paint?

Ethereal

*E*thereal. *Extremely delicate and light in a way that seems too perfect for this world.*

Was that Abi's mother? Was that how she saw herself? Too Perfect? So where did she go?

Exosphere. Outermost region of a planet's atmosphere. Ha! Maybe that's where. She couldn't stay near water so she flew on the wind, up and up. A woman carried by the wind.

No, she left on her own two feet. There was nothing to stop her. Nothing to hold her.

No matter how hard Abi slams the dictionary, Dad isn't going to move today.

But it's heading into the middle of summer and the wind is pretty still. Does that mean it's going to drop something on them?

"He said he knows you!" Rhodes's voice chirps. "Funny though, he thought you lived up 60th. He seemed surprised when I pointed out your house!" On she goes, words Abi doesn't want to hear, something about "right by the bus stop." "He even suggested a mechanic for Betty." She fishes a piece of paper from her bag. "May I use your phone?"

Abi nods.

She can tell by Rhodesy's end of the conversation that the mechanic is too behind to help out old Betty. That is, until Rhodes says, "Horace the bus driver gave me your number." Then it's different. Then she can bring Betty around later in the day.

"'Why didn't you say Horace sent you?' That's what he said." Rhodes does well with imitating others; she could be a one-woman show. It takes her a while to put everything back in her bag, an extravagant fabric affair that appears to be made from ancient curtains, with roses and hummingbirds all over it.

"And Horace said for us to see his railway train track, as soon as Betty is on the mend..." She breaks off. "Abi! What's wrong?"

"Nothing." Abi looks away from her.

"No, something is." Rhodes walks round so she's in front of Abi.

Abi stares back at her. "Okay," she says at last, "I just don't want to see some old guy's choo-choo set." Trains are supposed to be for kids.

"Well," says Rhodes, "Dr. Seuss said that adults are obsolete children. Maybe your friend Horace is not so obsolete. Hmm...besides, he made it sound as if you two were friends."

"Yeah, well." Abi can't think what else to say. She doesn't like when Rhodesy does that "hmm" thing. And when she looks hurt.

Rhodes's voice is soft. "You do have friends, don't you, Abi?"

"Of course," Abi says quickly. "I have...Jude. And...there's kids at school," she adds. But a picture of Fiona comes to her mind and she has to look away from Rhodes's eyes.

"Who do you laugh with?"

Stop poking at me like this! Makes Abi want to poke back. "I don't need to laugh."

"You do," Rhodes says. "More than anyone."

She reaches into her bag and pulls out a crumpled paper bag. "Your colour," she says.

Abi reaches in and pulls out a ball of yarn.

"Red?"

"I couldn't bring myself to bring black," Rhodes says. She fetches the needles from Abi's room, and then sits, sets about looping the yarn around the needle, the fingers of both hands moving in a fluttering figure eight. There's something quite beautiful about those hands, something different. Abi's never noticed before, and she's surprised she hasn't. Those, and her dancing hips. But these thoughts seem to be only in Abi's mind; all of Rhodes's attention is on the matter in her hands.

"It's called casting on. I'll show you how to do it with the next project. Now, I want to get you started." She stops, counts the stitches under her breath. "Enough for a scarf."

"It's July."

"Good – it'll be ready for winter!"

"Planning ahead?"

"I like knowing exactly what's going to happen tomorrow, yes."

There's not a speck of laughter in her as she says this. In fact, her tone is so different that Abi stares. Maybe it's just that she's counting the stitches as she speaks.

"Exactly?" asks Abi. "No surprises?"

"None," says Rhodes. "Now, come on!" She puts the needles in Abi's hands. "Keep your hands busy, and free your mind."

"My mind is free, thanks."

"I don't think I believe that," says Rhodes, "but we'll just go on."

Of course, quickly she realizes that being left-handed, Abi knits in a backwards sort of way. So Abi makes up the lemonade iced-tea Rhodes brought, sets out the cookies on a plate, while Rhodes attempts to figure out how to show Abi this wondrous womanly art.

"Like this!" Rhodes is triumphant after ten or fifteen minutes. Abi brushes cookie crumbs off her hands onto her shorts.

Almost an hour later, Abi has about two centimetres of a scraggly red, stitches twisted, two dropped — Rhodes finds them, brings them to heel.

"Just why is it we're doing this?" Abi holds it out at arm's length. *This is ugly, face it.*

"My mother always said that every girl should know how to knit."

"Really?"

"Really."

"Why?"

Rhodes pauses. In her thoughts and words, that is; her hands keep moving. "It's as I told you: you keep your hands busy, and your mind can be free."

"Free?"

"Of what's around you. Like in *A Tale of Two Cities.*"

"Dickens wrote that." Abi knows that much.

"Yes. It's during the French Revolution, and atrocious acts are happening all around...and what do the women do?"

Abi shakes her head.

"They knit and knit and knit!"

Rhodesy! You're too much for me! She's certifiable, that's for sure. Wacko. But all the same, there's something infectious about her enthusiasm, her earnestness.

"So you're saying that we should knit and knit and knit while atrocious things go on?"

Rhodes knows Abi's laughing at her, and she sighs. Abi's words finally cause her to set her knitting down. "A woman in the southern States began a project. With young men convicted of drug offenses. And to provide some comfort for the babies of drug-addicted women. She went to the prison with needles and yarn, and she taught the young men how to knit, and they knit sweaters for the babies. It started out as an act that the court ordered – so many hours of knitting – but many of the men couldn't stop after they began, and they continued on, making garments for the little ones. The sweaters warmed the babies, and the knitting soothed the unhappiness of the young men..." She breaks off. "You don't believe me?"

"No, no!" Abi protests. "I believe you. You being you and all..."

Rhodes raises her brows as Abi goes on.

"I have a hard time imagining it, that's all."

"What do you mean by 'you being you'?" Rhodes asks slowly.

"You wouldn't lie. You know. You're very...very *earnest*." There it is. "In fact," Abi goes on, "maybe *that's* what I will call you...Ernestine!"

Rhodes smirks. "Ernestine?! I'd feel a bit less as if I was in the army then. All this surname stuff." She nods.

There's a great snurfling sound from The Chair.

Ernestine – yep, it suits her – looks up, alarmed.

"He does wake up once in a while," Abi whispers. To her amazement, Rhodes – Ernestine now – sort of shrinks away as he stands. Of course, he doesn't even look at them as he makes his way to the bathroom.

She reassembles her bag while he's in there, sets Abi's knitting out on the table, prepares to leave. Her hands are busy, picking up, putting away, pulling the same item out again. Then as the bathroom door opens, she's perfectly still, as if she might blend in with the mildewy walls.

But Dad doesn't look toward the table and makes one of his infrequent trips out the back door.

"He's going to stand out there and stare at the river for about twenty minutes now," Abi tells Ernestine.

Her brows crimp anxiously around her eyes. "He does that often?"

"No, not often."

Abi doesn't tell her about the extra nails she hammered into the railing not long ago. He always leans too far over.

"I'd better be off," Ernestine says then. Motions to the straggly knitting. "I expect you to be half finished next time I come." She attempts to sound funny.

"You're not coming back for a long time then?"

Ernestine pats Abi's arm and for just a second, her hand rests there. "Make it a short scarf, Abi."

Farce

 F *arce.* It's not a new word. Abi's heard it before, but can't remember exactly what it means. Maybe it was something on stage. *Something ludicrous*, the dictionary reads. *An empty show.*

Farce. An empty show. Dad in The Chair.

No, that's not how it is at all. Dad is exactly what he is. He's not putting on an empty show. He himself is empty, like a shell left hollow after some bug has withered away: tap him too hard and he'll crunch inward, a brittle husk of a person. But he's not pretending to be anything else.

J ude said he'd call on Saturday.

By noon, Abi's knit about forty centimetres.

By 2:00, she has one third of a scarf. It's making a warm spot on her lap. The stitches have grown quite smooth and even. When did that happen? She holds up the fabric she's made, and feels strangely proud. She has an urge to show it to someone.

The phone rings and she leaps up, feels the yarn pulling at her ankles.

"Hello?" says a voice. "Mr. Bekell?"

"No – no! I'm not Mr. Be...whatever you said!"

The voice is squeaking "so sorry" as she thunks the receiver back into its place on the wall.

There is yarn across the floor. She gathers it up. The stitches hang from the end of the needle. One little pull, one little step farther, and it would be out. She jams the needle in, holds up the third of scarf, and looks at it with a critical eye.

Yes, there it is. The point at which her new-knitter muscle warmed up, and it began to feel somewhat natural. Must have been just after noon.

She pulls the needle and begins to unravel the wool. It feels good, stretching her arm out as far as it can go, scooping up more yarn, pulling it out again. It's all over the floor, like crimped hair, a wild Raggedy-Anne-of-Green-Gables gone crazy with hair-cutting shears.

She manages to put the needle back in when she gets to the last couple of rows. She has an idea that she might not be able to figure out all that about casting on. By the time the afternoon has hit the doldrums – no wind, no bugs, no birds – she's back to about thirty centimeters.

When she goes to sleep there is half of a Christmas-red scarf next to her bed. Her fingers feel as if they've been wrapped around a baseball bat and stuck in the freezer for a month.

The phone hasn't rung all day, except for the one call for Mr. Whatever-his-name-was.

My Beautiful Sunday

The sun comes up on Abi's side of the house, and it wakes her the next morning, and it brings a memory: when she was really little, and Dad singing, "This is my, my, my beautiful Sunday, when you say, say, say, say that you love me..." It seems as if he began every Sunday with those words. And Mum would laugh, wouldn't she? Or would she? Abi wants to remember it with her laughing; she likes it better that way. If she lies really still – doesn't make a move to get up – she can almost hear the sound of that laughter. No, it's the river, carrying mud from one place to the next.

The sight of her scarf takes Abi by surprise. It seems like a dream, the day before.

Then she remembers the waiting; the phone not ringing.

What's a promise, anyway?

Abi takes up where she left off with the needle and yarn, and leaves bed only when a hunger headache threatens.

It's hard not to think of Colm and Fiona every time she opens the cupboard now. She can hear Colm, all "chipper" as Horace would say, and she can see Fiona's miserable scowl.

Cereal, and back to the scarf. She can feel the sun warming the east side of the house, rising over the roof. Dad gets up, dumps cereal in a bowl, looks vaguely for the milk.

"Fridge," Abi reminds him. Click, click, click, go the needles. She likes the sound. She suddenly realizes the TV's off. "Hey, what's with..." she starts to say, but then shuts up. Why remind him?

He sits at the table. Still seems to be looking for something or somebody.

"Dad." Abi speaks as if he's a songbird just landed on the windowsill. "Dad, eat."

He does, tentatively.

They sit, almost like any other daughter and father, eating breakfast. "Did you sleep well?" she asks.

It's supposed to be the question the parent asks the teenager, and it's supposed to annoy the teenager.

"Huh?" he asks. "Oh. Yeah."

Does he remember what I just said?

"I could make you a cup of coffee," she says, her mind scrambling to think of where some might be. "We could sit out back." Dangle our legs over the edge, listen to the water on the move.

He stares at her blankly. She wishes he'd wear his glasses. She imagines what she looks like to him. Something like the way his one and only honeymoon photo looks to her: fuzzy.

The ring of the phone is so loud they both jump. Is this the call that was supposed to come yesterday? Is he going to say something about forgetting? What is she going to say? Should she just let it go? She doesn't get it until the third ring, and she's still not sure.

"Abi?"

"Jude."

"Are we still on for today?" he asks.

That was yesterday.

"We can drive in to Vancouver, walk in the sun, have an ice cream."

That must mean Dyl will be with them. Probably means ice cream will end up on her shirt.

"Sure," is all she says. Dad's not even going to notice she's gone.

There's a summer skirt somewhere in Mum's drawer, and a T-shirt, comfortably stretched and white. She knots it in front. Pulls on sandals. Pretends her hands aren't shaking.

He's just a boy. Pushes the knitting under her pillow, though she has no intention, ever, to let Jude see this hole of a room.

Dad's still sitting at the table when she comes out. Not waiting for that coffee she mentioned, is he? He's looking toward the door, his face with no expression. None Abi can read. What's he thinking when he's like that? Almost seems to be listening to voices in his head. Whose voices? Mum's? Abi's when she was little? His own mother's? Father's? Or is he just sitting, listening to the silence, now that all those people are no longer here?

She looks through the screen door. No blue pickup in sight. Not yet.

In the cupboard there's a small jar of instant coffee. She puts the kettle on the stove. Jude will probably be here before the water boils. Dad won't miss the coffee, she suspects.

A watched pot never boils.

If you watch it long enough, it does.

She makes the coffee and sets it in front of Dad. He says nothing at first, then he wraps both of his hands around it as if he's cold on this hot July day. His hands are big, capable-looking. He murmurs a thank you, as if he's suddenly remembered some part of himself.

"You're welcome." She watches as he slowly drinks the coffee. After each sip he peers into the mug, hands still tight to the ceramic. Makes her think of a little kid – Dyl, with his glass of juice.

Maybe that's why Jude is taking a long time: something's happening with Dyl.

Then she hears the churn of gravel, the honk of a horn. Dad looks up. "I always said, if a boy comes calling for my girl with a honk of the horn, I'll..." He drifts off, trying to remember his threat. Then he goes on. "I'll...rip out his wires. That's what I always said."

He's left Abi speechless. Motionless, too. She can't seem to move from where she is – halfway to the door, but he makes no move either; so much for his threat.

Jude's horn sounds again. Twice. Impatient.

She's out the door and hauling herself up the passenger side of the raised pickup.

"Starting to wonder if you were going to come through that door," says Jude. He's smiling, but she's not.

"I was starting to wonder if you were going to *come*!" she says.

He reaches over and clasps her kneecap. "Didn't think I'd stand you up, did you?"

"No." She pauses. "Not really."

He starts the truck. "My mum's sick again. I had to settle Dyl down with a video and convince Mum she'd be okay for a while."

"Why didn't you bring him then?"

He'd put his hand to the stick shift to get into gear, but

abruptly he reaches out to Abi and crushes her in his arms. She can hear his heart beating fast, she can smell deodorant, a faint smell of smoke, paint thinner, and yes, a whiff of apple juice. There's an urgency in his hug.

"I was hoping we could be alone," he says as they move apart, and he shifts into first with such a determined push, pulls the truck out into the road, shifts to second, quickly to third.

She's certain he can hear her heart clear across the truck over the open-window traffic noise. She looks out her window. Isn't this what ballet dancers do to keep themselves from falling over when they turn quick pirouettes? They fix on a point, find it with their eyes, hold on it, hold, hold...

"How about you?" asks Jude.

"Me what?"

"Weren't you hoping we could be alone?"

"Me. Yeah. Sure. Of course," she adds. *Fix on a point. Hold. Holding.* She can't look at him right now; she's too full, might overflow. *Yes, of course that's what I wanted.*

For some reason, she can see Mum, that time she cried. She pushes the mental picture away.

"You're shivering!" says Jude. "What's with that?"

"Just the cool air blowing in the window, I guess."

He's doing that looking-at-her again.

"Watch the road; you make me nervous."

She thinks of Horace's bus driving. *Why are all these people converging in my head at just this time? GO!!*

They drive all the way into the city, where different smells rise from the summer pavement, where there's a pulse.

"Let's go to the ice cream place at the beach," Jude says, tapping the steering wheel in time with the music.

They drive, looking for a place to park. The beach is covered with people. There's the springy thwacks of tennis balls in the courts, and a guitar picks out a tune − she can hear it through thin strains of radio. Jude takes her hand as they walk slowly between the strolling and wheeling people. He walks ahead of her as they thread through to the food stand, and she follows, their arms stretched.

"Does the vanilla have the little black specks?" she asks the boy behind the counter.

"Black specks?" Jude raises a brow.

But the boy knows what she means. He grins. "You mean, is it *real* vanilla! Yes, it is." He gives her an extra scoop.

Jude orders black cherry gelato, whatever that is.

On the other side of the food stand, there's a grassy hill. The benches are full, but there is a big tree, too broad to wrap your arms around, with thick roots bunching into the ground. "Let's sit there." Abi leads the way, sits on the ground, back to the trunk, elbow resting on a root. There's enough room for Jude beside her. It's comfy; the shape of the tree, and the late afternoon sun. Jude stands over her, gives the tree a quick look, then shades his eyes to see farther down the beach.

"I told some friends I'd be here," he says, and starts off.

She feels suddenly foolish in her tree roots and moves quickly to stand. The T-shirt snags on rough bark, and she tugs at it, hears the fabric open. Jude is halfway down the beach. She hurries after him. "I thought you wanted to be alone," she says, as she reaches him.

He flashes that smile, that brilliant, beautiful smile. "I want my friends to meet you."

She reminds herself not to skip.

There's a group playing volleyball, who look as if they've been here all day. Girls in tankinis, surf shorts; boys with bare chests, red cresting their shoulders.

"Jude!" Two of the girls cry out. "Man — where you been?" says a boy with a bleached flat-top. "We been waiting for you!"

Jude wraps an arm around Abi. "You know how it is," he says.

The volleyball boy looks at her as if he hasn't noticed her before. And he probably hasn't. "Oh, yeah. How it is," he repeats, and smirks at her. The two girls come closer, look at Abi carefully, unsmiling. Another girl nears too, but she's staring at Jude, and a puppy wriggles under her arm. She's not letting him go, though, no matter how much he wriggles. "Where's the Dyl-boy?" is her question.

"With Grandma," says Jude shortly.

"I brought Mortimer here to play with him," the girl goes on. She's the only one of the group not in a bathing suit. Rather, she's wearing an old sweatshirt, with the sleeves cut off in deep circles, and a piece of Indian fabric tied around her round hips. Her legs are sturdy. The puppy fits easily in her hands. She turns her eyes on Abi. The girl's eyes are round too, and big.

A feeling comes over Abi, a feeling she wants to put words to: *No matter where this girl lives, you feel at home there. If you're a friend.*

But the girl says nothing to Abi.

"You're on," says the flat-top boy, throwing the volleyball to Jude. And that's it: Jude's out in the sand, and it's just Abi and...

When they're standing alone, the girl holds out her hand. "I'm Amanda."

"Amanda," Abi says. "I was just thinking of you as Mortimer's Mum-person. Now I don't have to."

Amanda laughs, a loud, wonderful laugh. "You're all right!" she says. "So what are you doing hanging out with Jude Arden?" There's a coldness in her last words.

The suddenness of the question surprises Abi. Before she can think of an answer, Amanda asks, "You've met his son, Dyl?"

Abi nods.

Amanda scratches the pup's ears, floppy and golden. "Sit with me," she says. She has a bright red blanket, looks like an old bedspread, with a pile of softcover books spread at one end. Every one of them looks as if it's been read many times. One cover has been torn off and then mended with tape.

"A dictionary!" Abi says. There are pieces of paper hanging out the edges, covered with ink and pencil scribbles.

"I've found a few good words in there," says Amanda.

Abi nods, and picks up a book of poetry. Someone named Jan Zwicky.

"Is it good?"

"Oh yeah," is the answer. "You like poetry?"

"It kinda scares me. But I do read the dictionary."

"Nothing to be scared of."

"Not understanding something," Abi says, "can be scary."

Amanda picks up the dictionary with one hand, and takes the book of poetry from her with her other. "Poetry's sort of like...a dictionary of emotion. You can find definitions of stuff that's hard to define, and you can understand it. Sometimes it's just not anything you're looking for...then, you say you don't understand it."

Amanda had put Mortimer down on the blanket. Now he makes a curious snuffling noise, and they realize he's fallen asleep, and is snoring. "Puppies are babies," says Amanda.

"They nap just the same." She sits beside the puppy and strokes him gently with two fingers. "Having Mortimer makes me wonder what it's like to have a little guy like Dyl." Her hand doesn't stop moving, but she does stare out to the volleyball net. "Maybe I'd run away too," she says, almost more to herself than to Abi.

Abi wants to make sure she understands Amanda. "You're talking about Dyl's mother?"

She nods slowly. Then says, "But I couldn't − I just couldn't run." She pulls the sleeping Mortimer onto her lap, upsets his sleep. "That's why," she says fiercely, holding the poor waking puppy, "that's why I will not get pregnant. I won't."

"Ever?"

She shakes her head. Again, her movements are jerky, vehement. "I don't think so, no. It's such a crappy world to bring another kid into!"

She's talking downward, to Mortimer, and Abi's glad for it; she's shaking suddenly.

"You think that?" she asks. "That the world is that bad?"

Amanda stares at her, and Abi wonders if anyone ever makes her stop and think about what she says. Finally, Amanda speaks. "Well, I know *I* don't want to make one more kid for this place." She reaches out to scratch the puppy's ears and he twitches in his sleep.

"Why don't you just let him sleep?" Abi asks.

"That's what they say, isn't it?" Amanda laughs. "Let sleeping dogs lie."

"That's not what I meant," Abi says, but Amanda's not listening. Abi doesn't like her laughter. She doesn't remember ever liking and disliking one person so many times in such a short time as this girl. She wants to grab the puppy from her arms, knock her over, and run away. Instead, she picks up the dictionary, and says, "I'm going for a walk," but when she's one log away, down the beach, she falls into a jog. Then she goes until the bunch of them – the skinny Barbie girls, Amanda, the volleyball gang – are out of sight. Here, the beach narrows, the sand is gone. It is rocks, rocks with edges and rocks rounded from tumbling, that she sits on with her feet in the water. She looks out across the water to the other side of the inlet, to where she can see expansive rooftops of homes with wide, deep windows. Of course, it's too far away to see anything in the glass, but Abi imagines what it must be to be on the other side of the window...bare feet in thick carpet, hands wrapped around a mug of real coffee, looking out to the view of the water, the city, the wooded Stanley Park, everything green and blue, and everything else blue and green. No river brown. No grey cement industrial buildings.

Abi becomes aware that she is clutching the book in her

hands so tightly that her fingers feel strained. She opens it to the letter G.

Gilgai: a hollow where rainwater collects. Hmm. Here's one: *geodesic. The shortest possible line between two points on a sphere.*

Like mapping out the flight of a plane when you're traveling the earth, Abi thinks. She looks closely at the book, and then across the water again. *The shortest line...between herself and that thick carpet between her toes.* Well, that would be directly across the water. But that's not possible. That is the nature of water: you have to go around.

"Here you are!" It's Jude, and he's not happy. His voice is angry when he crouches beside her. "I feel like an idiot, marching around the beach yelling out 'Abi!' Why didn't you come when I called?"

"I didn't hear you." She closes the dictionary. She's not going anywhere today.

Blinking in the Light

It's not as if they had much to say on the way to the downtown beach, but on the way home the silence is different. Jude pulls the steering wheel tightly and brakes too quickly. With each of those fierce tugs, Abi feels something in her tighten, and tighten again.

She has to break the silence. "That girl I borrowed the dictionary from..." Jude hadn't been too happy when Abi had to find Amanda to return it before they could go.

"Amanda," he says, his voice similar to Amanda's when she'd said "Jude."

"She doesn't seem really part of your group."

"She's not really part of any group. She just plunks herself down. Some of the guys call her 'hen.'" He laughs. "She's definitely not a chick!"

He looks sideways at Abi. "You know what I mean? She is. She's a hen. Looks out for everybody. Won't let anybody DUI – drive under the influence. Not even just a couple of beers! She'll take your keys away from you, wrestle you to the ground if necessary, with those big arms of hers! Makes sure you don't swear too much when little kids are around. Offers you books to read. The dictionary!" He laughs again. *This time at me*, Abi thinks. But it's better than the scowls and silence.

"Does she have a boyfriend?" Abi doesn't know why she asks this; maybe because of Amanda's vehemence over pregnancy.

"Who? Amanda?" His tone is enough.

"Right," Abi says, and looks out the window. "She's not a chick."

Who's a chick? Am I a chick? Is it something I want to be? Something tells Abi that Amanda just might strike a blow to anyone calling her that to her face. But "hen" wouldn't sit so well with her either.

It's talk-talk after that, chip-chipping away at the ice between them until it feels as if it should be gone. "Where's this?" she asks, as he pulls up in front of a house, an orange house with a yellow door and window frames the same. Jude looks at her blankly.

"My house," he says. He gives himself a gentle swat on the side of the head. "I'm supposed to be taking you home!" He shifts back into reverse.

Abi sees a blur of face at the wide front window, a pale smudge against the dark draperies, and then it's gone, and that bright door bursts open.

"It's Dyl!" she calls out, and Jude brakes sharply.

"Don't go!" Those little arms hammer at the door. "Don't go!"

Jude leans out the window. "Buddy," he says, "I have to."

The boy bursts into tears, and as Jude turns the engine off a woman comes to the door. "Oh, you're home," she says, relieved. She puts an arm up to the door jamb and she leans her head into her elbow: a sort of vertical hammock. She'd be pretty if she wasn't so tired looking. She begins to cough, and the coughing makes her eyes water and she swipes at them with a Kleenex. Jude puts his head farther out the window and tries to speak, but she waves her hand at him as if to say "Don't bother me – wait."

Abi pulls at the truck door handle. "I'll walk to the bus stop," she tells Jude.

His shoulders slump and he pulls the keys from the ignition. "Okay." He warns Dyl out of the way and swings open the door. "Dyl and I'll walk you."

Abi looks back at the woman in the doorway, the woman Jude has not introduced her to. The woman lifts her hand in a tired wave, and shakes her head slightly before turning away.

Something tugs at Abi. It's stupid, she knows, but she wants to do as Dyl does, and shout "Don't go!"

But Dyl starts after the woman. That is, he makes a few quick steps in her direction, then back to Jude, back to her, back and back again. It would be comical except for the look of distress on his face.

Finally he dashes to the woman, grabs her limp hand. "Danma. Boat lady."

She turns and looks at Abi. "Is that you?" she says. "Are you the girl on the river?"

Mud girl. Back again. Abi nods.

"Come," says the woman. "Please. I need you to show me how to fold a paper boat."

I need, she says.

Behind Abi now, Jude mutters, "There's always something," and he follows her into the house.

The inside is much like the outside. Bright, full of colour, crayon box colours. Forest green and orange afghans. A mash of daisies in a jug on the painted table is the only white in the room, and all that colour makes the white almost seem like a real colour. Abi always used to throw the white crayon away. All it ever did was pick up chips of real colour from the others, and if she did use it, what would appear on the paper was streaky something-or-other, but never white. Here the daisies glow with petals white-white, centres yellow-yellow, and stems green–green. She can't stop herself; she touches the petals.

Jude's mother smiles at Abi and she has the most beautiful smile. Slow and spreading. "I'm Lily Arden," she says, and puts out her hand, and even though her hand is cool and fragile, there's still a strength to it. Maybe it's just in the extra moment she holds on.

She has a collection of paper that looks like the sort flowers are wrapped in at the grocery store. "I always buy myself flowers and I always save it," she says. The paper is thick, greeny-blue, with a slick surface.

Abi begins to fold. There is no time to lose; that's the sense Lily gives. Beside Abi, she begins with a second piece of paper. Dyl stands across the table from them, and Jude waits by the door, arms crossed over his chest. Abi can feel him watching, and her hands begin to shake.

Lily pauses, and Abi knows that she has noticed her hands. Makes her shake more. Then Lily looks up at Jude, and it's hard to know what she's thinking. It's not good for a mother to look at a son like that, though, with one brow lifted and her eyes cold.

"Boats!" Dyl reminds them.

They keep on, fold for fold. There's an odd quality to Lily's motions and her silence: an urgency, and at the same time, a holding back...no, a conserving of energy. Something about her scares Abi. She follows Abi's motions and there's no need, at the end, to check if she got it.

"I need to lie down now," she says, and leaves the room. Just like that.

Dyl watches after her. "Danma sick," he says. He picks up both of the paper boats and settles himself into a wide upholstered chair as if he is going to wait for his grandmother while she sleeps.

Some part of Abi wants to sit and wait with him. Instead she says, "I'll take the bus home now." When Jude looks as if he might protest, she says: "It's not far."

"Okay." Jude follows her to the door, and pulls it closed behind him. Outside, he kisses her, a quick hard kiss, something that leaves her feeling as if she's never going to have what she wants.

Sundress

The sun is going down. Makes Abi think of being caught in the flush of a tipped-over glass of apple juice, all warm-coloured and yellow. But before the bus comes, the colour is gone and she begins to feel a little creepy out by the roadside in the murk of late summer evening.

The swing of the bus door sounds almost familiar, though she knows that can't be: one bus must be the same as the next...but yes, there's Horace.

"Abi, my girl!" He motions to the seat up front and across from him, where he can turn and talk with her when he has the chance.

"I met your friend Mary," he says.

Takes her a moment to remember who Mary is.

"I like her," he says.

Abi decides she likes that about him, that he can say it like that, straight out as a little boy would, Dyl even, and it's not until then that she realizes she thinks of Ernestine as not really having any friends, a sort of island, all on her own.

He's looking at Abi as if for a reply of some sort, but then the road calls for his attention. At the next light, he turns back to her. "You've had a bit of sun, Mary told me. Are you all right now?"

She nods.

"Though you're looking a bit red today."

She glances down at her shoulder and sure enough; she pokes at it and the spot stays white for too long.

"You've been having a busy summer," he says. "Too busy to make it to an old man's train set. I told Mary to bring you along. She said she'd see how it goes and all." The wistfulness of his tone catches her.

How it goes and all. What was it she said to Ernestine about Horace? Nothing, really. She'd turned her back on the whole subject. Abi never thought she'd be blocking the path of true love.

Horace stops the bus at the stop that is almost directly in front of her house. He says nothing about it, though; just his usual cheery wave. "Bye now, Abi!"

She should have known this about Horace – she should have known he wouldn't care where she lives. Just the same, as she steps down onto the step that causes the bus door to open, Horace peers out his window towards her house front. It's dark.

"Anybody home?" he asks, and Abi ignores the concern in his voice.

"I'll be fine," she says.

Dad hasn't turned on a light yet, and again the television is off. The silence is sweet and waiting for someone to say something.

"Dad?" begins Abi.

Has he been there all afternoon? With that coffee mug in hand?

When she turns on the overhead light, she notices a second mug, and then the cookie crumbs that dot the gold-flecked Arborite tabletop. Dad blinks in the light.

"Did you have a visitor?"

Dad looks up at her, and his eyes seem blank. It's as if, inside his head, someone's packing boxes and is moving out, taking him away bit by bit.

"Dad?" Abi asks. *Just leave one piece, just one.*

But his look is still blank, even with a vague nod, and she backs away into her room and closes the door, doesn't even bother to turn her own light on. She takes off her skirt, slips her bra off from under the T-shirt, and climbs in between the sheets.

When she closes her eyes, she tries hard not to see that man at the kitchen table. Instead she tries to wrap her mind around the moment that Jude kissed her...or the moment he said he wanted his friends to meet her...but the memory won't stay still. Strangely, all she does see is Dyl settling into that chair, waiting for his grandmother.

At last she hears Dad get up from the table and plod to his room. She hears the creak of his old metal-frame bed, then all is still. It's very dark outside the window, with that alive stillness of summer night, the gurgle of the river water.

The sun wakes her again. Again, she sees the red of the scarf on the over-turned box beside the bed. She pulls her pillow up behind her, and sits and knits. It takes a couple of rows to feel comfortable, to find a rhythm. She likes how her breathing and thoughts follow the pace. From the living room, she hears the morning strains of "O Canada." From under the house, she hears the river.

Why did my mother leave?

She puts the knitting down and pulls on shorts, leaves on the T-shirt she wore to bed.

There's a thunk at the front door, the phone books that are delivered every summer. The heavy white pages book that includes all the city listings and the slim local white and yellow. Here there are job possibilities.

She sits at the table, with a bowl of Muffets and milk between herself and the book, and flips through the pages. She sees a full-page ad for the lunch place, Mack's Coffee. It's in the Industrial Park, walking distance. Oh well. Rule out that one. There are a lot of other businesses in the Park. Maybe she should just walk there and take the résumés. Dad used to work there, at the Milwood Homes place. Abi doesn't like the idea of running into any of his old workmates. Hadn't thought of *that* when she phoned the coffee shop. Maybe it's just as well she never got to the interview. Still. There are only so many jobs around here, and if she gets something that doesn't require bus fare, it's like earning an extra half-hour's wages.

There's the recycling place, the ice arena — they probably have a concession. How about driving the Zamboni? Ha! The tire store — can't be anything there for her. All those auto places. RV rentals. She could work the desk and then, when she hears someone plotting a trip to the Maritimes, she could stow away. *Dreamin'!* Then there's all those big windowless buildings with BIG orange or red names — words like BAMCO or LIDSCON. Who knows what. Does anyone actually like working in those places? Maybe they really enjoy the lunch break at Mack's. Maybe she should go and talk to the manager, and explain to him about Jude, and having to look after Dyl. No, she couldn't; it would be just too embarrassing.

She plops her bowl and spoon in the sink, rinses them out, puts them in the dish rack. There's a paper boat caught in the wires of the rack. She pulls it out.

She crumples it into the garbage.

Dad doesn't notice Abi passing in front of his chair, going into his room, rustling through his clothes closet. There's another skirt. Denim. Almost new. Here's the white shirt. The juice stain still shows. She goes through the other clothes and finds a summer dress she doesn't remember. It'll do. It'll have to.

She takes it to her room and puts it on. Her mirror doesn't allow her to see anything below her waist, so she can't really see what the dress looks like, unless she stands on her tiptoes, close to the mirror. She's suddenly conscious of her hair, untrimmed and longer than it's ever been. She remembers how Mum always pulled it into a loose sort of ponytail, doubled up in an elastic, and she tries to do the same. It'll have to do.

She puts the résumés in the folder that the Career and Personal Planning teacher gave out, and slings the purse over her shoulder. Last: Cinnamon lipstick.

It's about twenty minutes to the Park. What a thing – to call it a Park. On her way, she passes two houses, with windows and doors boarded and development signs out front. That would be her house – if they didn't live in it. If Abi's mother had had her way, that would be their house. And where would they be? *Where would we be, Mum, if it had all been up to you? Would you have taken us with you?* The answer is obvious, but Abi doesn't want to let the word into her head.

The parking lot of the ice arena is filling with cars, and kids – mostly boys – are piling out of the vehicles, geared up for hockey. SUMMER SKILLS SCHOOL, reads the large sign over the door. The kids look about seven or eight. "You have to go," Abi overhears a mother say. "I've paid over three hundred dollars for this!"

Abi steals a look at the boy's face. His expression says "So?"

"And I have to go to work," adds the mother. She climbs back into the car. "I'll pick you up at four." She zooms off, leaving the kid at the door, hockey bag at his feet. He waits until the car is out of sight, then with his big hockey gloves he twice swipes at the ground where his stick has fallen. Abi picks it up for him.

"Thanks," he says, not looking her in the eye. Then makes a swipe at the bag. Abi picks it up, slings it over her shoulder, and opens the door for him. He lumbers in on his skate guards.

A man meets them at the opening of a hallway. "Adam!" he greets the boy. "You're with us again this year."

The boy mumbles something and grabs his bag from Abi before he clumps into a dressing room. The man turns to her. "You must be the big sister."

She shakes her head. "No. I'm just...looking for a job," she blurts out. "I was...thinking of the concession stand."

The man is moving away. "No openings there," he says. "Too many schoolgirls working there. We hardly have enough hours to go around. I believe we do need a bartender, though, up in the restaurant." He's walking off to the dressing room.

"Bartender?" she echoes.

"Leave a résumé upstairs," he calls over his shoulder as he disappears into the room. As the door closes, she glimpses red and blue uniforms.

"I'm not..."

But he's gone before she can tell him she's not old enough.

She reaches up and touches the ponytail of hair, tugs at a strap the dress. So. He thinks she's old enough to tend bar. He can't have looked very closely at her. Still. She feels a bit strange, walking back out into the warm summer day. She's never thought that she looks older than she is. No one at school has ever noticed. If so, they've never said anything. But then, when does she ever speak to them?

Abi leaves résumés at three of the windowless places.

She's passing Mack's Coffee, her head turned away from the window, when she hears her name.

"Abi Jones!" Someone has stepped out from the door of the coffee shop. Takes her a minute to recognize him: Seth MacGregor. He worked with Dad at Milwood Homes. He used to come around after Dad was laid off. Even when the others stopped. Seems to Abi he even came once after Mum left.

"It is Abi, isn't it?" He peers at her, looking somewhat mystified, nervous even, and she realizes she needs to say something.

"Yes."

Now Seth is beginning to look as if he regrets saying anything. "So. Um." He waves his thumb into the door of the coffee shop, just to let her know someone's waiting for him.

She steps back. *Go if you want.*

"How's your dad?" he asks. Because he has to.

"He's..." What can she say? "He's the same." He'll know what that means.

He nods vigorously. "Well. That's...how it is then, I guess." He gives her a funny, tired-looking smile.

"How are you?" she remembers to ask.

More nodding. "Fine, girl, fine. Took a while, but I got a position at West Coast Cedar." A happy flash of smile, then he remembers who he's talking to and he looks somewhat embarrassed and clears his throat. "Your dad will find something...when he's ready. A man of his abilities can't go too long without something."

Abilities.

"Want to join us?" he asks.

She looks in Mack's and sees half a dozen vaguely familiar faces. "I can't," she mumbles. "I'm busy at the moment."

Seth squints at her with washed-out blue eyes. "That's right," he says. "I heard you were looking for a job. Mack said a word to me...about an interview..." His voice falls away. Now he *really* has nothing to say.

"Bye," she says. One of them has to.

"See you around," he says.

So. Mack told Seth she had a job interview. She can hear him now: "Yep. She's like her old man when it comes to work."

Her face burns with shame.

She can imagine Seth saying, "At least she tries," and old Mack harrumphing at that.

Abi hurries away, tries to run from the memory pushing into her head. They'd all come over that day. Gotten their pink slips and gone to Billy's for a beer. Mum had made sandwiches. Abi remembers how Mum set the plate down with a thunk and walked out the back door, to the greenhouse, and she stayed there for hours, until long after the last of them had left, after all their EI papers had been filled out, until every last rotten anecdote of a rotten boss had been threshed out. Abi remembers Dad's voice, his strong laugh. He didn't have a rotten story – he'd just been one of the numbers sent out the door – but he knew exactly what the others were talking about.

After they'd left, there'd been silence. Was that the last time Abi had heard his laugh? That's when Dad moved into that chair. Seems he's never gotten out. The silence settled over all three of them. Even the river rumble seemed subdued – as if Abi had on those big old earmuffs, as if she'd wrapped herself in a thick wool felt blanket. Mum was on the other side of that blanket. Maybe in a blanket of her own. She always did feel a little pulled-away after that. That was the beginning.

Abi had gone down to the greenhouse as the sun was setting.

"Uncle Bernard," Mum had said, not looking at her. "He's going to be Uncle Bernard."

Uncle Bernard had lived his entire life in this house. He was sixty when he died, and left it to Dad. There was no one else to leave it to.

"Who?" Abi asked, even though she knew what Mum's answer would be.

"Your father." She peered through the floorboards, to the river. "He's going to turn into Uncle Bernard now, and I don't want to be married to Uncle Bernard," she said. That's how it had been; that was the other time Abi saw Mum cry.

"I don't remember much about Uncle Bernard," Abi had said. Mum had looked at her with sad, sad eyes.

"He was a dreamer," she said. "Always sending off letters in bottles, never going anywhere – when he did go somewhere, he was always late. He always wore these old clothes – rags, really – never bought any new clothes."

"Why?" asked Abi.

Mum shook her head. "He said new clothes were itchy. So. He just sat around this little rotting house. And then he died." Mum looked up at the blue of the back wall as she finished speaking and her eyes could've set the whole rambling shack on fire.

A giant mill truck sweeps by Abi at the side of the road, and Abi remembers how that look scared her. Maybe that look was one of the first answer-pieces Mum gave her. She really did loathe the house. It wasn't home. Nothing in it was *home*.

Abi can see the house now. She wishes she had other shoes, more comfortable for all this walking. She remembers something else now. One of few memories of Uncle Bernard. Memories of him aren't complete: they're usually just an image, or a snatch of song, the feel of a soft flannel shirt in a hug. This memory is Christmas, and mostly what Abi remembers is candles – everywhere. She's never been in a church, but since that Christmas she's been quite certain that must be what it's like. If it's not, that's what it should be like. She recalls the walls and the windows behind all those candles, the layout of the place. It was the house she lives in now.

Makes her stop for a minute, pause to look at this place she's grown up in. Really? *This* was the candle house?

She pushes the front door and the screen slams behind. Dad turns in his chair.

"Mary." He speaks in a clear voice, clear as a crystal bell, cutting as a fine-edged metal blade.

Her mother's name makes Abi go cold.

But when she looks at him, his eyes aren't on her; they're on the dress, and then she understands.

By the time she's halfway across the floor, she's pulled the elastic from her hair, and as soon as she's inside the bedroom door, the dress is off. She pulls an old sweatshirt over her head and gathers up the sundress. She leans out the window and throws the dress down into the water. She doesn't have to run to the other side of the house to watch it disappear. She knows exactly how it looks, the river pulling it, pushing at it, the cloth swaying, rushing away. She buries her head on her arms there on the windowsill, and hair spills over her face, the summer wind catching it.

She hears a sound she's never heard in all these months. If Abi thought she went cold before, now she's ice.

Her father crying. No. Sobbing. Dad sobbing.

Abi holds on to the sill until he stops and it feels safe again.

Manila Envelope

Dad is leaning over the railing, looking into the water below. He'll be there for a while, Abi knows.

She goes into his room. The window is closed even on this hot day, and the curtains hang across the window. It smells musty-warm. Abi would like to pull aside the curtains and open the windows, but she doesn't. The light blanket on the bed is rumpled on one side. The other side is perfectly smooth. How does he do that? Sleep without pulling at the blankets that used to cover Mum?

She opens the door of the narrow wardrobe that is his closet, and the hinges squeak.

He should have done this months ago, no? She reaches into the far end and gathers Mum's clothes into her arms.

Mum's not going to wear a one of them now, and they can't be doing him any good. Abi takes them into her own room, and then goes back for the bits and pieces – the wedding shoes in their box, the belt, a scarf or two. She didn't take much with her, as far as Abi can tell. That would make you think it was a spontaneous decision, but Abi knows better now.

In her room, she pushes it all into a large plastic garbage bag. Maybe Colm will take it away next time he's here, to some charity. Will Dad notice? Yes, but when? Will he care? Should she ask?

She ties the top of the bag into a solid knot. She's not going to ask; she can't stand the thought of those sobs that poured out of him last night. This has to go, that's how it is. Then she has to fight her own sobs, because the funny thing – and no, it's not funny at all – is that it's Mum who taught her how to be at moments such as this. "Tough," she'd say. "Sometimes there are things you must do...and you do them. Because you must. That's how it is." And she'd get this set to her jaw, a jaw that was square enough already.

Before Abi lost her first tooth, the thing hung in her mouth for several days. She was terrified to lose it. She couldn't sleep for two nights, or was it three? Then Mum had that look. "It has to come out." Abi can still remember the terror she felt as Mum took hold of the tooth with a towel wrapped over her fingers, and with a gentle twist it was out.

The terror turned to relief. Dad had had to leave the room. "Just let it be," he'd said. "It'll come out on its own." But when he asked if it was safe to come back in, and he saw Abi and she proudly showed him the gap, he gave her a hug. He said he was happy for her. He'd smiled at Mum. "Glad you can do that," he'd murmured. What had Mum's smile been? Somewhat superior? Sad?

There are a few of Mum's things in a bottom drawer, too. Abi checks to make sure Dad is still at his post before she goes into his room again.

Underwear, winter socks, two pairs of pajamas, and underneath, a thick manila envelope. She stops at this; she hasn't seen it before. She doesn't take it out right away, but debates.

Her mother owes her answers, she decides, and she lifts it out, carries it to her room. Still, she takes her time opening the envelope, carefully spilling the contents over her bed. Here are photographs. Surely there'll be some answer here.

She rakes her fingers over them, spreading them out, then slowly picks them up one by one. Then faster, and faster, not caring about the edges, creasing some.

Trees – old trees, gnarled trees, stumps, bleached beach logs. Dried grass in late-summer-dead fields. Sunset burning over the water. Landscapes, scapes, escapes. Not a soul in any one of them. Not a one. *This is her heart*, thinks Abi.

There's a slim envelope among the photos that causes Abi to realize she was hoping to see even one of those slim blue airmail envelopes that came from across the Atlantic once in a while. But no – just this one white regular envelope. She opens it. Finally. A human being in one of the photos. A picture of Dad, taken from behind his chair. In fine ink, the word *dreamer* is written across the bottom of the photo. Across the wall, in the background, are Uncle Bernard's and Dad's collected replies to their bottle messages. Dad's head is tilted so that he is looking at them. Sunlight streams into the window from behind the photographer – Mum. The beams catch at Dad, try to lure him.

Abi fills the envelope and pushes it under her mattress. She puts the clothing from the drawer into another bag and knots it too.

What is the answer in all this, she thinks. She can fit piece after piece together, but ultimately she is always left with the two disparate people who are her parents. The south pole and the north. The hot and cold. The apple and the orange. There is nothing to compare. There's just her mother, with her need to be on time and live in a house with a deep foundation, and her father, who'd just as soon be adrift. He's a seagull, and she's a stone garden figure – of what? Together they had Abi. And what is she?

As far as the Rockies

They're knitting, Abi and Ernestine, sitting on the old car seat out front, away from the sun at the back of the house. They have to raise their voices to speak to each other when the vehicles pass by. But it's not even mid-afternoon and the traffic is a bit less than usual.

"What do you think, Ernestine?" Abi asks her. "Do you think that if you never fall in love, then you'll never have to feel pain?"

When she looks at Abi, Ernestine's eyes are clouded, and she doesn't say anything. For the briefest of times, Abi can see her face as she'd looked that night of fireworks, at just that moment when she realized that Abi had come, but not with her. But this is something more, something that makes Abi want to back away.

"It just seems to me," Abi mumbles, "that it might be like that." Then she picks up her knitting again.

Abi doesn't tell Ernestine about Jude, coming to the door the night before, just as the sun was setting, how he'd caught her arm, gently, but not letting go. "Let's go for a walk."

"Dyl?" she'd said.

"With his grandma."

She didn't ask how the grandma was; she didn't dare. There was some part of her that wanted not to feel this disquiet, some part of her that wanted to grab his hand and run, and if pain came later...Well. Let it be. It would be worth it. But no, there it was. That word of Dad's: *Mary.* It was like the little sounds that bats emit so they can listen for echoes, and know where they are. *Mary, Mary, Mary,* there between them, her and Jude.

So when he caught her to him, just round the blackberry bushes, and pressed himself against her, she fought. She pushed him, she pulled away.

"What's the matter?" he asked.

"I'm not ready," she said.

"You're old enough."

She hated to think there was something mocking in his tone.

"It's nothing to do with age," she said, wondering what it did have to do with.

She realized how she'd been longing to curl up in his arms and just stay there. She hadn't realized it until that moment, and then she knew she couldn't. At least, not then.

As if he was reading her thoughts. "Then when?"

"I don't know." It shouldn't be this confusing.

Mary, Mary, Mary...

B ut that was last night, and now Ernestine isn't knitting with her, she realizes, at the end of the first row.

No. Ernestine is looking out to the roadway, her hands moving in her lap as if she should have needles and yarn there to occupy her fingers. "Oh, my," she says, as always, but there's a truly desperate edge to her tone.

Don't get weird on me, Ernestine. Last night, Jude, was enough... Don't.

Then Ernestine says, "Maybe this wasn't a good idea. Maybe I shouldn't be here."

Abi has poked at something in her; she's not sure what. She doesn't say a word. Last night, she pushed Jude away. She moved without thinking. Now, she sits still. Very, very still.

Even though Abi's not looking at her, she can feel Ernestine's eyes suddenly on her.

Ernestine finally says, "Do *you* want me here?"

Abi finds herself nodding dumbly, feeling pretty much like Dyl. Abi looks at her; Ernestine is pale and slow.

"Well," she says, "then I'm here. This is about you, not me. So I'm here."

When she says that though, Abi feels sad, even though she knows that's not Ernestine's intention.

Ernestine doesn't look at Abi as she speaks. "I'm not much for talking about love," she says softly. "Not much at all. Though I expect you are. Being sixteen and all."

"Seventeen...in the fall."

"Seventeen," Ernestine repeats, and then her eyes are on Abi. "I remember turning seventeen," she says, and Abi feels an odd twinge of fear as she sees Ernestine's eyes change. The clearness – the steadfastness – is not there. Instead they are flat and dull. Abi feels panic pulling at her stomach, and pushing into her lungs.

Ernestine goes on, and her voice is different: bitter. "I thought the world was going to open up when I became an adult. I thought I'd travel, find my vocation..." Her voice drifts off, then abruptly she asks, "Do you know what a vocation is?"

"A career?"

She shakes her head vigorously, and not a hair moves. "It's so much more. It comes from the Latin verb – *vocare* – to call.

It's a calling. I wanted a job that felt more than just 'good.' I wanted work that felt 'right.' When it feels 'right,' that's when it's a vocation."

Abi suddenly realizes that Ernestine's never told her where she works, and she's never asked.

"Did you do it? Did you travel? Did you find your vocation?"

She laughs, a hollow sound. "I took a bus from Princeton to Vancouver. And I have a job I like."

"Which is?"

She motions to what's in Abi's hands. "What do you think? A sewing and yarn store."

Of course. Abi doesn't need to ask if it's "right." She knows it keeps Ernestine's hands and thoughts busy.

"What else did you think?" Abi asks.

"I thought I'd find a wonderful person to share with, and we'd have a family and we'd have a house that felt like a home."

"And?" Abi persists.

"You know...I've never been even as far as the Rockies," Ernestine says.

Friday, Jude waves to Abi from the field at lunch hour, and she grabs an apple and the blanket and goes to meet him. He takes the blanket and spreads it over the grass that has finally stopped growing and is now browning in the July heat. They sit, and he opens his bag, takes out his sandwich. Swiss cheese again. "Trade you half for the apple," he says, and she does. He takes the apple from her hand. "You know," he says, "this was it."

"What?"

"What started it all. Eve gave Adam the apple, and that was it – they knew they were naked." His voice is playful, teasing.

And they knew right from wrong. That's what comes into her head, and she likes to think it's a thought that comes from Ernestine, not from herself. At least she didn't say it aloud.

"There's blackberry leaves," she says, pointing them out. "You could cover up with them."

He grimaces. "You don't really believe all that, do you?"

She shrugs. "It's an old story. Maybe there's a bit of truth to it. More likely it was Adam gave Eve the apple, and whined for her to make a pie."

To her surprise, he bursts out laughing. She can see the fillings in his upper teeth, and when he looks back at her, his eyes are bright. "I like you, Aba-with-one-b Jones. I like you muchly." The words explode from him. Then: "I'm sorry about the other night. I didn't mean to scare you."

"I know," she says, though there are other words she wants to use; she can't think what, though.

He touches her fingertips on the blanket, and her body is suddenly alive. *Is this just "good" or is it "right"?* Maybe that's the question, not "Is it right or wrong?"

Strangely, it's Jude pulling away this time. "What?" he whispers.

She shakes her head to silence him, and leans over and kisses him full, like she's never kissed anyone. She wants to hear those voices coming back to her. *Mary, Mary, Mary... Just good...or right...or just good...or right...*

She doesn't hear a damn thing, because the river suddenly roars. Wind catches the front of Jude's hair as they pull apart. He flattens it, his hand moving slowly.

They look at each other until she wants to look away, *has to* look away.

"I want to be...just us." Jude's voice is husky.

She's a piece of glass, sitting on a window edge in Mum's greenhouse, waiting, watching the water rush away underneath, knowing she's going to fall any minute. There's no direction anymore. There's only down, and then along with the river to the west. When did she decide she has no choice?

"I know," she says. It's not the same as saying what she wants, but for Jude it's enough. They gather up the lunch bag, the blanket. He takes her hand, releases it slowly as he walks away. By the time his fingertips leave hers, her entire body is trembling. She's the piece of glass, falling now, falling into the current.

She doesn't want to have eyes that are flat and dull.

Leave 'em 'til They're Crunchy Dry

Halcyon – *a period of time that was idyllically happy.* And there's a second meaning in the dictionary. *A mythical bird that breeds in a nest floating at sea at the winter solstice. Charming the wind and waves into calm.* So it's summer, and it's a river, running away to the sea. Close enough.

"**T**here's something different about you," says Ernestine. She has a forearm crossed underneath her bosom – NOT a word Abi uses regularly, but with Ernestine it *is* a bosom. *Amanda* comes to her mind. Another possessor of *bosom*.

Then Ernestine uses the back of her hand to prop up her forearm which in turn props up one side of her face. Abi has the feeling that Ernestine really does need all this propping up just to contemplate Abi's face.

It is *serene*. There is something stopped in her. She no longer feels a sense of franticness. There is something in her that usually sits up with teeth bared and ears pricked. Now...it wants to stretch lazily in the sun, roll over, go to sleep. She's moving slower.

Abi smiles at her, a smile that stretches loosely, and Ernestine looks more worried. Abi doesn't tell her that she doesn't need to: let her worry.

Ernestine holds up a bag. Is there relief in her motion? "Skeins," she says. "I need help rolling skeins into balls." She pulls thick green wool, dark and rich, from the bag, definitely winter colour.

"Here." She takes Abi's two hands and pulls them out in front of her. She untwists the skein and pops it over Abi's hands, pulls them apart to make the yarn taut. Her movements are so quick, so familiar, so thoughtless. Then she takes the end of the yarn and wraps it around her own hand and begins to form a ball. As she pulls the yarn from the skein Abi feels a tug on first one hand, then the other.

"Go with it," says Ernestine, and she tugs harder, until Abi's hands begin to swoop like swallows over a field, anticipating her smooth pull. Swoop, swoop, swoop, and they turn the five skeins to balls.

"You could start a sweater," she says as she plops them into the paper bag.

"No," Abi says. "It'd take too long."

"Then a little sweater," she says. "These five balls should just do it. I'll bring a pattern next time."

She shows Abi how to cast off the stitches of the scarf, and it feels strange, off the needle, the piece of red fabric it's become. Ernestine bundles it around Abi's neck and the sudden warmth after wearing a halter surprises her. Makes her feel she's had a chill all day.

They've been sitting out on the car seat by the front door, and now Abi slams through the screen to show Dad. She bends over in front of him, his eye level. "What do you think?"

He reaches out and touches the scarf, all that bright colour. Then he looks puzzled. "It's not Christmas," he says.

Abi laughs. "Ernestine thought it would take me forever." There's a boastful tone to her voice that she doesn't mind at all. "I made it," she adds.

He still appears puzzled. But eventually he says, "That's good. Yeah, that's good." His face smoothes with recognition. Abi has to struggle with how that makes her feel, and as she stands, she pats him on the head as if he's a little child, and has a thought: maybe she can make a big sweater instead of a little one, and he can have something to bundle up in for the winter in his chair. But no – it'll be all she can do to finish a little one. She's not even sure what makes her want to do that.

Back on the porch, Ernestine is busily casting on, starting her own project. "How's the job search coming along?"

"Not too bad," Abi says, suddenly glad she left those résumés in the block buildings with letters on them. *Which were they?*

"Do you feel you have a vocation?" Ernestine asks Abi. The wool she's using is pale yellow. On skinny needles. Funny – Abi always thinks of her as a bright yellow person.

"Not really," Abi says. Hasn't given that part of her future a thought really. All she's been thinking of is a job, and to get out. Doesn't matter what the job is.

"Because you know..." Ernestine goes on. *Click, click, with those skinny needles...* "If you don't have love in your life, it's good to have work. Work that means something to you."

Abi hopes her silence will help Ernestine to pick up on the fact that she's stunned.

Finally, Abi gets a few words out. "I thought you weren't supposed to say stuff like that anymore. I mean, aren't women supposed to be able to have everything now? That's what they always say at school."

"You sound too cynical," Ernestine says, "for sixteen."

"You started it," Abi says, "and I'm almost seventeen."

"Well." Ernestine sniffs. "We're not supposed to knit either."

"But those guys – those convicts in the South – they knit."

"So then it makes it okay for women to knit again?" The look Ernestine flashes at her is an angry one, but Abi knows she's not angry with her.

"I'm only saying that if you don't have the family you want...well, having a job you enjoy can make a difference in your life."

"Does it for you?"

Never once have Ernestine's fingers stopped moving. Now, if anything, she knits faster. "Well..." she begins. And ends.

The answer is no. Abi backs down from saying it aloud and she doesn't want to hear Ernestine make something up. Not for Abi's sake. So Abi's glad when a vehicle comes to a sudden stop by the blackberry bushes. A cloud of dust rises, and she can't see who steps out. A semi-truck's horn blows; someone's not happy about the sudden stop.

A voice calls out. "SORRY!" after the truck. As if the driver can hear! The cloud begins to settle, and someone comes their way. It's Amanda from the beach. *The hen.* "I had to track down that Jude," she begins, "to find *you*." She points to Abi, then holds out her hand to Ernestine. "I'm Amanda," she says.

Ernestine gives Abi a look of surprise. "I'm Mary Rhodes," she says. "Very pleased to meet a friend of Abi's."

"Likewise," says Amanda. She straightens her back and adds about three inches to her height. "I need you," she says, turning to Abi. "Your help. With my work. I have three houses to clean today. Got double-booked with one, and lost my partner. Can you do it?" She speaks all machine-gun fire now, her loose friendliness put aside.

Abi hesitates – she still isn't sure how she feels about this person – and Ernestine speaks up. "Don't let me stop you. Maybe this is what you've been looking for."

Abi has to laugh. *Aba Zytka's vocation has come a-calling. Somebody's taken note of my sparkly Saturday kitchen, and as it turns out, it's my Destiny.*

But at her laugh, Amanda steps back and looks through narrowed eyes. "Hmm," she says. She speaks to Ernestine. "I have a hunch Abi's a cleaning machine."

Ernestine gives a nervous, quick smile and pushes the screen door open. "See for yourself," she says.

In goes Amanda, and Ernestine pushes Abi after her. They follow burly Amanda, and Abi is relieved to see that Dad has gone to his room. With the three of them standing in the kitchen, the house feels very full.

Amanda's eyes take in everything, and she speaks. "Jude said something about you two having lunch today. I told him that that wasn't today – must be some other day." She ignores Abi's gasp.

How could she? Is she just a little crazy? Is this something Jude already knows about her?

But Amanda's quick bobbing movements make Abi curious, and the grin on her face does warm her.

"Oh, look at this faucet," Amanda says, wiping her finger around the base. She peers into the sink. "And your sink! Quite glorious!"

A titter of laughter escapes Ernestine.

"Windowsills." Amanda checks. "Corners." She peers into the corners of floor and wall. "Oh, yeah, baby!" and her tone is jubilant. "You're on!"

"I'm on what?"

"You're hired!" she shouts.

Ernestine whispers. "I think you just went through a job interview." But she does look perplexed, too.

"Mind if I whisk Abi off?" Amanda asks Ernestine.

"Seems to me," says Ernestine with a smile, "that you do whatever you need to."

"That's right." Amanda's nod is a snap of her neck, and she leads the way out of the front door, down the walk to the ancient Dodge van parked out front. Abi follows — not sure if she should be thankful or resentful — and Ernestine is close behind, thrusting yarn and needles into the knitting bag.

Abi peeks into the back window. Everything's in there.

"Yep, fully camperized," Amanda says with a grin as she opens the passenger door. "It's my mum and dad's."

"Your Mum-and-Dad's?" The phrase rolls off Abi's tongue. *Does anyone have a Mum-and-Dad? Not a mum or dad, but a Mum-and-Dad?*

"Yep." Amanda closes the door after her. Abi waves to Ernestine, who stands nearby, clutching her knitting bag to her belly. She does have a funnily round little tummy, Abi notices. Abi waves back.

"You live with your Mum-and-Dad?" she asks Amanda as she plops into the driver's seat.

"Oh, yeah. They're the best, my folks."

Funny to hear that warmth in her voice. Makes Abi feel even colder somehow.

"We've done a lot of camping in this." She motions to the back, to the miniature stove and sink, the icebox with the Mac-tac front, the nubbly plaid seat cushions with the foam showing through at the corners.

"You and your Mum-and-Dad?" Abi asks. She just wants to hear those words from her own mouth, but if her tone is different, Amanda doesn't seem to notice.

"My brother too," she adds.

Abi looks at her as she drives. She's checking her side mirror, changing lanes, all thought on the road. *Does she have any idea how lucky she is?*

She goes on. "Me and my brother drive it now. My dad doesn't want it to go over the mountains again, 'cause it'll need another tranny, and he's tired of putting a new one in every time."

Abi's thoughts are away over their own mountain. *Why, if a person had a vehicle such as this, they could live in it. Travel. Imagine hearing the highway hum under your floorboards.*

"You just shivered!" Amanda looks at her for just a moment, and she has a frown on her face. "You're not ill, are you?"

"No," Abi tells her. "No, I'm just fine, really."

Amanda looks at her, unsure. "We have a big day ahead of us."

Abi's on the borderline of feeling truly annoyed now. First, this girl comes after her for help, cancels her date, and now she seems to be ready to drive her back home.

"I'm up to it," Abi snaps, pulls herself up in the seat and looks ahead.

"Okay," says Amanda easily, and begins to slap a tune into the steering wheel.

They drive on, getting closer to the part of town where the houses are in rows, big houses with no trees between them, only fences. High fences. These houses are not on the bus route.

"So what exactly is this big day?" Abi asks.

"As I said. Three houses. Mr. Stewart's. The Ralphs'. Last, Grinsteads'. Two or more hours each," Amanda says. "Without you, it'd take me four, and I couldn't do it. I've never let a customer down." She speaks this last quite fiercely as she pulls up in front of an enormous mint stucco house. The front yard is jam-packed with oddly cut bushes and cement figurines, and not one, but two fountains.

"Is the inside as cluttered as the outside?" Abi asks.

Amanda grins. "And they say you can't tell a book by its cover!" She laughs and swings out her door. Abi follows and Amanda pulls open the side door. "Take this." She hands Abi a large bucket filled with cleaning products and rags, sponges and rubber gloves, and an odd plastic and metal contraption. Abi isn't at all sure what it is, but Amanda must see her questioning look.

"That's my robot arm. It's supposed to be a kid's toy, from the toy-store." She picks it up and demonstrates how the lever on one end works to move the robotic "fingers" on the other. "You'll see what *this* is for!" She plunks it back into Abi's bucket, then grabs a mop in one hand and hefts the old Filter Queen vacuum easily to the door. "Let me know if I work you too hard!" She grins. "I think I did poor old Brad in."

"Brad?"

"Yup. He was my right-hand guy until this morning."

"What happened?"

"I don't know. He didn't show. I waited half an hour, then I couldn't wait anymore."

She seems so cut and dried. But maybe not. She adds, "I'll talk with him tonight."

"So I'm just filling in?" Abi asks, suddenly realizing that somewhere in the back of her mind she'd been adding up hours and dollar figures.

Amanda looks keenly at her. "For now." She's opened the door and pushed through the scraggly potted plants to the kitchen. "You might not even like the work," she says.

Does it matter? "I'm not looking for a vocation."

Amanda turns to her at that word. "I thought vocations come looking for *you*," she says.

"Is that how it works?"

"I've heard."

"This isn't yours, then?"

Amanda looks thoughtful, and she pauses in the doorway. "I don't think so," she says.

Abi follows her and she points to several boxes on the table.

"This place is the worst." She says it quite cheerfully, though. "Mr. Stewart leaves stuff everywhere, and before we can even clean, we've got to go round and pick up all the junk, put it in a box. We leave the box in the room so he can put it wherever it does belong." She lowers her voice as if someone – Mr. Stewart – might hear her. "I don't think he ever does put it back." She points to a stack of books on a chair. "I'm positive that pile was on that other chair last time

I was here. That vase with dead flowers in it was in the middle of the table with different dead flowers and very smelly water..." She pauses to sniff at the vase, half an arm's length away from herself. "Yep. Smells like the same water to me!" With a quick movement, the flowers are in the garbage, and she's poured the offending water down the drain.

"And oh, yes! There's the note. I save Mr. Stewart's notes." She reads aloud.

Dear Ms. Blake, I must ask you again – DO NOT THROW AWAY the flowers here on the table. I'm trying to come up with a dried flower arrangement to have on a permanent basis, and every time my flowers reach a perfect point, VOILA! you throw them away, and I must begin again!

Amanda sniffs and pulls the sheet of paper carefully from the notepad, folds it, puts it in her pocket, and begins to write on the next piece.

Dear Mr. Stewart,
Recipe for Dried Flowers:
Cut 'em in the thick of all their Bloomin'
And Hang 'em by their Toes
Leave 'em 'til they're Crunchy Dry
And we'll have No More of these Woes.

Abi peers around her to read the words. "How'd you come up with *that*?"

"Oh, I don't know," Amanda says airily. "Mr. S seems to bring it out of me." She reaches into Abi's bucket and pulls out the robot arm.

"Now you're going to show me what that's for," Abi says.

"Come this way," says Amanda, starting down the hall. "We're going to find his socks. There are always a few in the bathroom corners, gathering up the spiders' webs for me."

Abi follows, armed with the toilet brush, and they make a parade, like two kids, Amanda with a swagger. Abi can't imagine doing that with anyone else in her life, and when Amanda reaches the bathroom and opens the door with a flourish and motions Abi in, Abi can't help but give her a grin, which Amanda returns. "Make sure you never tell anybody how much fun we have doing this!" she says.

Amanda sets a big jug of vinegar on the toilet lid. "Mr. S actually likes that we don't use all those poisonous cleaners."

"Okay," is all Abi can say. So maybe she does know how to shine a kitchen, but she does have much to learn.

"I have to argue about it with some of the customers..." She breaks off. "See? Look at this!" She reaches with the robot arm behind the door, and comes up with at least five socks, dust all over them. And long hairs.

"Oh yuck!" says Amanda, but there's almost a happy tone, as if she really does enjoy her work.

"What's with the long hair?" Abi asks. "I thought you said he lives alone."

"He does," says Amanda. "He has a ponytail. There's long hair all over the house. Must be balding. He sheds like a dog." She releases the lever on the "arm" and the motley socks drop into the hamper in the hallway – overflowing with clothes – then begins to work on the bathtub.

Abi finishes the toilet and sink; Amanda does the floor.

She begins to hum a tune as she works. Together they move into the bedroom. Feels a little weird, cleaning some guy's bedroom. But Amanda's all business. Picks up the book he's reading from where it was dropped to the floor, its covers splayed. She finds a bookmark, marks Mr. S's page, and sets it on the bedside table.

"Must read himself to sleep," she comments, and hands Abi a bottle marked "glass cleaner" for the mirrors. Smells a lot like lemon.

Dad used to read in bed, before he started to fall asleep with the TV. When did the reading stop? She can't remember, and scrubs extra hard at the mirror.

Amanda's humming is drowned out by the vacuum cleaner, but Abi can see her lips moving, so she's singing now.

Abi dusts, and they move down the hallway, the vacuum in Amanda's wake.

The next house, the Ralphs', is spotless.

"Why are we here?"

Amanda shrugs. "Dusting, vacuuming, you know."

"Does anyone actually live here?"

"Mr. and Mrs. and two kids, a boy and a girl. If you look at their picture over there on the mantel, they look like a laundry detergent ad. You'd never know they *live* here." Amanda's voice has the same tone as at the beach when she asked what was Abi doing hanging out with Jude. Must be the tone she reserves for people she doesn't think much of. Abi would like to ask her about Jude – why does she call him *that Jude* for instance? – but something stops her.

In this house, there are no reasons for Amanda's toy-store robot arm.

It's surprising to Abi how much there is to do, really. Different things. Vacuum the furnace area. Pick up the ornaments to dust. Lots of framed photographs. Sort the Tupperware. Mrs. Ralph has left a list with items checked off. The list is a computer printout. Amanda checks the list frequently and crosses off each item as they do it. She doesn't hum at this house.

At Grinsteads', she begins to again. Mr. Grinstead cooks for the family, and he's left a note that tells them to finish off the Chinese takeout in the fridge, and to try the English trifle he's made. Abi's never tasted trifle — a mix of cake and whipped cream and fruit and custard. She'd like to make something that makes somebody feel this good.

Amanda stretches out for five minutes after they eat. Then she's up, the food like fuel, and they fly through the house with a rhythm, as if they are the left arm and the right arm of the same body.

"We're a regular team," Amanda says, as they climb into the van when the day's come to an end. She reaches under the seat to where she's stowed her bag, and she finds a cheque book, writes in it, makes a notation.

She hands Abi a cheque for sixty-five dollars. "You have an account to put that in?"

"No, but I'll get one." Abi stares at the paper in her hand before she folds it and tucks it in her pocket. She looks over at Amanda, and sees that she's grinning again. Abi grins back and suddenly it hits her that every muscle in her body is screaming bloody murder. It even hurts to relax her mouth as the grin collapses.

But Amanda's just gets bigger. "Hard work, isn't it?"

"Yep," Abi manages, and that's it until they near the house on the river.

As they park, Abi sees a figure rise from the field and come through the blackberries toward them. *Jude.*

"Better go!" Amanda's tone is tight. Doesn't seem as if it comes from a person who hums.

"What was that tune you were humming?"

She looks surprised, and has to think for a minute. "You know – I think it's a Christmas song," she says sheepishly. "*Il est né le divin enfant.*"

"Which means?"

"Something about the divine infant."

"It's July!"

Still sheepish, she says, "Christmas is an all-year thing, no?"

They laugh, and when Abi turns back to the house, the suddenness of Jude's face in the window startles her. He seems bigger somehow. Abi wants her laughter to move away this silly thought, but he smiles, and that does it. Back to size. She suddenly realizes she's been holding her breath, and breathes again.

He opens the door. "Here you are," he says, "the Housekeeper from Hell!"

Abi wonders which of them he's speaking of.

Amanda's voice is clear. "How long did it take you to come up with that?" she snaps. "All afternoon?"

"Pretty much," he says smoothly. "Since *lunchtime*," he emphasizes.

So he was upset Abi missed lunch.

Amanda speaks. "I thought your girlfriend was looking for a job."

Abi can hear the anger burbling under her words.

The two of them face each other as if Abi's not even there between them, and suddenly she's angry with both of them. She pushes past Jude and stumbles into the screen door.

"Abi!" She hears behind her.

"Bugger off!" she hollers. "Both of you!"

Jude says something to Amanda, but Abi doesn't even care to know what. She finds the way to her room, and closes the door. Her aching muscles won't even let her lie down in a normal way. She's a tent, and someone's yanked a peg out of the ground. She collapses onto the bed.

No one follows her, though she hears a mumble of voices for a while before all is still.

Halcyon days are over.

Cow's Belly

I.

The letter I is next. The first entry in the I section is, of course, I.

Me. Back to where I started, is what that feels like. See? It is dumb, this idea that having a vocabulary will take you somewhere. It's still me — I — in this bed, with the river mud churgling away beneath me. If I disappeared, even then there'd still be the river mud. Churgling: the pamphlet didn't say anything about where made-up words will take me.

Last night, Abi fell asleep with her clothes on, and her teeth feel horrible. Now before she goes to brush them, she reaches into her pocket for the slip of paper. Seems like a dream, though her muscles tell her it really happened. The sixty-five dollars on the cheque is real, and so is the scrawl that says "Amanda Blake."

Abi's never had a bank account. Today that'll change. She puts the paper into the old purse, and then goes to brush and scrub the grime. She's finished the bath and wrapped herself in Mum's ugly old terry housecoat when she hears the voices, the screen door slam.

"Will!" It's Colm. Must be food bank day.

"Where do you want this box, Gramps?"

Oh no. That'll be Fiona. Abi can picture her out there, standing in the kitchen, in the middle of the room, as far as she can be from the possibility of anything actually touching her. Abi has noticed that in her home Fiona does everything with long arms. She sets a box down, leaning over. She doesn't want so much as her skirt to brush the cupboard, the door with the paint all chipping off. Doesn't matter how clean it is. There are patches of paint completely missing and it looks horrible. Then there's the counter that Abi scrubs. There'd be no explaining to Fiona that every mark on it will not come off – Abi has tried. Whatever those stains are, they've been there since the time of Uncle Bernard, Abi is sure, and they'll be there until the whole thing floats away. Same goes for the ancient table. But there's no telling Fiona that, no way. Abi wonders what Colm gives her to convince her to do this? It's got to be something; there's no other way she'd do it.

"I got a little something for you," says Colm, "something a little more mind-bending than checkers." Abi hears his sandals on the walkway outside, with Fiona's following.

Abi peeks out the bathroom door to see if all's clear, and scoots to her room.

"We're not staying, are we?" Fiona's voice, peeved. Abi can hear her from outside and she feels a flush of embarrassment. Then anger. She pulls on some clothes and opens the door a crack. What *does* Fiona do this for? Does she *like* making people feel ashamed?

Colm answers her, but Abi can't hear his words in the screech of the front screen door.

"Doesn't anybody oil this thing?" Fiona holds the door for herself and looks at the offending spring hinges. She slowly closes the door and it obeys her with not so much as a sigh.

Again she takes up her position, standing behind her grandfather as he pulls out a chair and reaches into the bag he's brought. Dad gets up slowly – God, he moves like an old man – makes Abi's throat go all tight, makes her want to kick him – and he sits down opposite Colm at the table. He looks a bit nervous, Dad does, but he almost smiles. Or something like a smile.

It's chess. Abi can see the set between them, a child's set, with bright green and pink plastic playing pieces. Colm shows Dad where he mended a piece, and Dad looks closely. "Hardly shows. Like new. Got it at the Hospital Thrift Shop. I've been watching for one of these. Waiting. They don't come up often."

Fiona snorts when he says "thrift shop," and as he begins to explain the various moves of the pieces, she goes back outside, not caring at all about the door. The slam seems even louder than usual to Abi. Abi moves out into the room, and through the front window she can see Fiona, looking back at the house, hands on her hips. Then she turns away, slinks to her grandpa's car and leans on the fender, checking her nails.

Colm is talking about the knight's move. "Two spaces in one direction, then one in another. They're the only piece that can pass over others."

Dad's nodding, nodding. He seems to be getting something out of all this. He's found his glasses and put them on. Those glasses always age him in a comfortable way – a way Abi is used to. Her earlier anger fades.

Colm goes on. "The bishop moves diagonally. The rook –" he holds it up – "in straight lines."

She'll wait until they're gone to sort through the groceries and put them away, but he sees her.

"There's milk there, Aba – it'll be wanting the fridge for sure." There's a formality to Colm; he always calls her Aba. Maybe someday she'll ask him to call her Abi, but in the meantime, she likes how he says "Aba." She appreciates how he can bring food to their home, food she thinks of as a "handout," but she has the feeling that's not how Colm sees it.

But then there's Fiona, and Abi's next thought is how it's amazing that manners and kindness can come and go with just a generation or two.

There's a sound from Dad, and she looks at him. "Could you make some...coffee, please?" he asks. He looks at her through the black rims, and she feels as if it's the first time in too long that he can actually see her.

"Of course," she says, hoping the quickened beating of her heart isn't too obvious. She can't help but stand there and stare at him for a moment before putting on the kettle. *Coffee. He asked for coffee.* She puts spoonfuls of instant in a couple of mugs, pulls down an extra for herself. Celebrate! Then goes back to putting the milk in the fridge, and a tub of margarine.

She wonders if Colm doesn't add a few things to the boxes. Probably does it in such a way that Fiona wouldn't know. Can imagine her yelling at him – why would he do such a thing?

When Abi looks out the window again, there she is, in the car, smoking a cigarette, blowing smoke rings through the open window, moving her head in time to the music. She turns quickly and sees Abi watching and a small smile comes to her face. Abi moves away from the window, wishing she hadn't been spotted, and moments later there's the slam of the car door, and Fiona is in the doorway, hand on hip, and looking even more impatient than before. She watches her grandfather and Dad, a sneer on her face.

"So," she says. Her voice is low, but Abi knows she's talking to her. "You know Stu Stevenson?"

Abi has to think for a moment. Stu – he's in English class too. The guy with the bleached-out yellow hair and the shy smile.

"Well, do you?"

Abi nods, unsure of what to expect from Fiona.

"I've seen him looking at you in class," she goes on. "I think he likes you."

Abi is quite certain that no matter what she says, Fiona is quite capable of turning her words into something she never intended. So she says nothing.

"He's a loser," says Fiona. "But even you probably know that already. Do you know he lives in a foster home? And he's lived in more than you can count. I don't think anybody wants him." The way Fiona moves her eyes around the kitchen and the living room cause Abi to think that Fiona feels the same way about her.

Abi tries to put together what she knows about Stu. Stu struggles, that's what she remembers most. He does exams with the principal because he needs twice the allotted time. Now Abi remembers the word dyslexic. And he always chews his nails when Mr. T, English teacher, asks questions. Except Mr. T never asks Stu, so he doesn't need to go without those nails.

"How do you know that? About the foster homes?" is all Abi can think of to say to Fiona.

Fiona's eyes rest on her now. "Everybody knows that," says Fiona.

"Not everybody," says Abi. "Only the people who have nothing better to do than to stick their nose into other people's homes." She's surprised even herself.

Fiona turns to her grandfather. "When are we getting out of here?" And she stands, glaring at him as he goes on with his chess move and explains some other part of the game. He waits for Dad, who takes a hand from his temples to move a pawn.

Fiona huffs and puffs. *Won't take much to blow this house down.* Abi likes how Colm ignores her, even as she edges toward the door.

Another huff.

Colm moves a knight, one, two, three.

And a puff.

"Okay, girl," he says grudgingly. "You can hitch up the horses."

Fiona flounces off back to the car, and Colm looks up from the table to meet Abi's eyes. "Don't listen to her, and don't be taking any of her words to heart. I like that young man, Stu. He lives near our house." He stands and rests a hand on Dad's shoulder. "I'll be seeing you, Will. Practice with Aba." He nods at her, his eyes entrusting her with something, though she's not sure exactly what.

She waits until they're gone to open the cupboard door. Dad moves another pawn, and sits waiting. He takes off the glasses and massages the bridge of his nose, rubs at his eyes.

"He's gone, Dad," she says. *Please, please, put those glasses back on.*

"Oh, I know," he answers easily, sliding the glasses back into place. "I'll be ready for him next time."

Abi warms up his coffee, pours in more fresh whole milk. Dad smiles at her, as close to a real full smile as she's seen in too long. As they drink, she sees his eyes sliding to the side of the table where he's pushed the chessboard.

"Are you trying to figure out what move Colm is going to make next?" she asks, and something in her feels like a wriggling puppy, so happy his mind has a crack, an opening.

He nods, sipping. "He's going to do something with that knight." His hand hovers over the little green horse head. "Then I could move my bishop here...like this, see?"

She sees a light in Dad's eye and hears something in his voice that she hasn't heard for a long time. Something is awakening in him.

The screen door swings open behind her. Dad raises his head to look. Abi sees a flash of his awake eyes. Then:

"You!" he exclaims. "Holy Mother of God – it's..." And he stops, as if he can't say the name. "You," he says again.

Abi goes cold.

Ernestine stands in the doorway, her face the colour of tripe.

Mum used to boil up a piece of tripe now and then. Cow's belly. The colour of grubs. She always ate it alone. This is the thought that passes through Abi's head when she sees Ernestine's face. The colour of tripe.

Ghosts

Dad walks around the table with a hand placed on the Arborite. Then he gets close to Ernestine. *Close*, standing right in front of her as if he doesn't believe she's there. One of those "touch it and it'll disappear" things. She looks him squarely in the eyes, but Abi can see she's shaking as if a winter's gust followed her through the door. With those heels, she's not much shorter than he is.

Suddenly, Dad shakes his head. Hard. And he turns back, this time to his chair in the living room and pulls his glasses off as he sinks into it. Looks out toward the river, through the back window. Abi watches him like that for long seconds, until she realizes she's waiting for him to turn around, until she realizes he's not going to. When she turns to Ernestine, she's not moved – just a horrible look has come over her face, sort of twisted and indescribably sad.

"I'd better go," she says in a whisper. "Oh, I'm so sorry."

She leaves, before Abi's numbed mind can think of anything to say, and after she's gone, there's a deadness to the house, with Dad sunken in his chair, TV still off, and Abi with this feeling that she'll never see Ernestine again. Maybe never see Jude again after yesterday. Or Amanda. Back to being just her and Dad. *Me. I.*

She moves that stupid knight of Colm's. Maybe he'll never come back either. That would make Fiona happy! Oh yeah, it would.

Can't say how long she sits at the table. Abi finds she's watching Dad, waiting for him to move, waiting for that light in him to come back. It hadn't been only in his eyes; it had been in his movements, too, in the crinkle of his lip in a half-smile. Made her remember that he used to be even funny sometimes. Now it's darkness and stillness.

She remembers talking with Ernestine about falling in love, and about the pain of it…those odd words of hers: "*Maybe this wasn't such a good idea…maybe I shouldn't be here…*" Those words had something to do with this; there was something between Ernestine and Dad.

So why had Ernestine – no, *Mary* – shown up that first day on the wharf? All that Big Sister talk…it was all *rubbish*, as Mum used to say.

Abi feels a sudden thrust of yearning to hear that word again. *Rubbish...*and you could still hear the touch of accent Mum had worked to erase.

Images come to Abi now: Ernestine's face all twisted over Dad, deaf in his chair that day, or all anxious as he leaned over the river. So *why* had she come along? Why?

Adults did just whatever they wanted to do. They acted as if they cared, but there was always something else going on – something they thought you were too young to hear or you wouldn't understand.

Abi understood all right. Or enough for now. Enough to know that she didn't really matter. Everyone thought she was old enough to care for herself – and she was. But you could be old enough, and you could still *matter*, too.

When Abi stands, her chair falls away behind, and she jumps at the crash. She didn't know that her push had so much force. Somehow it makes her even angrier, and makes her feel better too. Angrier and better.

She throws things into that old purse and SLAMS the door. She doesn't bother peeking in the window; she knows he hasn't moved. She doesn't slow until she reaches the bus stop.

The bus arrives, and the driver isn't Horace, and she realizes some part of her was hoping to see him. For what? Some reassurance that there is one adult in her life who is truly grown-up. No. *Mary. Mary, Mary, quite contrary, what's up with you, Mary???*

"Where's Horace?" Abi blurts out. It scares her how her own voice sounds all bleating like that.

And even more so, when she hears the calmness of the driver.

"Horace just started his four-week vacation," he says evenly, pointing out to Abi that she hasn't yet taken her transfer.

Four weeks!?

She takes a seat toward the back, and leaves the transfer in the dispenser. It bugs her that she feels alone like this. As if she could stand on the bus and shout, scream at people, then pass out, smash her head on the metal tubing that passes over the backs of the seats...and nobody'd care. Somebody – eventually – would drag her off through the back door. No, she knows it wouldn't be like that, not really. The driver would have to rush back, people would hover over her, someone would punch nine-one-one into their cellphone, but the only reason any of them would do it is because, if they didn't, somebody would sue them. Who? Dad?

Abi doesn't realize she's snorted out loud until the thirty-something guy next to her turns to stare.

"Something funny?" he asks, and his voice isn't sarcastic. He actually looks as if he'd like to know what's funny enough to make her laugh out loud.

"Not really," she says, but wishes there was something to share with him. Even if she could just tell him he makes her hopeful.

He splits a half-grin before he goes back to looking out the window.

"It's an ugly river, isn't it?" Abi says.

"The river's the river," he says. "People have built ugly things around it." He doesn't turn around again.

She thinks of her dad painting the back of the house, the river side, that blast of blue. *Nothing can make this house pretty*, Mum said.

The bus turns onto the brief stretch of highway, and then into town, and she pulls the bell when they hit the first string of stores and a bank. She doesn't stop at the first bank, though. She has to walk to the next. Only then is her breathing regular, and she thinks maybe she can get the right words out. *Sometimes you need to do things – even difficult things.* She can hear Mum's voice.

She lays her identification out on the high counter and the woman behind it shows Abi how to fill out the forms. "A chequing account?" she asks.

It's going to cost her almost fifteen dollars for the cheques, but Abi wants them. She likes cheques, she's decided. She wants the plain green-striped ones that look businesslike. No, she doesn't want an address or phone number on them. She doesn't want to live there, but she doesn't tell the woman that.

"Do you like your job?" Abi asks her.

The woman looks up at Abi from the forms she's filling out, and she pauses before answering as if it's a question she's not thought about in a long time.

"Good benefits," she says.

"Benefits?"

"You know – medical, dental, insurance, pension plan, vacation. I'm up to four weeks paid vacation now," she says, pointing out where Abi's to sign. "I go to my folks' cabin for almost a month and lie in the sun."

"They pay you to do that?"

She smiles. "Pretty soon I'll have so much maternity leave coming to me that I think maybe I will have a baby after all!"

Abi doesn't know what to say to that. Nothing is probably best.

"Do you want a passbook or would you like a monthly statement sent to your home?"

"A passbook, please."

She fills in a little book, puts it into the computer, which spits numbers onto the first page, and hands it to Abi. "That's it."

She looks at it. There's the sixty-five dollars, the fifteen eighty-nine for cheques, and the forty-nine eleven that's all hers.

Outside, the hot wind hits as she walks to the corner, the corner of Trunk and Fifth. She realizes she's not far from Horace's.

After about ten minutes, the corner is too hot, and she crosses the street...just as the bus sweeps down the road and she misses it. Abi doesn't want to go home yet. She crosses again to the shady side and in not much time she's at his corner. Must be the house with the hedge. She has to walk around and around again before she can find the gate. Then she wonders how she missed it. There's a hand-carved sign that reads "Ladner Junction," and even as she pulls on the latch string she can hear a low toot-toot and the sound of wheels. There are also a lot of birds, she realizes, especially for this time of day and the heat. The number of birds might have to do with the number of feeders in the shade.

She's a giant here, and the birds are huge beasts. It is a land of miniature. The pond, with giant fish, is a lake with a bridge running over it, an old-looking trestle structure, and then she sees the train coming out from a tunnel, a tunnel she hasn't even noticed, built as it is into a mountainside, all mossy.

After she checks to make sure no one is actually around, she bends down to look inside. The tunnel is long and dark. When she looks, she knows exactly how it feels to be a train passenger going through. But the train has gone on and it is out of sight in a grove of trees, both giant and miniature. The miniature trees — are they what is called "bonsai"? Those Japanese miniature trees? Abi thinks they're pine, and they're gnarled and in perfect proportion. Again, she has to kneel. By then the train has gone on. She follows it to where it pauses at a station, red brick and all the doodads you'd expect at a station. Behind it is a string of houses, all bright colours, and she has to scrooch down to look closely at the tiny front porches and in the front windows. There's a swing with two children sitting on it. She gives it a gentle push and sets them in motion.

She hears a chuckle and turns. "Their names are Fred and Wanda," Horace says, and it takes Abi a moment to realize he's talking about the children in the swing.

"Will you join me for a cup of tea?"

She nods and rises to her feet and follows him as he steps with care through "Ladner Junction."

"I've been expecting Mary for the past hour or so," he says. "It's not like her to be late."

Is there a question mark in his words? When he turns to look at Abi, can he see in her face that she might have an answer for him?

"No, it's not like her," she mumbles. "What kind of tree is this?" She points to one of the miniatures.

He pauses as if her question has stumped him. Then: "Why a Japanese black pine, of course."

It's kind of flattering really, that he'd expect her to know.

He has one of the heritage homes left in town. It's painted a deep red, and there's a lot of wide, cream-coloured trim around the windows, the doors, the gables and porch. Deep window boxes are filled with geraniums. If Abi breathes deeply, she can smell their cinnamon fragrance.

"I grew up in this house," Horace says. "Come – I'll show you." He crosses the wide painted planks that make up the porch, and goes in through the front door.

Inside, the walls are all cream, except for the beautiful panels and mouldings – wainscotting, Horace calls it, again speaking as if that would be something she knows. The furniture is all as old as the house, and as loved. Upholstered in brocade – now, there's a word she does know, thinks Abi, and at last she can attach it to something! The rugs on the hardwood floor are all in many colours and intricate design.

"The back porch is where the sun is this time of day." Horace leads the way to the kitchen, and Abi stops in the doorway. The room is huge. Counters run around three of the walls. The windows are tall with the high ceiling, and around the table are more chairs than she can count in a quick glance. She has a sudden image in her head, and the question is out before she can stop it. "Do you eat all by yourself at this table?"

Horace gives her a long look. Then he nods. "But I have happy memories and good ghosts. I used to sit at this table with my brother and sister." He sets an enormous kettle on the old gas stove. "This was a farmhouse. Still is, except now the farm's gone." He laughs at his bit of a joke. Then he assembles tea things: a tray, honey pot, creamer, a plate of cookies and crackers, three thick pottery mugs.

"Mary will know we're in the back." He leads the way out the door, which has been standing open, letting the bright July sunshine pour onto the old floor. Even as one part of Abi recognizes a certain wistfulness in Horace's voice, another part of her suddenly sees the cracks in the ancient linoleum.

"Does Ernestine...I mean, Mary...come here often?" Abi asks.

He sets the tray down. He doesn't answer the question until he sits and looks at Abi. "Sometimes I just don't know what to do with Mary. She makes me feel like a little boy, and I want some other little boy in the class to go over to her and tell her that I like her..." He breaks off, smiling. "Does that still happen in schoolyards, I wonder." He goes on without an answer. "Then other times she makes me feel that I'm an old, old man." He stops again. "You can't possibly know what I mean, can you?"

Abi doesn't want to tell him that the only thing she does know is that this morning she saw a look on Ernestine's face like she's never seen on anybody's face before, and she doesn't know why that look was there.

Finally he answers her question. "Yes, she comes over often. She stays and stays. Then all of a sudden, she'll leap up, looking as if a gremlin's whispered in her ear, and within half-seconds, she'll have her sweater on and her bag gathered up and she's gone. Once, she was gone so fast she left the door open behind her. And she runs, she almost runs away." He's shaking his head at the end of his words. "Now today, she doesn't come at all."

"Maybe something came up," Abi says, her voice low.

"Maybe," he says, swirling the tea in his mug, looking down his nose.

Glum, thinks Abi. Horace looks glum. She resists her own sudden urge to leave. Instead she refills her mug, squirts in too much honey. There's never honey in the food box.

Horace notices her fondness for honey. "It's good on these chunky crackers too," he says, handing her a thick Norwegian-style cracker. That quick his glumness disappears.

When the crackers are gone, and the cookies, and the tea that is still in the pot is cold, Horace disappears around a corner for a moment and then returns. "Watch this," and from the far side of the house Abi hears a *whoo-whoo* whistle, an echo of the real thing, and along comes the train, smoke pouring from its funnel.

Abi can't help it: a little rush passes through her, something magical. She feels a bit silly about it, but when she looks at Horace — and he is staring intently at the little engine, a smile on his face — she doesn't feel silly at all. Obviously, he feels the same way, and he's probably seen this hundreds of times. He is definitely less obsolete than some adults she knows.

"You're smiling!" says Horace.

"Something Er...Mary said to me once."

"Yes." He nods. "She has a way of warming your soul. Not just with those knitted beasts she's forever working on, either!"

"Beasts?"

"Beasts, yes. Those scarves and sweaters, they take on a life of their own, as far as I'm concerned. Frankly, I think she's a bit obsessed."

Abi motions to the train running around his yard. "And you're not?"

"Me?" He feigns shock. "Not me!"

The train — engine, passenger cars, and caboose — chugs by and heads off into another tunnel. Abi realizes she's been sitting on the porch and hasn't even seen the valley with its bakery, library, and string of houses. She stands, moves closer, and up over the small rise of land she can see that one house actually has a clothesline with tiny garments and a string of cloth diapers on it. "Reminds me of my mum's," says Horace.

"Does the train go all the way around your house?"

"All the way." Horace is proud of his train, Abi can tell. They wander around the yard, and Horace points out other houses, and a barn set in the midst of an "orchard."

"See?" Abi says. "The farm *is* still here."

Horace laughs, and Abi hopes that, at least for now, just this moment, he doesn't miss Ernestine quite as much as he did earlier. She watches for his train to come around again. She's heard it go round, the sound growing fainter, fainter, then growing clear, clearer. She gets down on her knees, and wonders: *How many people have waited at a train station for someone, not sure if they're ever going to show up?* What would it be like to count on someone? To *know* you can count on them?

She looks over at Horace, watching for his train to appear from under the hedge, and the lump that's in her throat is so big it hurts, makes her eyes water.

The sun has that waning summer afternoon feel, when the heat is gathered and still. "I should go," she says to him.

"I'll drive you home," Horace says.

For a minute, she thinks to say "no," then she remembers that he does know where she lives. So she says "thanks" instead.

He drops her off close to the front door, even though she can hear his Honda being scraped by the blackberries. "I'm glad you came to see my garden train," he says. "Come again soon."

"I will."

He waits until she goes inside, and she waves from the window as he pulls away.

Dad's exactly where she left him, asleep. Abi makes herself a sandwich, and a second, which she leaves on the table beside him. She places the bishop from the chess game beside the sandwich. *Tell me something about Ernestine. Give me one more piece of the Mum-puzzle. You're up, Dad. Make a move.*

Forgiven

Thursday is a prison.

No Jude in the field.

No Mary. Or even Ernestine.

No Amanda.

Abi works on the sweater. She'd like to have a little chat with Ernestine right about now. Knitting might keep your hands busy, but it doesn't do anything to free Abi's mind. With one row, she feels anger. With the next row, confusion... Maybe if she knits to the point at which she needs help, Ernestine will show up. That's something Ernestine would do, Abi thinks. So she knits the back and front of the sweater, all the way to the armpits, to where the pattern says to cast off two stitches, then two more with each row. As she knits, she tells herself stories. Or at least, words come and go in her mind. Like the tide, she thinks.

What do I know about Ernestine? She needs to do something with her hair. And there's something in her, something that hurts, something she hangs on to, won't let go of, something that scares me. But not as much — no way as much! — as it scares Ernestine herself!

And what, what do I know about Dad? What did I used to know about him before he sat in his chair?

She knits through an entire row before a picture comes to her. A picture of Dad in his boat. *His boat? What happened to his boat?*

She stops the rhythm of her needles. She'd forgotten about his boat. He must have sold it when he lost his job. How is it she knows nothing about the sale? Dad loved that boat. He used to spend Saturday fixing it. It was kept down at the marina, in a berth. *I'll check next time I'm in town.* But she knows it won't be there, and the thought of that empty berth makes her begin to knit again.

Then there's Mum.

Abi's mind suddenly blanks, and in the silence, she can hear the water under the house. The tide is high. Dad hasn't turned on the TV — funny it's even off — but there's the water, moving away, away. Always rushing away. Always never changing. She always thought Mum hated it. Now Abi wonders if Mum was afraid of it. How it always changed and how it always stayed the same. Why did Mum marry Dad if what she really wanted was for him to change? Doesn't seem right, really – wanting that about somebody.

She wonders if Ernestine has called Horace. Why would she run away from Abi's house, and then not show up at Horace's? What could be so wrong?

Abi casts off two stitches, hoping she's doing it properly, knits through, casts off two more, knits to the end, and throws the whole thing down.

What is it that goes wrong between people? Why did she feel so angry with Amanda and Jude?

Jude. How is it that one minute she's feeling all roiled over him, and the next minute she wants him gone. Only she doesn't really. She just wanted Amanda and he not to fight, not to push and pull at her like that. She couldn't stand that sense of being in the middle and at the same time so just not *there* – others looking out for her – but not really.

So Jude. What does she know about him?

The water passes under the house. Abi hears it between her thoughts, and she hears in it a mocking tone. *Sor-ry, sor-ry,* it says. Yes, she needs to say that to Jude. *Sorry I let Amanda tell you I wouldn't meet with you for lunch. Sorry I told you to leave.*

That's right, that's right, says the river.

SHUT UP, Abi says, but her voice doesn't carry, not like the river's, *away, away.*

She stands. Washes her face. Jams on a wide-brimmed floppy hat, sets out down the road.

Abi knows Jude sees her as she walks into Hood's, but he half turns away and chats with the customer. Then they walk by, to the window, with hands full of paint chips. "Come to the natural light," she hears Jude say as he pushes through the front door, and on the way back in, his hand brushes hers as he passes. He looks back over his shoulder before turning to the customer, an older woman with a Martha Stewart haircut and flappy hands. "It's like this, like this," she says over and over. He smiles at Abi, winks.

So we're all right, then! Abi sits on one of the chairs near the door and waits. And she thinks of his words last Friday. *I want to be just us.* What would that be like?

He's behind the counter now, putting brushes and roller sleeves into a bag, and his eyes meet hers. She can feel herself flushing.

The Flappy Hand woman dithers on, and Jude takes his time explaining. She leaves, and he stays behind the counter and Abi wishes she wasn't sitting. He stares at her, a dreamy look on his face, and she feels more and more uncomfortable. He pulls his artist's brush from his pocket and, in the air, he paints her face, taking pains to trace her brows perfectly with such concentration on his face. He paints her lips and even though there's five metres between them, Abi feels the caress. "Am I forgiven?" he asks.

"I thought it was the other way round," Abi says softly, but he hears – because he wants to, Abi thinks.

"No." He shakes his head, but doesn't say anything about what it is she's supposed to forgive.

"Come back at six?" he asks.

She nods.

"We'll have a fire on the beach." He looks at her closely as if trying to read her mind. She doesn't want her mind read.

"Six," is all she says.

In the back of his truck, Jude has a box, and in the box there are a few sections of newspaper, kindling, and several heavy, hewn logs.

"You carry the blankets," he says as he hands her two thick, striped Mexican blankets. He carries the box.

"Is this always in your truck?" she asks.

"Never know when I might get lost in the woods," he says and laughs.

It's not the weekend, so of the half dozen firepits, only one is in use.

"Not quite as wild as Point Roberts, but not full of bodies like the city beaches. Just right," says Jude.

Just right for a fire, too. It's been a rather cloudy day, though not cold. Some children are playing in the waves and quite a number are out where the water is deep, their heads bobbing about, their parents huddling by huge logs, shivering in hooded sweatshirts. It crosses Abi's mind to ask Jude if he ever brings Dyl here, but she doesn't. Seems she's asked him a few questions like that now.

"Let's get some food," he says. The fire is leaping up, the blanket is just right. Abi can feel the sand – warm from the day in spite of the clouds – pushing between her bare toes, as Jude takes her hand.

"The food hut!" He motions to the old beach stand, painted with once-bright fish and sea stars. "Mediterranean food – they have these meatball things." And he nears the counter and orders two dinners. "I know you're going to like it!" he says.

Is it normal, Abi wonders...to feel this rush of emotion? It's like the opening move of a football game – not that she's ever paid much attention to that sport – with two sides tackling each other. One side has only a split second to begin to say something about, "Oh that's nice of Jude, to share his favourite food with you," when it's slammed to the turf, and the other side says, "But you can order for yourself...if he'd just give you time to look at the menu." Then the first side picks itself up, dusts the grass clippings from its bum, and says,

"But *somebody* cares about you – that's all it is – he *cares* about you." "*But* if he *really* cared..." the second side roars, and...back and forth.

Abi doesn't even want to hear the end of it. If she smiles right at Jude, looks right into his eyes – dark, dark, dark eyes – then the football voices go away. And besides – she bites into a spicy meatball – the food is *perfect*.

Their firepit is at the far end of the beach. By the time they get back there, they've eaten almost half the meatballs. They sit on the blankets. "The potatoes are good. What's on them?" Abi scrutinizes a chunk, edges deep golden brown with spiky pieces of darkened green on them.

"Rosemary," says Jude, rather carelessly. Makes Abi suspect he really doesn't want to talk about the food anymore.

"Your painting," she says. "Tell me about it."

Jude looks surprised at her question.

"I didn't notice any artwork at your mum's house. What do you paint?"

There has been a growing murmur from the football front again. Somehow her question silences it. But in the length of time it takes for Jude to respond, it starts up again.

"Oh, you know." He looks out at the ocean as he speaks. "Abstracts, I guess you'd call them."

Abi hates this – this feeling of struggling for things to say. She has so much to say. But it's not going to come out. She doesn't want to talk about Dad, or Mum, or her house. Obviously, Jude doesn't want to say much about his painting.

"I still haven't found a job," she says finally.

Jude finishes his meatballs and potatoes, and he folds the paper plate in half. "No?" he says. "Why're you wanting a job so much?"

Stopped again. "Same reason as anybody, I guess. Too bad the job was filled at your store."

"Yeah, well." He looks away for a moment. "That would have been hard."

"What would have been hard?"

"Having you working right next to me all day. I wouldn't be able to concentrate."

"Of course you would," she says.

"No, I couldn't. I knew that just looking at you, that first time in the store."

She feels shy, and at the same time, some flutter of anxiety; she's not sure exactly what he's saying. "Well," she says, "doesn't matter anyway. The job's gone."

"And now you're working for Amanda."

"That was just one day, filling in for Brad, who usually works with her."

"Hmm," is all he says.

"You really don't like her, do you?"

He reaches out and takes the paper plate from her hand. "No, I don't," he says as he folds it, places it next to his. Then he pulls her close to him. "But I like you." His lips are in Abi's hair. "Except sometimes you talk too much." He laughs softly.

She feels herself warm, and her shoulders melt. True enough. Maybe she doesn't have to talk or think, think about what to say. She leans into him, and they sit like that for a long time, breaking only once for Jude to put another log on the fire.

The kids straggle up from the beach and pass by, draped in towels, a couple of them in old terry dressing gowns, with their parents behind them, hauling folding chairs and coolers and canvas bags slung over their shoulders…coming back for things dropped or missing. Then they're gone, and except for the seagulls and snipes, it is quiet. Just a few older people strolling along the edge of the water, but mostly the beach is theirs. The sun begins to dip. Jude's hands seem to awake.

"Have you been thinking about what I said in the black-berries?" he asks after a while, and Abi can feel a finger, softly inside the armhole of her summer shirt, tracing so gently the outer round of her breast.

Now there are words inside her, warring again.

You don't want him doing that.

But I do. I like how it feels. Good. Soothing. I'm the centre of the world. I am the world.

Just where do you think this is going to go?

It doesn't have to go anywhere. Just here.

You think.

Yes — that's what I think.

I thought you weren't going to think...or talk.

I have to talk — back to you. Though if you shut up...

Think harder, girl. Think about this guy. What's he after?

Isn't anybody going to come by and tackle you, take you to the ground, put you out of the play? 'Cause I'm tired of listening to you...

But look: now his other hand is moving. I tell you — I don't like this one.

Well, I do. And he's waiting for my answer.

Think harder: he doesn't care what your answer is.

Abi puts her hand to the side of Jude's face, and kisses him, hard. She surprises him. She surprises herself. But his hand, suddenly inside the front of her jeans, surprises more.

You're sixteen.

Almost seventeen.

Okay, try this one: just what do you think this is about?

I told you — I don't want to think...

Her belly is jumpy now. What has been soothing is now...well, she doesn't know.

"OKAY KIDS," comes a voice. "The park SHUTS down at dusk. Time to put everything BACK where it belongs, pack up and GO."

She leaves her head buried in Jude's shoulder. She doesn't want to look up. The owner of the voice sounds tall, and he's standing right over them. Abi doesn't want to know what he looks like, and she doesn't want him to know what she looks like. More than anything, she doesn't want to feel ashamed. She shouldn't feel ashamed, shouldn't have to.

"We're not bothering anyone, sir – no one else is even around. There's got to be another good hour here in the fire – seems a shame to leave it..." Jude tries for the "sir" thing again, just as he did at the border crossing.

"Oh, there'll be another fire." Is there a slight mocking in the tone now? "But dusk is dusk and this is it. I'll fetch a bucket of water, douse the thing myself."

Jude stands awkwardly after the man leaves, and pulls on the corner of the blanket, pulls it out from under Abi before she's quite off.

"Sorry," he apologizes as she stumbles.

She folds the second blanket.

"We could go in the truck, I guess." Jude sounds grumpy. "But it's not very comfortable." He hands the folded blanket to her, and picks up the box with what's left of the wood, and he starts off to the parking lot.

"Actually," Abi begins, speaking to his back as she follows, "I think I'd better just go home. My dad'll be wondering."

Walk, walk, walk. Is he ever going to say anything?

"So your dad does that sometimes, does he? Wonder?"

The meanness stings. And the knowledge that he has seen Dad, has known, has never said – until now. But Jude stops and turns to her so quickly she bumps into him.

"I'm glad he wonders about you – that makes two of us."

How could she have thought?

It's a quiet ride home. Abi sends away thoughts, tells words goodbye. She just wants to smell the salt of sea, feel the sand that has fallen from her feet to the floor of the truck. And when Jude kisses her good night – mmm, more salt – he reaches under her shirt and she can feel his fingers through her bra. Her nipple is like a lost beach pebble inside her underwear, something foreign, something she's not familiar with. How can he do that?

"Next time Aba, next time..."

She stands on the porch and watches his truck pull out into the road. Even though she thinks it's supposed to be the other way round: maybe he should watch until she's in the house.

Rate of Effectiveness

What is the chance of Amanda asking her forgiveness?

Abi thinks she can count on the fact that, whatever Jude might do, Amanda'll do the opposite. So she decides that she should phone her.

"I'm sorry," Abi says. "I'm sorry I told you to go away."

Amanda's quiet for a minute. Then she says, "It's okay, Abi. I think you just did something you needed to do. We were both acting as if you weren't there, as if you had no thoughts about it even."

She doesn't say what "it" is, but she has said more than Jude did. "I've been hoping you'd call," she goes on. "Brad's gone tree planting. Would you like to work with me? It's about six hours a day, Monday to Friday." She stops, but Abi has the feeling she had more to say. Was Amanda going to try to convince her?

"You can think about it, if you..." she says, but Abi cuts her off.

"I'll do it," she says.

Amanda exhales. "Good," she says. "I'll pick you up Monday at nine." She pauses. "How is everything?"

That word *everything* is like another hand at Abi's belly. Instantly, it's all aflutter and then crumbly.

"Abi?" comes Amanda's voice.

"Everything's fine." Her voice flutes.

"Hmm," she says. "How about I swing by after I finish this next house?"

"If you want," Abi says, and Amanda flares.

"Say it, Abi! Say what you want!"

All this time Abi's been feeling that sense of spiralling, down-pulling, but Amanda's words pull her up. She's stopped with a realization: it's never been *Amanda* she's disliked. It's this: her way of pushing Abi, prodding her, that Abi's not liked. Yes, she's succeeded – at least for the moment – in halting that sense of inevitability – but now there's a crumbling in Abi that makes her feel uncertain.

"Sure – come," Abi manages to say. Amanda seems to be waiting for something, though – something more convincing.

But how can Abi tell her that she wants her for more than just to come over with a sandwich? Abi wants Amanda to tell her things. She has questions for Amanda. She wants to ask her what it's like to let a boy inside you. Even though Jude said she has had no boyfriends, Abi has a feeling that Amanda knows all about it. Maybe even more than Jude knows.

"Yeah, come after work." Abi tries to muster some warmth in her words.

"I'll be there at half past six. I'll bring a sub. What does your dad like on a sandwich?"

So everybody's noticed Dad. "Anything," Abi says.

"It'll be something good." Amanda hangs up.

There are other things that Abi would like to tell her. About Mum. About her fears of leaving Dad. Ending up somewhere she doesn't want to end up. But how can she put words to these thoughts? What words?

Abi finishes the body of the sweater, casting off two-by-two until the last six stitches. She checks through the book to remind herself how to cast off, and does it. She's glad Ernestine insisted on showing her how to do back and front together, because now there are only the sleeves left to do. Hadn't Ernestine said something about showing her how to do both of those together too? But then what's the rush? Abi tries to cast on. Tries again, several times, but there's something twisting and wrong about it, and terribly uneven. She pulls it off again, tries once more. Gives up. The body piece is quite good though, with even stitches. Would fit a very large doll, like the one Abi had when she was a little child. She took it everywhere when she was four; it was almost her size. Had it out back one day, on the wharf, and it fell into the river. Mum stopped taking her to the beach that year because she spent all her time looking to see if the doll had washed ashore. Mum had always said that things dropped in the river always came ashore. She stopped saying that after the doll.

D ad does look at the sandwich as Amanda sets it down beside him, but makes no move to eat it. Amanda looks out the window and then suggests she and Abi sit out back.

"Ever grown anything in that?" She motions to the greenhouse.

"That was my mother's. She was always trying to grow tomatoes in it."

Amanda passes Abi a sandwich. Thick cheese bread, garlic beef. Heavy slices of red tomato.

"Where's your mother now?"

"I don't know."

"I'm sorry." Amanda stares at Abi, her forehead wrinkled.

"She left a year ago."

Amanda pulls her shoes off, and puts her feet into the water. The current pulls at them, pushes them west.

"You haven't heard from her?"

"Not a word."

"I don't understand that," says Amanda.

There's a sudden loosening in Abi's chest. "I don't understand it either."

"And I don't understand that." Amanda motions back to the house. Abi knows she means Dad.

Abi just shakes her head.

Amanda knows when to stop. And she doesn't ask about Jude, at least, not directly. She says: "My brother's having a barbecue tomorrow. Do you want to come? I could pick you up in the afternoon."

Abi knows there is a challenge in her words, and it is: "Don't tell me you've got plans with that Jude because I know you don't. So...say yes to my invitation, and if he asks you later...well, snooze-you-lose, tell him!" Something like that.

Abi knows that Amanda won't let her say no. And – truth is – she doesn't really want to say no.

Still. Some part of Abi wishes that Jude didn't always leave things to the last minute. Or even until the next day

"Sure – pick me up," Abi says. Amanda's chin seems to tilt up a bit. Abi tries not to let the minor sign of victory bother

her. It's not fair: a new friend, a boyfriend, and they don't like each other. It gives her the same sort of feeling she has about having two parents, one in a chair, and one who-knows.

"Will your Mum-and-Dad be there?"

"Oh yeah," says Amanda easily, "Dad'll be throwing hamburgs around — as he calls them! — and Mum'll be zapping mosquitoes and flies with her new electric bug killer. I'm not sure what's worse: the contraption itself, or the kick she gets from using it. The bugs positively sizzle, and I swear smoke curls up from their poor little carcasses." Amanda is laughing, even though she shakes her head. "She does rescue spiders, though — even the big furry ones — and returns them to the out-of-doors. Of course, they might die of starvation if she continues to kill off their food source!"

After she leaves, Abi tries to put together a picture of Amanda's family: bug-zapping mother, hamburg-throwing father, university brother, and Amanda, with her robot arm. At the moment, it's more of a collage than a picture. But that'll change when she sees them all together, she's sure of it. Then they'll be a picture.

Abi takes the bus to the drugstore, and finds the aisle marked "fem. hygiene." Yes, the birth control is in this aisle too. So are the pregnancy tests in their bright pink and blue packaging. She tries to remember what they said in school. Condoms have to be used with something else, otherwise they're not enough. Spermicide. Can't imagine asking – no, telling – Jude about this. "Here, put one of these on." Abi thinks of Amanda's voice, and can hear her new friend in her head: *snooze-you-lose*, she'd said. What would she say about this? *Wear-it-or-forget-it-baby!*

Abi remembers overhearing a conversation in the gym washroom, one girl saying to another, *I told him: you wear a raincoat, or we're not going out to play!*

Was making love supposed to be about threats?

There's a square box with a pretty picture. "Feminine condom" it says. Rate of effectiveness: 92%.

There's a woman standing next to Abi now. Abi tries not to watch her, in the hopes that the woman is not watching her. But still, she sees the woman's hand moving up to a slim box. "Personal lubricant."

What?

It's as if she hears the question. She turns to Abi. "You doin' okay here? Need any help?"

The expression on her face is open, kind. Her hair is cartoon red. She's not a hidey kind of person.

"No – I'm fine. Just need some of...these." Abi grabs the pink box of condoms.

"Well, they're not much good without this," says the

woman evenly, and hands her another slim box, this one of spermicide.

"Right," Abi manages to say, and she's away down the aisle toward the checkout. At the checkout, she opens her wallet.

"We don't take cheques without identification," says the clerk.

"Identification?"

"Driver's license, credit card. You know."

Abi shakes her head, and the clerk sweeps the two boxes under the counter. "There's a bank machine just down the street," she says. The man behind Abi harrumphs.

"But," she starts to say.

"I'll keep it here at the counter for you," the clerk says, and she pulls back a piece of hair that is not long enough for her ponytail, not short enough to stay out of her eyes. Abi doesn't bother telling her that she doesn't have a bank card yet. The impatient man is now plunking his purchases down on the counter. Abi flees.

Blackberry Tears

Jude hasn't called by three o'clock when Amanda picks up Abi. The Dodge rattle calls her to the door. "Sounds as if someone forgot to finish putting the engine together before they plopped it into the van."

Amanda laughs her round laugh. "Yup — exactly what it sounds like! Maybe they did!"

This time the puppy, Mortimer, is with her. He has an over-sized pillow in the back of the van, a space hollowed out in the centre of it. He wiggles and yips as Abi climbs in. She's happy to see him. Already he's bigger than he was the first time she saw him. He gnaws the side of her hand with his sharp puppy teeth.

Amanda drives through the town, past the two grocery stores, one on either side of the main street, each flanked by a string of stores. She drives on, past the high school, the library, on to where the road meets up again with the river, now a little closer to where it joins the ocean. "You ever go to the marsh?" Amanda asks.

"The marsh?"

"Yeah," says Amanda. "There's a baby salt marsh out here, at the end of the dike."

"A baby marsh?"

"Just forming. Something my geography teacher went on and on about last year. She dragged us all down there to show us birds and poisonous plants."

"Things living in river mud, you mean?"

"Pretty amazing what lives down here, really." Amanda pulls into the driveway of a small rancher.

The front yard is square and surrounded by a wide planter-fence. That is, an almost waist-high planter, about seventy centimeters wide, made of wood fence slats. The planter goes all around the outer edges of the front yard, and the ground in the middle is covered in smooth flag-stones. There is a curving concrete ramp that leads to the front door.

Abi climbs out of the van and pushes through the gate for a closer look. The plants are amazing; she's not at all sure she knows the names of any of them. Everything is golden and red, green, silver, and white, and very fragrant.

In the middle of all this, is a pond, the sides of which are the same height as the planter's. The pond is filled with lilies, and as Abi goes closer, all at once water begins shooting out of a fountain. She turns to see how this has happened, just as the door bursts open and a woman with long and wild black hair comes rolling toward her down the ramp, like some crazed skater kid.

"You're Abi!" she cries out, and Abi wonders if she can possibly stop her wheelchair in time before she sends herself hurtling into the pond. She does, and grabs Abi's hand.

"You!" she repeats, "are Abi. I'm so pleased to meet you. I'm Bobbie," she adds with a laugh. She waves her long arms around. "You're admiring my garden!"

It makes sense then. It's an accessible garden. Even the lilies in the pond can be tended from Bobbie's chair.

"My koi – the fish. Have you seen them? Tom, Dick, and Harry. I had them for three years before I realized they're all male."

In the heat of the afternoon, the fish are deep in the pond, trying to hide in the shade of the lily pads. Abi bends over the water and can just see flecks of gold and cream as they move lazily from her shadow.

"You both might want to go round to the backyard and join Jon and his pals."

Amanda leans over and kisses her mother's head, and her mum hands her a long bright scarf, which Amanda takes and ties loosely around that full crinkly hair. It's amazing, really; a person would be more likely to be caught staring at that hair than at Bobbie's chair. Her smile would be enough to distract from anything, Abi thinks, with those cheeks as round as Amanda's.

Bobbie's eyes twinkle as she says, "There are some rather nice-looking boys back there." She motions behind the house. "Just generally *nice*, too," she adds. She looks at Abi and lowers her voice. "That's Manda's thing, you know: they have to be *nice*." She mimics: "'But is he *nice*, Mum, is he *nice*?' Surely, she is the only nineteen-year-old to say such a thing!" Even though Bobbie's words are mocking, there's no mistaking the pride in her look toward her daughter.

Amanda grumbles. "Maybe that's why I never have a boyfriend, though, eh Mum?"

"Oh, go round back!" her mother commands.

So they do. The back deck is big, full of more bright plants in big, tall pots, and there's a built-in brick barbecue, a fireplace, really. Out in the yard — a quarter-acre of grass is what it looks like — there's a three-on-three volleyball thing happening. Behind the property is farmland.

And yes, it's mostly boys. "That's my brother, Jon." Amanda points him out, a tall skinny guy with reddish-brown hair. She explains that the others are mostly his university friends. And there're a few girls. One stands out because she flits. Here, then there, back, around. She's off. Hard to even see her features, except Abi notes a lot of light-coloured makeup on a rather tanned face, and hair with heavy streaks.

"Who's that?" she asks.

Amanda says, "Jon's girlfriend," and her voice is so neutral that Abi thinks if she knew her better she would know Amanda was saying she doesn't quite like this person. Then again, maybe not. After all, she doesn't like Jude and she's not afraid to let everyone know *that*.

"Come help me make fruit salad." She leads the way to the kitchen. It's a small kitchen.

Amanda notices Abi looking around the tight space. "Jon and I do most of the cooking, and Dad some. Though Mum loves to bake cookies." Amanda points to the collection of ancient-looking cookie cutters on the wall. Underneath them is a hook holding a longish rod. Abi guesses that Bobbie uses it to reach up and pull the cutters off the wall.

Amanda works on canteloupe, and hands Abi a colander of freshly-washed strawberries. She begins to carve the tops out and cut them in three or four. Then grapes, mangoes, honeydew. They add their cuttings to a giant glass bowl. Bobbie joins them, working at the far end of the island. She hums as she works, and the sound makes Abi smile.

"Do you know Amanda hums while she works too?" she says to Bobbie. "Christmas songs, even."

Bobbie laughs. "She learned them from me!"

The screen door slams.

"That'll be Jon," says Bobbie, and she's right.

"Beer," he says, and dances around his mother's chair, heading for the fridge. Then he sees Abi. "Whoa! You must be Abi! Amanda's friend. Good to meet you." He puts a hand on her shoulder as if he's Abi's brother too, and gives her a smile. It matches Bobbie's smile. An unwavering smile. Abi has the feeling that she could tell either of them anything about herself, and the smile wouldn't change. Strange thought. What would she tell?

So Abi's smile does falter a bit with this thought, and yes, his doesn't. "We've been hearing a lot about you. You're gonna be Manda's right hand!"

"Abi's left-handed," Amanda interrupts.

When did she notice that?

"Okay," says Jon easily. "You're gonna be Manda's...left hand."

His mother hands him a knife. "If you're going to stand around and chat, you can chop."

"Like I said, I'm coming for beer." He opens the fridge. "Besides, I made breakfast *and* lunch today."

"Fair enough," says Bobbie.

He's not finished. "Two loads of laundry, even folded. That's the worst part," he adds as an aside to Abi.

"Don't let Manda work you *too* hard," he says as he leaves the kitchen. "She will try."

He leaves both his mother and his sister shaking their heads after him, and the air is warm with affection. Abi's mind scrambles for the words to describe this – if she can name it, she can hold onto it – but she can't find quite the right words, and she just wants to *be* the feeling, hold it as a wordless thing, for as long as she can. Sometimes you can't snap a picture quickly enough, and you can't record a moment in any way that will preserve it. It's enough, it's all it can be, to be there.

It's a perfect day, really. The hamburgs – as Amanda's dad calls them – are delicious, hot, tangy with spice and tomato and Bobbie's "chutney," whatever that is. They have a crazy game of croquet. Abi comes to know that the lawn only looks smooth: it is actually full of dips and tufts, places for the hard wooden balls to lodge. With lots of laughter, balls are sent flying to the edge of the property by other players. At one point, one game has nothing to do with the wire wickets, and everything to do with a wild zigzagging gambol through the field and across a narrow ditch that runs beyond the length of the property. (Try rolling a ball over a rough old two-by-twelve, and not dropping it into the deep ditch full of thick-bladed grass and thistles.)

Then it's evening and the air cools somewhat, especially off the river, and Rick, Amanda's dad, builds up the fire in the fireplace. Bobbie wheels easily across the deck, with something on her lap. A guitar, which she hands to Jon. "Best part of a summer evening," she says low.

"That's why you paid for all those music lessons." He tunes it for a few minutes, then begins to play some ballady piece that Abi doesn't recognize.

Jon's girlfriend, Kristen, tries to scoop up Mortimer as he rushes past on one of his puppy excursions, but he dodges her and somersaults in the process. She tries again, and he skitters off to the side. Seems funny to Abi that Kristen, herself a flittering person, wouldn't recognize this need in another.

"Leave him alone," says Amanda finally, after Kristen's third try, and Kristen scowls and sits next to Jon. Bobbie looks from Amanda to Kristen and then to Jon, and then she begins to sing along, and one after another joins in. Even Kristen after a while. She looks quite pretty while she sings, Abi thinks.

The guests finally begin to leave. A few have had too many beers, and Rick fills his car to take some home. Amanda, or Manda, as her family calls her, fills her van too, but saves the front seat for Abi. She drops Abi off last.

"It's late," she comments as she pulls in to the blackberries. "You should have just stayed."

But Abi hardly hears this. She has seen the back end of a truck pulled over a way up on the side of the road. She just hopes that Amanda hasn't seen, and if she has, that she won't say anything about it. The warmth of the evening is gone, and there's a knot in her.

Amanda seems not to have noticed. "I'll pick you up Monday morning just before nine," she says. "It's going to be good, working together."

"Yeah, it will be." Abi tries to sound as if that's the only thing on her mind. She forces herself to turn and look at Amanda, to give her a smile, to say, "I had fun...Manda – thanks."

The knot in her stomach is growing.

"Monday," she says, as she climbs out of the van. She has to extricate her foot from the wash bucket and sponges that are on the floor.

"Monday," says Amanda, and Abi knows her friend will wait until she goes into the house and closes the door. So she does. Pretends she doesn't see the truck there in the dark. Amanda turns onto the road and is gone.

Aba Zytka Jones stands behind her door, and waits for the knock she knows is coming.

He doesn't knock, but she knows he's there. She can almost hear his breathing. How long can she stand, not opening the door?

There is only silence from the living room. The house is silent. All she can hear is the river. And that breathing. Or is it her own? She opens the door slowly. Then the screen door, and there is a hand on her wrist. The hand is gentle, though. What is she afraid of?

"Come," says the voice, the voice that is everything she thought it would be. The hand leads her across the porch, through the path between the blackberries, down to the willow. How can he see in the dark?

He lights a match, shields it with his hands, looks at her briefly, his eyes full. Full of what? Full for her, she thinks, and at the same time, empty of something. Empty for her, too. He's waiting. There's a place for her, just her size. A perfect fit in those eyes. He lights a candle set in a glass holder, and then his eyes hold hers longer – until she can't stand it, and she looks around. They are inside the tent of the willow. The river is at their feet. There are old quilts that make a nest.

"I've been waiting for hours," he says, and he pulls her close. She has a deep, sudden sense of wanting to cry. Instead, she kisses him, hoping, hoping the feeling will go away.

"Where were you?" he asks the question of her neck.

"Does it matter?" she says with her lips in his hair. She wishes she hadn't worn a skirt, but he has his head at her belly, and his hands are under the fabric, and he is pushing at her to lie down. The quilts are soft and comforting, a place where she'd like to sleep for long hours. But he is all over, and her shirt is open. Where did his pants go?

She thinks of the drugstore, sees the woman asking her, "You doing okay here?"

"What about...protection?" Abi asks. She hardly hears the words herself. Sounds as if they are asked by someone else. *You're not going to have any, and we'll have to stop.*

He does pause. Then he finds his pants, digs in a pocket, pulls out a packet.

"Is that all?" she asks.

"Comes with the works," he says.

The works. What exactly are "the works"?

She can't help but stare as he kneels in front of her. Something in her responds to this, something she'd like to control, but she'd also like not to. That spiralling sense again, down, down. Or maybe not "down" but "away." Yes, more of an "away" thing. Here is a chance, to forget where she lives, to forget her father in his chair, her mother – damn her anyway – that look on Ernestine's face – oh, all those looks on Ernestine's face – all that lumpy throat feeling over the warmth at Amanda's house. Just for a time, she can forget it all, and she can be with this person by the river. There will be a connection. She can be a part of the world. She can be the centre. The knot in her belly is almost gone now. Her muscles are soft. The sound of the river rises, and nears to carry her away. She is the piece of glass, she is almost to the river, *come, come* it says...her mother cries in the greenhouse, her head bowed, her shoulders moving with sobs...*no, that picture must go...*

Abi sits up.

"What?" His voice isn't so soft now.

"I can't." The words are choking her.

"But I have protection. Nothing's going to happen."

"It's not that," she says.

"What then? What else is there? First, you're not ready. Then. What?"

She's on her own after all. Always was. This need in him has nothing to do with her. Or anyone for that matter.

He's angry. "It's not fair," he says.

"It's how it is." Her own voice surprises her. She buttons up her shirt, pulls at her skirt. "I don't know when I'll be ready."

"Maybe you'll be like your friend," he sneers, and at first she thinks he's talking about Amanda.

"You know – the balding one."

Ernestine.

Then Abi does start to cry. But she can't let him see, so she scrambles to her feet and doesn't stop running until she's behind her own door.

When she wakes up in the morning, her legs are caught in the sheets, stuck with blood from the blackberry tears in her skin. When she gently pulls them free, they begin to bleed all over again.

Fire Music

When the sun is up, and before she eats, Abi pushes softly at the screen door, lets herself out, walks between the blackberries, feels as if she's in a dream, really – floating – except for the dried fragrant grass that catches at her toes, and she thinks that perhaps, like the river, it is trying to tell her something. She already knows, before she reaches the willow and draws aside the feathery strands, that there is nothing there, and she wonders if it even happened, but she knows it did.

It's over. She'll not see him again.

She thinks back to when he was *My Boy*, out in the field, eating his lunch alone and she could watch from behind her window. But she did all her crying last night. Now it is time for breakfast.

Muffets and milk, and she questions which chess piece to move, but doesn't touch any. Dad, in his chair, is listening to the local events channel, and there is the sound of dull film fireworks. So unlike the real thing, she knows now. A monotone voice says something about *Fire Music*, the annual celebration of fireworks, an international competition, first weekend in August, blah-blah-blah.

Oh, shut up. She thinks back to July 4th.

Abi wanders into her room. Picks up the knitting needles. If only she could cast on. Old Ernestine, with her sprayed hair and sky-high heels. And then those hips. Ernestine, Ernestine. Mary. *You.*

Abi stuffs the ball of yarn and the needles back into their paper bag and shoves it into the bedside-table-box. Here's her notebook and that stupid pamphlet *Expand Your Vocabulary*. Right. *You'll go places.* Where are we at now...let's see...the Brooklyn Bridge? The Eiffel Tower...no, the Sphinx. No, again. We're at the letter J!

Abi flops onto her bed and opens the dictionary. *Jamboree.* Where could she go for a jamboree? Was that at Amanda's, last night? Brother Jon with his guitar? *A large celebration or party, boisterous.* Yeah, that would be it. Then it was over. How about *Jekyll, Dr.?* There's a word, a name. *Jekyll and Hyde. Or was that*

Jude and Jude? Here's another – *jetsam: material that has been discarded to lighten the vessel.*

Abi jumps up from the bed, carries the pamphlet, the notebook, the dictionary, out the back door, and tosses everything over the railing into the water below. "Go then!" she calls out. "Go some place!" She watches them swirling and poppling away. Does she feel lighter? For a minute she wonders about jumping in after the papers and books – though of course, she knows better.

Sundays can be long. *This is my, my, my beautiful Sunday, when you say, say, say, say that you…*

Abi hears the Dodge pull up at 8:45, and she's out the door, in some comfy old overalls and a т-shirt.

Amanda – *call me Manda, she'd said at the barbecue* – grins at her. Abi grins back, and while the newly-hollowed space in her doesn't quite fill, it does feel easier to carry.

Amanda talks about how she started her business. "My mum taught me and Jon how to clean the house. In grade ten, I didn't want to work in a restaurant – I didn't want a boss. It wasn't easy finding my first customer. I had to prove to a few people that a teenager could be responsible and do a good job. It's tough, being young and doing things that are supposed to belong to the adult world."

"So, how'd you do that?"

"By leaving them with the shiniest house they ever had!" Amanda laughs her big one. "First, though, Jon made me some business cards and flyers and he helped me put up posters around a couple of neighbourhoods. The first call was from someone who knows Mum. She was so happy with my work that she passed my name along to the Georges. Mr. Stewart asked about me, and phoned me. We've only ever talked on the phone and left notes. You know how it works: they tell two friends, and *they* tell two friends, and so on. I've never had any complaints. Now, I charge by the house, instead of by the hour, and I have a bank account for university tuition, so next year I'll take a few courses while I work."

She sounds so proud, just bustin' with it, thinks Abi.

"Only two houses today, but they're big," says Amanda. She's right: the first is unlike anything Abi has seen.

"I'm going to get lost," she whispers. The hallways are wide, ceilings high, and it still feels like a maze of walls and more walls.

"You're whispering, but you have a silly grin on your face!" says Amanda.

"Do I?"

"You do. You don't know that?"

Abi thinks for a minute. "I guess I do."

Amanda stares at her for a minute. "I have the feeling that you could get through a lot, Abi, with a grin like that, a grin with a mind of its own!"

"Maybe," says Abi. She'd like to tell Amanda what she's thinking right at this point — that she feels connected with her in a way she's never felt connected with anyone before — but she can't. Just gives Amanda another grin that she's quite aware of and says, "Which way is the bathroom?"

Amanda laughs. "The Syens have five. You'll have to be more specific!"

The morning passes, the five bathrooms are almost clean.

"I lost one of Mrs. Syens's earrings back in that corner." Abi points to a fancy bit of shelving that the little clump of pearls fell in behind when she was cleaning.

Amanda purses her lips in thought. "Guess we'll have to kludge something together for a rescue."

"Kludge?"

"You know — put some odds and ends together. A coat hanger and a bit of wrapped-around duct tape, most likely."

But Abi's stuck on the word. "Let me guess — kludge starts with a 'K,' right?" Was that just yesterday she threw away the dictionary?

"That's right — a 'K.'" Amanda's peering behind the shelf.

"I'll find a coat hanger." Abi trots off, shaking her head.

The kludging works, and Amanda shows Abi a few other

cleaning tricks she's learned. Best, the house is so big they can play two different radio stations full blast, listen to tunes of their choices, and hardly hear each other.

Then it's over and they put their gear together. Amanda empties the vacuum filter into the garbage, and they stop in a park to eat the lunch she's brought along. "I'll supply lunch," she says. "And how about if you empty the vacuum from now on?"

"Doesn't seem quite fair," Abi says after a bite of sausage sandwich. She knows why Amanda is offering this. "How about if I take out the garbage too?"

"All right," Amanda agrees, after a moment. She seems to realize that Abi likes to hold her end of a deal.

At the end of the day, Amanda writes a cheque. "This is just for today. I'll start to write them out every second Friday, okay?"

"Okay," says Abi, again aware of the exhaustion in her muscles.

Amanda looks at her keenly. "Make sure you drink enough water while we're working. Maybe with some lemon in it. It's hard work, Abi. Go to bed early tonight, okay?"

Abi just nods.

"And thanks," says Amanda. "I think we're going to be a great team."

"I think so too," Abi manages to say.

At home, after Amanda has dropped her off, she lies down on her bed – just for a minute, she thinks – and when she awakes, it's dark, the middle of the night. In the fridge are some milk, an apple, a few slices of bread and some cheese. She leaves enough milk for cereal, and eats everything else. Now it's tough to go back to sleep. She can hear the river without the constant hum of traffic, and her own thoughts seem too loud. Ernestine keeps coming to mind, accompanied by a memory of the anger that Abi had felt toward her. *You can come back now, Ernestine.*

The thought of Jude comes too, but she pushes it away.

From the paper bag, she takes the one complete piece of sweater, tucks it under her pillow, keeps her hand there, and at last falls back to sleep.

By the time Thursday rolls around – it's a slow roll – Abi's muscles are getting used to the work, and she's able to eat supper after work before she goes to sleep. The cupboards have some food in them, and the fridge its own stock.

She's missed Colm's and Fiona's Wednesday visit, and she's happy for that. She's not happy to see that the chess set is untouched, though. "Dad?" she says, but he doesn't answer. He's hardly spoken since Mary-Ernestine walked through the door that day, and the empty pop bottle has been on the floor beside his chair for days now, untouched. Abi leaves him a bite of food, as usual, washes his bowl from something-or-other that he's made himself during the day. She finishes her own food, and sits watching her dad, then can't stand it. The summer evenings are getting shorter now, but they're still long when you're alone.

She catches a bus and takes it down River Road, gets off where she needs to, to walk to Horace's house. He's on the front porch as if he's been waiting for her.

"Abi! You've come for tea," he says.

The train is already circling through the garden. He's added a couple of buildings, she notices, a library, and out over the pond, a house not unlike her own.

"My house," she says.

He nods. "Do you mind?"

"No," she says slowly and kneels for a closer look. It is different though. There are bright curtains in the windows, and the whole house is blue. How did he know the back of the house is blue?

As he pours tea, he asks, "Have you seen her?"

Abi knows who he means. "No – have you?" Ernestine must have told him about the blue.

"No." He sips his tea and the train runs by their feet. "I've phoned and phoned, but she never answers, and she has no voice mail."

"Do you know where she lives?"

"These days, I'm wishing I was at work instead of here with my four weeks vacation to get through." He shakes his head. "I've sat in front of her house for an entire day, and not seen hide nor hair of her."

"Nor hairspray," adds Abi, and he looks at her in surprise.

"Nor hairspray nor bright yellow-and-black," he says.

So he's noticed the bumblebee thing too. They share a laugh, a sad laugh.

"What's happened?" he says.

"What about the shop where she works? Do you know the name of it?"

"I phoned there twice," Horace says. "The first time, the person who answered told me that Mary would call back, and she never did. The second time, they told me she wasn't in."

"How about if I try tomorrow?"

Horace nods. "Okay. I'll give you the number." He finishes his tea. "What if she's not there?"

Abi looks out at the world he's created – *Ladner Junction*. There's something changed, apart from the two new buildings. "You move the people around," she realizes.

"Sure," he says, "you can't always stay in the same place."

Whoo-whoo…whoo-whoo…

"You don't suppose she's left town, do you?" she asks.

"You don't think she'd do that, do you?" he asks. Neither answers the other.

That's it, until Horace drives Abi home.

When Abi calls the yarn shop in Vancouver – *An Olde Yarn* – they tell her the same. "She's not in today."

"When will she be in?"

"We don't know. She didn't say."

Abi has the feeling they're not telling the truth.

Dad's watching the local events channel again. No, not watching. He has it on. That's all.

Abi can hear from where she eats her supper at the table.

It comes to her: there is one place Ernestine will be, if she's still in town. There is one place.

Jar of Buttons

Saturday is the first night of the international fireworks competition downtown. If Ernestine is still in town, that's where she'll be.

Abi can imagine Horace shaking his head on the other end of the phone.

"But how, oh how, are we going to find her there – if she's there – in all those people?"

"There are four nights of competition. We'll search a different area each night."

"It's dark." Horace doesn't sound despairing; Abi knows he just doesn't want to get his hopes up, only to bring them back down again. Hopes are kites.

"We have to try," she says. She has a couple of questions for Ernestine.

"I'll pick you up at six," says Horace. "That'll give us almost four hours of daylight before the fireworks start."

"Sounds good," says Abi. The hours stretch ahead. She wishes that Amanda worked Saturdays too. But by Saturday, most people want to finish their work and enjoy their clean house. She thinks of the thirteen houses they've cleaned. Right now, half past eight on a Saturday, everyone's eating breakfast, preparing to go to the beach, asking a dad to set up the badminton net, still in bed, reading a book with a mum popping in, asking "What would you like for breakfast?" What about that Mr. S, all on his own? What would he be up to? Not picking up his socks, that's for sure. Maybe he takes an hour to make breakfast, something with cheeses she doesn't know the names of, and he knows how to cut fruit to make it look like something she's never seen. Then he reads three newspapers from three different cities, leaves his dishes in a heap, hoping someone else will do them, and goes for a long bike ride, down to Mt. Baker with its summer snow peak…okay, she's being silly. Funny thing to think about: what other people do on Saturday morning.

An engine comes to a sudden stop outside, dust rises. Before Abi can get up from her chair, there's a frantic scramble outside the door, a hard knocking, and the door opens.

Jude and Dyl.

Jude's face is pleading. "Abi, I've gotta ask you one more time. Please. I've gotta leave Dyl with you. My boss needs me to work today."

"What about your mum?"

"She's sick." He pauses. "Real sick."

Abi looks at Dyl. His little face is scared. As scared as his grandma is sick, Abi suspects.

She stands straight and looks at Jude, holds his eyes. "What time are you finished work?"

"My boss said I'd be able to leave at 4:30."

"Okay," says Abi, "I'm not working today, so I'll take care of Dyl. Because I like him," she adds, "and because your mum is sick. But be back on time, because I'm going out."

He looks contrite.

"4:30," he says.

This time, Dyl seems to accept that his dad doesn't hug him goodbye. He stands in the middle of the kitchen, his arms hanging at his sides, and says nothing. Abi stands by the door, looking at Dyl, wishing he'd do something, but knowing that if he did, if he ran to the door, screamed, called after his dad, burst into tears – if he *fought* – it would break her heart.

She slams the door shut after Jude and then slows, picks up Dyl gently. "*We*," she says, looking into his face, "are going to have *fun* today."

"Boats?" he asks, filled with hope.

"Lots of boats!"

So this is what some people do on a Saturday morning: fold dozens and dozens of newspaper boats. So many that the pile of papers actually does shrink. They fill the bathtub, and float the boats, but after a while the bath looks like a busy port. Grey streaks of newsprint wash up the sides of the tub. Dyl doesn't seem to notice her scooping up the saturated, sunken boats, and slopping them into the bucket by the tub. Because there are more and more. All those classified sections, with their red circles around job after job, and Abi doesn't need them anymore. Fold, fold, fold, and in they go. Join the troops.

Dyl doesn't say much, but he laughs, and Abi is happy to hear that sound. When she wraps her arm around his narrow shoulders and pulls him close, he doesn't back away or clench his bones. The morning passes.

For lunch, Dyl nods when she suggests scrambled eggs, toast, apples cut up, and they eat on the wharf out back, but after a while it's too hot.

Abi tries to remember where there might be a few books for little kids. Mum used to have a box somewhere. There's a stack of a few boxes in the corner of the living room. It's the one on the bottom, the heavy one, and there are a few books from when she was little, and a lot of old books that probably belonged to Uncle Bernard. They take the kids' books into her room, and sit on the bed. The first one Abi pulls out is about a bunny whose family is trying to decide what he is going to be when he grows up. The bunny is a baby and can't say what he's going to be, but he knows all the time that he wants to be a daddy rabbit. The last few pages are about the kind of daddy he's going to be, and when Abi finishes the read, she looks at Dyl and he looks at her, and she thinks, *If I have to lie, I'd sooner lie to an adult than a kid.* She has no idea what he's thinking, but guesses it's something he can't even put words to because he doesn't know them yet. Not like that.

"Let's get out of here," she says. "We'll go for a walk. Go on an explore."

She finds a cap for him to keep the sun out of his eyes. It's too big, but she finds a pin and adjusts it, and puts one of her own shirts on him to protect him from the sun. It hangs down to his knees, and under the sleeves hangs like wings, so he flaps around a bit with a silly, shy grin. Abi puts on her own floppy hat, and she fills a bag with a blanket, a couple of water bottles, some crackers and a jar of buttons that she's had on her windowsill for as long as she can remember.

She holds his hand tightly and they cross the street. There's an undeveloped area behind some of the industrial buildings farther down. Maybe they can cut through a parking lot and get away from the river and the road. She's never been there before. Judging by the cracked areas of dried mud, it's not a place to go in the other seasons of the year. Now, in August, after weeks of sunshine, it's all right. It's safe. There are patches of grass, and the strong smell of warm chamomile. She puts down the blanket, and they look for the round yellow flowers of the plant, crush them in their fingers. "Smell," she says to Dyl. "We'll collect some and make tea when we get home." His eyes go round. "Tea?" She nods, and he looks.

They lie down on the blanket and pour out the buttons, make patterns of them, play games. Dyl falls asleep, and Abi lies beside him, feeling the sun, a warm friend. This feels good: a day off after five hard ones; listening to the at-peace sleeping-breaths of a little person; summer.

When they do return home, it is almost four-thirty, and Abi makes Dyl something to eat.

Then it's after five, and no Jude. Dyl is trying not to cry. Abi tries hard not to let Dyl see that she is upset. She re-packs her bag for the fireworks, makes a sandwich to eat later when she'll be hungry. Reads another book to Dyl, after skimming through it silently herself. Five-thirty. Quarter to. Horace is a bus driver: he'll be here on time. Abi looks up the number for Hood's Paints.

"Jude left at four-thirty," is the gruff answer.

She doesn't look up his mother's phone number. What if she wakes her?

Promptly at six, Horace is at the door. "Who's this?" he says. He kneels and puts out his hand for Dyl, who shyly takes it.

Abi explains. Horace seems to know what she's talking about, and she wonders what Ernestine might have said to him. Horace suggests they sit and have a cup of tea while they wait, and Abi tells him they don't have tea. He shakes his head. "That's a bad thing," he says. Then, "We should try to take young Dyl home. Do you know where he lives?"

"I've only been there once, but I think I can remember."

She doesn't know the house number, but it's the only yellow and orange house on the block – unmistakable. Once there, she peers into the living room window. There's Dyl's grandmother, under a light quilt on the couch. She's awake, reading. Abi taps softly on the window, and Lily looks up to see her and waves, motions to the door.

Abi goes to the door and opens it. "Hello, Lily," she says. "Don't get up."

"Hello, dear," says the woman.

"I've brought Dyl home. Is Jude here?"

Abi feels badly when she sees the pained look that passes over Lily's face.

"I haven't heard from him," says his mother. "I don't know when he'll be here." Just with that much speech, and a brief attempt to rise from the couch, her face is pale and her breathing is hard. Abi fights down a feeling of panic. She turns around to realize that Horace is right behind her.

He whispers too, even more softly than she. "She's the grandmother?"

"Yes."

"We can't leave the child with her alone."

Abi shakes her head. Lily shouldn't have been left alone either, but she doesn't say this aloud. She says, "You need to find Ern...Mary, I mean. You go."

At first he starts to say no, then he reaches in his pocket for a cellphone. "I'll give you my number, and you call me. I can pick you up and take you home after Jude gets back, or I can drive back in a hurry if you need me." He writes out the number.

Abi asks Lily for her number, and tells her she's going to stay with her and Dyl until Jude comes home, and Lily just nods, a once-up-and-down motion.

Abi says goodbye to Horace. "Good luck," she says. When the door closes after him, Dyl goes over to his grandmother, and very carefully snuggles near her knees. "Grandma's all sore," he explains to Abi. Lily strokes his head.

"How's your day been, my Dyl?"

"We made boats. And buttons. And tea!" he suddenly remembers. He pulls enough out of his pockets to make a pot full.

"We *could* have had tea!" Abi laughs. But she's glad they didn't wait for Jude at her house: this is where they should be.

She fills the kettle with water, and asks Lily, "What have you had to eat today?"

"I'm not particularly hungry, Abi."

Abi looks through a few cupboards. "How about some soup?"

Lily says no thank you, but Abi makes it anyway, thins it with water, serves it on a tray that can go across the woman's lap. She gives a bowl to Dyl. Then comes back with mugs of tea. The mug is too heavy for Lily, and Abi finds a child-size tea cup in a high cupboard.

She pulls a hassock closer to the couch, and sits. Is it her imagination, or does Dyl seem to calm when she's nearby now?

"My grandson likes you," says Lily softly. Each word is work. "You're all he talks about lately."

"I like Dyl."

Now Dyl has remembered that in his other pocket are some of his favourite buttons, and he takes them out, arranges them on the hills and valleys of his grandmother.

"How old are you, Abi?" asks Lily.

Abi has to concentrate on her words to hear them. "Almost seventeen."

Lily has closed her book. Now she puts her head back and closes her eyes, and Abi thinks she is drifting off to sleep.

"Your last year of high school?" comes her faint voice.

"Yes."

"Then what?"

"I'm not sure," says Abi. "I just started to clean houses with my friend Amanda. She's saving money to go to university. Maybe I can go with her." She hadn't put that thought into words before, hadn't even realized it was resting in the back of her mind.

Lily gives that faint nod again. "Yes," she says. "Education is good."

They are quiet for long minutes. There's just the click-click of Dyl with his buttons.

"And your family?"

The question usually throws Abi. "I live with my father. My mother left us."

Lily's eyes open slowly. "She did."

"Yes."

Lily continues to look at her.

"Almost a year ago. We don't know where she went. I woke up the morning that school started, and my dad was sitting at the table, and when I came in the room, he said,

'She's gone,' just like that. She left sometime in the night. Could've fallen in the river for all we know. Except she took the car."

"Did you report her missing?"

Abi has to think for a minute. "No – I don't think Dad ever did." She stops, wondering now why he didn't. Wondering why she hasn't questioned it before. "It's almost as if Dad expected this to happen someday. He didn't seem surprised." *And why hadn't he?*

Lily stares at her still, and Abi wonders why she's telling her all this – this woman she really doesn't know.

"You know Dyl's mother left." It's a statement, not a question, the way Lily says it.

Abi nods. "Jude told me."

"Yes," says Lily. "He likes to tell that story to anyone who will listen. I sometimes wonder when I'll see him on some talk show."

So...Lily knows all about her son's oily tongue. It occurs to Abi to wonder what Dyl's mother's story is after all. It could be anything, really.

Abi speaks, with hesitation. "I used to think that being a mother was a sort of promise."

"What sort?"

Abi ponders her words. "A promise to *be*. To be there, stay there. In person. And in heart. I thought there had to be some connection." She's not sure if she's explained it well, this idea she used to have.

"Do you miss her?"

The question catches Abi. "I thought I did. Now, I just want to leave too."

"Where will you go?"

"I don't know right now."

"Well, Abi," says Lily, and she sips her tea, "you hold on to your thoughts about a promise. Sometimes you have thoughts that others aren't thinking. Sometimes it's those thoughts that you need to keep for yourself."

Lily again sips her tea, but then sets it down as if it's too much for her. "Do you love my son?"

Abi feels as if she's been hit from the other side now, and she struggles for an answer. "I wanted to," she manages to say finally.

"I wanted to, too," says the woman, and suddenly there's nothing separating them, and that's when Abi knows – *knows* – that Lily is dying. They wouldn't be sharing these thoughts otherwise.

"I really wanted to," says Lily, eyes closing again, and she might be speaking the words for Abi, too.

Can a mother really want to love her child, and not be able to?

"You sleep," whispers Abi. "I'll take care of Dyl."

"Thank you."

Her eyes close with a heaviness, and within minutes her breathing signals sleep. Dyl plays with his buttons, all his attention on the colours and the stacking and the patterns. Abi looks around the room more closely than she was able to the previous time. If Jude paints — abstracts or whatever — there's no evidence of the work here. Mostly, there are black-and-white photos.

When Dyl yawns too many times, Abi asks him where his jammies are. He can't find his toothbrush, but he does bring out an old Archie comic book that seems to be a favourite. Abi feels silly reading it to a two-year-old. She stays with him, remembering strings of words from sea-songs Dad sang to her when she was little. She rubs his back as he falls asleep, until his breathing is even. The house is quiet. She pulls her hand away from his back, and can still feel his warmth with her. She sits on the front step, with the door open behind her. The sun sets and another hour passes before Jude pulls up.

He doesn't see her until he climbs out of the truck and comes round the front. Then he stops short and swears. "What're you doin' here?" He turns back to the truck and gives it a solid wallop with his hand. "Oh, Abi, I'm sorry. I forgot about you!"

"And Dyl," she reminds him.

He stands there shaking his head. Puts his hands in his pockets. Pulls them out again. There's a small shower of sand from somewhere – his pockets, the cuffs of his pants perhaps. So he's been at the beach. She does catch a faint drift of woodsmoke. But he only stands there, no word of explanation, just shaking his head.

Abi motions to the house. "He's asleep now. So's your mum."

He heads to the house. She wants to tell him to stop shaking his head – just don't bother. What? Is he *surprised* he forgot them? He shouldn't be.

He looks into the living room at his mother, curled up on the couch, and he closes the door as he steps back outside. A jingle of his keys, and he says, "Come on, I'll drive you home."

"You can't drive me home," says Abi.

"Look, I know you're mad at me, but I can still drive you home. I'm not a bad guy, you know. I won't hurt you." His voice is filled with impatience.

"You can't leave your mum and your son alone in the house."

"It's not for long."

"I'll take a bus. Or I can call Horace – he'll pick me up."

He stops. "That's right," says Jude, "you were going out tonight. With this guy? Horace?"

She says nothing.

He sits down on the steps and puts his head in his hands, rakes through his hair, his fingers catching in the thick, brown, uneven waves. "I'm not, you know."

"Not what?"

"Not a bad guy, like I said."

Again, she says nothing.

He looks at her, pleading. "It's not easy being a dad. I'm barely twenty. I gotta work. I gotta take care of my mum. My kid. I gotta cook some food when I get home. Go shoppin'." He sighs. "I gotta have a *life*. I *deserve* a life."

Abi's tone is grit. "*This* is your life," she says, motioning to the house.

He stares at her, and his face clearly says, *You don't understand.* "I need a little freedom. Can't always be tied up like this."

Abi doesn't want to hear more, and she passes him, goes into the house, finds the phone, dials Horace's cell number. When he answers, she can hear the hum of an engine in the background. "I'm about two kilometres away," he says. "I'll be there soon."

She can tell from his tone that he's had no luck with Ernestine, but in spite of that, his voice gathers her in and warms her after Jude's coldness.

She goes outside to wait. "Are you working tomorrow?" she asks Jude.

He leaves his head in his hands as he answers. "No, my weekend starts now. I have a couple of days off."

"That's good," she says. "Take care of your mum. Make sure she eats."

They wait in silence, but when Horace pulls up, Abi hears a sort of snort, an exclamatory sound, coming from Jude. "You didn't tell me Horace was an old guy!"

"He's a friend." She climbs into the seat after Horace comes round and opens the door for her. He says nothing to Jude, just gives a sharp wave as they drive off.

"She wasn't there, was she?" Abi asks.

"No," says Horace, checking over his shoulder for traffic. "But thousands of other people were."

"Maybe we can make a sign – a big one – and post it on the beach. We can go even earlier tomorrow."

"You want to go tomorrow with me?" Horace perks up.

"Yes. We'll find her."

"If she's there," he says.

William Then

But they don't find her on Sunday night, nor on Monday. Tuesday is the Grande Finale, the night when the winning country is announced, and the pyrotechnics are theirs.

"On the final night, every one who has been here on one of the previous nights comes again...and they bring all their friends!"

Abi has to make a grab for Horace's long T-shirt so that she doesn't lose him in the crowd, and she can barely hear his words. She hears enough to understand, though. Not that she needs anyone to point out that there are an incredible number of people here. Already it's difficult to move, and it's not even eight o'clock.

Abi pulls the signs that she has made from her bag, and starts to tack them to the sticks she's carrying, but Horace puts a hand on her arm. "Let's not, tonight. We might scare her."

She packs the signs away again.

Horace goes on. He's stopped moving now, and he's speaking directly into her ear. "I have this feeling...that she's been here every night, and we miss her. She sees our signs and she goes the other way."

Abi nods. She can imagine Ernestine doing that. What she finds difficult to understand is how Horace can know that, and yet not give up hope.

"How about we separate?" she suggests. "You go that way, and I go this." She motions to the far end of the beach, away from the tennis courts and the food stand, down where she'd wandered that day with the dictionary.

Horace points to a huge elm tree. "We'll meet there when the fireworks start at ten."

Abi doesn't tell Horace what her thoughts are, but they're something like this: it's Abi who Ernestine really doesn't want to see. Maybe if she thinks it's just Horace who has come, she'll be all right. Maybe she'll even talk to him. Or she'll think he's on his own, and she'll head in the other direction.

Maybe. Maybe. Maybe. Maybe if Abi goes right to the very end — even beyond the end...

Takes a while to push through. At one point, she sees a woman in a wide-brimmed hat, and she has a certain roundness to her. Is it? Abi moves over, closer, around. No. She stands there, feeling somewhat foolish as the realization of just how much she'd like to find Ernestine strikes her.

At the far end, she sees a few stragglers. Here the beach narrows, is suddenly caught up into a stone wall that grows higher and higher, becomes private property. The beach itself – the shoreline – is narrow. Rocks rise out of the water. The retaining wall is now the height of a house and it curves away. Abi didn't go this far last time. She follows it, enjoying the sudden quiet from the throngs behind her. She'll go back soon, she thinks.

And there she is, right in front her. Ernestine. Sitting on a rock, with a full skirt draped around her in the water, eating a sandwich, her great fabric bag piled on her lap. Cat's-eye sunglasses hide her eyes, but there's no mistaking her.

She's just taken a bite when she catches sight of Abi, and she stops, then chews furiously.

Abi moves toward her, and feels shy suddenly, uncertain. The tide is coming in, and the water swirls around her calves, licks her rolled-up jeans.

Ernestine wraps the rest of her sandwich and puts it back into the big bag. When she looks up and speaks, her voice is shaky. "I'm so sorry, Abi, that I ran out on you."

"I'm sorry too," is all Abi can think to say. There is too much she doesn't know. She sits on another rock close by, and they look at each other warily. *Don't run away again.* Ernestine is trying to make a decision. She makes it.

"A long time ago," she begins, "I knew your father. He was William to me then. Now...I don't know who he is."

"How well did you know him?" Abi asks.

The pause is long. "I'm not sure I knew him at all, now that I think of it." Another pause. "We were engaged to be married."

Abi blinks. "What...happened?" *There was something between them...there was a lot between them.*

"On the morning of the wedding, his friend brought me a letter – a note, really. He said he'd...changed his mind. There was someone else. He was already married to her."

"My mother?"

"Yes. They'd gone away the evening before, and they'd married." Ernestine's words are soft and smooth as a stone rolled over and over in water and other stones. They are words she's had to think and say again and again. Abi suddenly feels the heat of the setting sun on her shoulders. She needs to be in shade, but there isn't any.

"He didn't tell you to your face?" she says finally. "He wrote you a letter?"

Abi doesn't realize how angry she sounds until Ernestine

says, "Don't be so angry with him. *You* don't need to be angry with him."

Abi's voice comes out in a screech. "I'll be angry with him if I want to be! He's a big bloody wimp, that's what he is. *Writing a letter! Running away!* Big bloody *wimp!*" Her breathing is heavy, and she pulls her arms across her face, like a child, to dry her nose of tears pouring down it. Where'd they come from? There's more she wants to say; the words want to pour out of her. *Big bloody armchair wimp. You deserve to have someone write* YOU *a letter – a note – and run away!*

"Abi!" Ernestine's voice is low amazement, and she's looking strangely at Abi.

Abi realizes she's shaking – an angry, icy tremble, a glacier in spring thaw. She feels as if she's going to pull away with a great roar.

"Abi," says Ernestine again, and she stands and comes close, through the water, wraps her arms around Abi, and they huddle together. The great roar urge eases through Abi – maybe something to do with the gentle lapping of waves coaxing it away. The water reaches Abi's knees, before one of them speaks.

It's Ernestine who does. "He wasn't always like this, you know," she says softly.

There's an ache in Abi. Something like how you might feel taking a first bite of food after fasting for several days.

"He used to be full of laughter. He drew people to him. He was a light. I don't know where the light came from. He never did enjoy his work and he had no family to speak of, except that odd old uncle who left you his home. We used to have Sunday lunch with him every week, you know. William never missed. He said he was all his uncle had."

Abi and Ernestine begin to walk slowly down the beach, and Abi is glad for this. It means that she can hear Ernestine's words without looking directly at her. Now Abi thinks she has some idea why Ernestine's eyes are as they are: she's looking for your word, looking to see if she can hold you to it.

"One time, I said to him, old Uncle...what was his name?"

"Uncle Bernard," says Abi.

"Yes. I said that old Uncle Bernard was all William had...as far as family, that is. And William said, no, that wasn't true any more – now he had me, and I'd be his family." Suddenly Ernestine is quiet, thinking she's said too much to the daughter of the man she's speaking of.

Abi speaks up. "My mum has no family, except a couple of cousins far away. And she didn't like Uncle Bernard at all." Then she wonders if she should have said anything. She steals a covert look at Ernestine. Ernestine has a frown, a thinking frown.

"I've always wondered," Ernestine begins, "if that was why William married her. She had no one; she needed him – at least, I think that's what he thought. I, on the other hand, came from a family of seven. I have three brothers and one sister." She laughs a hiccupy laugh. "My brothers wanted to track them down and do something *awful* to William. But I told them no, they couldn't."

Abi can't resist asking: "Do you sometimes wish you'd just let them?"

Ernestine turns to look at her, thoroughly surprised. Then she sees a shine in Abi's eyes and she does begin to laugh, again no more than that hiccupy chuckle, and she says, "Oh yeah, many a time I thought, *Why* didn't I let them go – they would have been like a pack of dogs!"

An evening gust of wind off the water manages to move a bit of Ernestine's sprayed hair.

Abi points to Ernestine's head. "Your hair moved."

"Oh my. Did it?"

"It's all right. Really."

Ernestine stops patting her hair and she looks a bit embarrassed. They wrap their arms around each other and move farther down the beach.

"Of course, my theory is probably all wrong," says Ernestine. "There are many reasons why people choose people, why people marry. Why people don't marry," she adds.

"And why people have babies," says Abi.

"And what people do when they discover they can't have babies," says Ernestine.

Abi would like to read more in her eyes, but Ernestine has dropped her sunglasses down over her nose, and she adds nothing to her statement.

"You know," says Abi, "I always thought my mother hated dependence."

"She might have at that," says Ernestine thoughtfully.

"How do you know what you know about my mother?"

Ernestine flushes red. "When someone replaces you with someone else, you want to know about them. And friends would tell me. Sometimes because I asked, and sometimes because they felt they should. The same friends who gave me the note from your dad all those years ago, phoned me when your mother left."

Abi tries to imagine what that would be like – all those years of tracing another's life. She wonders about Ernestine's mention of people discovering they can't have babies. Was she talking about herself? So how did she feel when she found out that Abi was born? What about Ernestine's own life? What about just getting on with it? The sadness of Abi's thoughts swells, and she's glad when they come to the people waiting for the fireworks.

The sun is setting, and the excitement is thick.

"We should look for Horace," says Abi. "I think he'll just be glad to see you."

"Abi, he waited outside my apartment for an entire day. He called me and called me, and I didn't answer. I didn't show up for our tea. How am I going to explain all that?"

"How *would* you explain that?"

"I was scared. I *am* scared. I've never told him about all this."

"Horace is probably scared too; I don't think he's ever had a girlfriend in his life!"

Ernestine laughs suddenly, a little laugh, but still a laugh with no hint of a hiccup. "Oh, Abi, I'm sure he's had quite a few!"

"No – all he has is that train."

"I love that train!" exclaims Ernestine.

"See? He has his train; you have your fireworks. You both have something that makes you shine. You're perfect together!"

"It's never that simple," says Ernestine, and Abi sees a shadow of that old face in her.

Maybe a couple of weeks ago Abi would have disagreed. Today, she says, "You're right; it's not." She touches Ernestine's arm, prods her ever so slightly, and they resume walking.

"Horace is a true friend," Abi says. "No matter what."

Ernestine nods. "Still. One doesn't want to ask too much of a friend." When she says that, it's as if a wall of playing blocks goes up around her. The kid in kindergarten, by herself, making herself a palace. Abi wants to knock down the blocks – send them flying!

When they are not far from the elm, they see Horace, and his face lights as he moves toward them. He gathers both of them in his arms.

"Abi knows your heart, Mary. She knew you were here. Are you all right then?"

"I'm all right, Horace," she says.

He looks at her keenly, but doesn't ask anything more. "Look – I've set out the blanket. Shall we watch the fireworks?"

They sit, Abi in the middle. It all takes so long, all this feeling our way through the dark, she thinks, and she is doubly glad for the pink and green, the gold-bursting stars, and weeping-willow-silver to the ground. Then there are the wiggling-white-and-spermy, screechy bits of fire, reminding her of a family planning video at school. She doesn't explain her giggle to Horace or Ernestine. But when Ernestine reaches for her hand, Abi gives it a little squeeze.

Eating His Soul

Abi gets home from work on Wednesday, and there's Colm waiting for her, sitting out on the car seat.

"Aye, there you are," he says. "I've got a lemonade here for you, Aba, and I'd like to chat with you." He hands her a large plastic bottle with a lid, which he pulls off.

Homemade lemonade, with a vague taste of tea, and globules of pulp that burst cold and tangy on her tongue. She sits on the other end of the bench. She's quite positive she's never tasted anything as delicious as Colm's lemonade. Would be good at the end of every workday.

"You're working hard?" he says, and she nods.

"Cleaning houses. With my friend Amanda."

He nods. "Took me two hours to get that out of your Da.

I couldn't believe he didn't know where you were. I kept asking him and asking him, and finally out it comes. He didn't know Amanda's name, though."

"This is very good lemonade – the best I've tasted."

"That's good, that's good, but Aba," he says, "I'm worried about him. Worried sick. I think it's time...we do something." He's looking at her anxiously.

"Do something?"

"Aye."

"Like what?"

"He needs help."

I knew that.

The ice in the lemonade hasn't melted yet, and she swirls it, listens to the cubes knocking.

"How old does a person need to be to live on their own?" she asks, still looking at the lemonade.

She looks up in time to see understanding come into the old man's eyes.

"There'll be a place for you, Aba, no worries there."

She's not convinced, and he knows it.

"You're almost living on your own here," he points out.

"But it's my home. Dad's here. Mum might come back."

"She'd be able to find you, no matter."

He probably has more to say, but she cuts him off. "Mum lived in one of those places once. A foster home. For almost a year before her folks could have her back. You put me in one of those, and she won't come looking for me. She won't go near it. That place probably taught her how to run away..." Now Abi cuts herself off. She's said more than she's ever wanted to. Her mother only ever told her about that time once, and Abi's pretty sure Mum never meant to tell her anything about it at all. She remembers how Mum couldn't even finish telling the story, how her voice was all cracked and her words broken. How she'd said that was why Abi must know how to take care of herself; she, Mum, had not been able to take care of herself. She'd never said more.

Colm seems stunned.

"Sorry, Aba. I was just thinking. Thinking about him being somewhere safe, where he could get better."

Abi nods. "I know." She's shaking. "You're his friend. I know."

"And you need to be safe too," he says.

Abi doesn't respond to that. In a low voice, she asks, "What do you think is wrong with him?"

"I think sadness is eating his soul."

"I think sadness already has," she says. *Guilt finished it off.* She downs the last of the lemonade. "I'm going to be seventeen in a few months. I think somebody once told me that if you're seventeen, and you have a job, you can leave home."

Colm sits nodding slowly, his lips pursed. "Maybe I can come around more often."

"What about a boat? Do you have a boat? Maybe he'd go out in a boat. He used to have one."

"Is that right?" Colm looks thoughtful. "I don't, but maybe I can do something about that." He stands, and reaches into his pocket for a pencil. "I'll give you my number if you need to call me, all right? And think about what I said about there being a safe place for you. Just because it was bad for your mum doesn't mean it has to be for you too. Remember, young Stu, who Fiona was talking about? He lives with my neighbour. You could talk to her." But Abi's turned away now. He writes on the card in his hand. "I'll leave this on the kitchen counter then," he says. "And now I'll go say good night to him."

"Where's Fiona?" It suddenly occurs to Abi that the girl's not come with her grandfather.

"Oh!" Colm gives an angry snort. "She owed me for one mischief or another. But we're done with that now. I told her to go back to shopping with her mother. Leave me to it!" The screen door slams behind him.

When Abi goes in later, the TV is off and Dad is out back, holding onto the railings, looking out to the water.

She goes and stands beside him, and he does turn to look at her.

"Aba," he says, as if he's all there.

"Colm came to see you," she says. It scares her, knowing he might shut down, turn away, at any moment, at any word.

Her father nods.

"Did you play chess?"

It's an easy enough question. Still, it takes her father a full minute to drag up an answer from wherever it is he stores his few words. After a time, he shakes his head.

Abi feels a stirring of that anger she felt toward him on Sunday. "Dad, come in," is all she says, though, and she takes his elbow and tries to steer him toward the house. To her surprise, he resists her, and grasps the railing. *Okay.*

She doesn't know how long he's out there; he is still there when she goes to bed, early so she's rested for work the next day. She lies awake longer than she'd like to, and still she doesn't hear him come in.

What was it like, all those years ago? Twenty years? No. Eighteen, it would have been. Two women and one man. Her mum and dad and Ernestine. Two Marys and one William. Bill. Will. Ernestine called him "William." The guys at work called him Billy. Mum always called him Will. Maybe he was a different person with each of those names. What does he think of being "Dad"? Does he think about it? What did he think about when he was filling out that form for a Big Sister? What did Ernestine think when she...*hey, how did that go?* Abi falls asleep with her mind in the maze of her own questions.

Saturday Tea

"So how was it, Ernestine? How was it you found me?"

It's Saturday morning, and Abi and Ernestine and Horace are on the back porch sipping tea and eating chocolate-dipped cookies that Ernestine made the day before.

"I'd applied to be a Big Sister, and I'd told them I wanted an older girl – well, not as old as you, they don't usually have girls as old as you. I was thinking a preteen, or early teen. I wasn't at all sure I could relate to a little girl. They gave me a sheaf of papers to look through. Then the coordinator pulled out your application and said, "This one's really too old." But as she pulled it away, I caught sight of your father's name and asked her if I could have a closer look." Ernestine stops to finish her cookie before going on. "I saw your name, your age, where you live — I knew that your father still lived at his uncle's old place on the river."

"When did my dad apply?" Abi asks.

Ernestine looks at her oddly. "He didn't. The signing name on the form was your mother's. The date was last August."

What'd she do? Have a list? "Stock up on underwear and tampons. Find a Big Sister. Leave a cookbook..." Abi can easily imagine her with such a list.

There are all the other questions, too.

"So...were you just curious?" *Or was it more? And don't make it up...*

Ernestine thinks for a minute, and before she answers, she looks over to where Horace is sitting on the steps, half-turned away from them. He's got a red kerchief wrapped round his neck, and Abi can see the sweat absorbed in it. She thinks how, with a striped cap, he'd look just like a conductor. And there's something else; some sense of being at a train station, coming back to a train station, and back again, always going somewhere, never getting anywhere. That's all it is — just a sense. Funny — she's never felt that before about Horace. He's always seemed so easygoing. No, *carefree*, that's the word. Free of cares. She's never noticed a sorrow in him before. She finds herself backing up from where she's been kneeling, at the low table of tea mugs, backing out of the sun and into the shade, closer to where Ernestine is, with her chair tucked into the far corner of the porch. Ernestine seems to be still thinking about Abi's question. Abi looks from her, back to Horace, who is sitting very still, and again to Ernestine, suddenly conscious that she is between them, just as she'd been when they watched the fireworks. The thought crosses her mind that that is how someone wants it. But who is that someone? Horace? No. Ernestine? Why?

"So?" Abi prods again.

"Well," begins Ernestine, suddenly seeming very much like that first day that Abi met her. "Well..."

Horace has raised his head ever so slightly. He's listening.

Ernestine clears her throat. "It's like this – I had this idea that if I could see William again, I could find it in myself to...forgive him. I've needed to for a long time."

She looks directly at Abi. "You once said I forgive too easily. You were so wrong; I don't seem to be able to forgive at all. And I never forget. I keep thinking that perhaps I can learn how to do just one of those things before I die."

Horace stands. "The train must be stuck," he says to no one in particular, and goes round the side of the house.

Ernestine stares after him. "Dash the man!" she mutters. "If he had any brains at all, he'd be running from me!" Her voice is quavery.

Abi watches Horace as he disappears from view. She'd like to think he wouldn't run away — she really wants to know that — but then what was it he just did?

"Okay," she says aloud to Ernestine. "Maybe Horace only walks away and then he comes back!"

"They always run away — why should he be different?"

"Maybe just because he is. Why should he be the same?"

Ernestine looks at Abi a long time. "Maybe," she begins, "because I'm the same. I don't seem to be able to change."

"Is that why you ran away?"

She nods slowly. "I think. Because it scared me. I thought I'd made a horrible mistake. I'd thought that if I did the unthinkable — became friends with you, the symbol of all I'd lost — that something in me would heal. At first, it seemed easy. It seemed that the person I was hurt by and angry at all those years was gone. Then, that day I walked in, and he was there — right there — and I looked into his eyes, and I just wanted to run. I realized I hadn't forgiven anything. The pain was as raw as on my wedding day. I felt afraid.

"Now I'm not so sure it was a mistake — judging by how you and Horace believe in me. But I can't say I share your belief."

"Why don't you?" Abi asks.

Ernestine just shakes her head.

It's not a good feeling, the feeling that is closing in around Abi: it's the same feeling she has around Dad. As if she's in a room with high walls, no windows, and no door. She doesn't want to be in there with Ernestine.

Ernestine reaches into a wide pocket on her skirt. "Here," she says, "you have this. I don't need it anymore." She hands an envelope with soft edges — *does she hesitate just a bit?* — to Abi, who opens it to find an old photograph. It takes her a full minute to recognize the man in it: Dad.

He's standing, laughing, he has on that white shirt — the shirt in the one honeymoon picture — and the sleeves are rolled up. His whole body is laughing, Abi can see.

Horace rounds the corner then, a train car nestled along his forearm and a tiny screwdriver in his hand. Abi stands and slips the photo into her own pocket.

"I think I'd like to go and see Lily and Dyl." She stops. "Well, it's not so much that I'd *like* to, but I think I should." *And I really want to get out of here...*

"Will Jude be there?" Horace asks. He sits on the steps again and puts the screwdriver to the train car and begins to fiddle.

"I don't think so. He usually works on Saturday."

"I could phone the paint store for you, and find out."

"You would do that?" Abi asks. She's surprised he even thought of such a thing. "No," she says slowly, "I'll go, and if I see his truck in front, I might be back soon..."

"I have an old bike in the shed. You can borrow it if you like," Horace offers. "Keep it for a while, even." He puts the train car and the tool down and leads the way to the shed.

He has to clean a few cobwebs from the bicycle. Ernestine makes a small bundle of cookies, and puts it in the large square basket on the front. Horace gathers an armful of gladiolas, wraps them in a moistened paper towel, and points out the quickest way. The house is about eight blocks away.

Abi leaves Horace at the end of his driveway. Ernestine has wandered out from the backyard, but she keeps her distance, her wave is feeble. As Abi pedals away, she suddenly remembers a strange sensation she had earlier in the day, in the early morning, just after her bath, when she'd bundled up in that thick old robe and stepped out onto the wharf behind the house, wet hair dripping over her shoulders. Was it a certain smell? The queer and momentary motionlessness? What was it? Fall coming? Or something else? It had been something that had pushed at her throat, made her want to do what her mother had done. Something that made her know – *know* – she couldn't. Ever. August was too early to feel fall, wasn't it? Even in the early morning? At this time of day – mid-afternoon – it felt as if summer would never end.

How had summer begun? With wanting to find a job. Get a bank account. Plot to leave. That plot hadn't had an Ernestine in it, let alone an unhappy, unforgiving Ernestine.

That plot hadn't had *My Boy In Person* either. *My Boy* was supposed to stay in the blackberry field where she could gaze at him and make dreams. That plot hadn't had a Dyl or a Lily. Or a father who was stressing out a food bank worker.

She's almost there now, and she slows as she approaches the bright house. Good — Jude's truck is not out front. The door is open in the August heat. She leans the bike against the garage, takes out the cookies and the brilliant red flowers, and knocks softly on the open door. Lily is on the couch in almost exactly the same position as the week before, except paler, if that's possible.

"Oh, Abi," she says. "You're not here for Jude, are you?"

"No. I came to see how you are, and how Dyl is."

Lily looks pleased. "Thank you," she says, her voice even weaker than the week before.

"Abi." Dyl comes down the hallway from the kitchen, and he stops in the doorway, tucks himself in beside the wall and peeks around the corner. His eyes are round again. He's always so in a knot, this kid.

"Hi Dyl," says Abi softly.

He raises his hand, makes a quarter-wave motion, then drops it to his side. He doesn't come close. For a moment, Abi wonders what she's doing here.

Has he forgotten their time with the buttons? By the end of that day he'd been so comfortable, and now...

They make a triangle there in that room, the young woman, the older, and the boy, in two doorways and the farthest corner.

"How about if I take Dyl for a walk?" Abi asks.

He backs farther around the corner, and looks over to his grandmother.

"Okay," says Abi. "How about we stay here and make some tea and soup again?"

He moves slowly around the corner out into the living room. He points to the small pile of buttons, still on the coffee table.

"He's spent so many hours with those buttons," whispers Lily.

Slowly, with his head lowered, Dyl crosses the room and kneels next to the table, disassembles the pile of bright buttons, moves them around, looks up to Abi, who feels rewarded. She goes into the kitchen and finds the teapot. This time she finds a small bowl for the soup, and a matching spoon.

When she goes back into the living room, Lily asks her to please turn the radio off. "Jude left it on this morning before he left for work."

Abi turns it off, a newscast of something or other.

"I don't need to know what's going on anymore, out there," says Lily. "I have enough in here to deal with." She

nods, and Abi assumes she means "here" in her house: her ill-
ness, her grandson.

Dyl leaves the room, announcing that he can pee in the pot.

"You're a big boy, Dyl," says Lily, as he leaves the room.
And after he's left, in a low voice, she says, "I worry about
him. He's lived with a sick woman for so long. He doesn't
know how to go around a corner without checking me. He
needs to go play in a park, climb things, be pushed on a
swing, but you come and offer to take him for a walk, and his
answer is no." Her voice trails off.

"He just needs to warm up to me. I'll ask him again later.
Or next time."

Lily looks sadly at Abi then. Abi wonders how she feels
about the words "next time."

"Should you be in the hospital?" Abi asks her in a hushed
voice.

Lily's voice sounds surprisingly strong when she answers.
"I need to be here," she says.

Dyl comes back into the room, hoisting up his elasticized
pants, T-shirt half in, half out. Abi can see a small wet spot in
front, but he doesn't seem to notice. He's back to the buttons,
and very happy to see a mug of milky tea.

They play a sort of checkers game, without a board. After,
Dyl still doesn't want to go out. He looks at his grandmother
and shakes his head.

Abi stays longer than she'd expected to. She washes some laundry that's sitting in a pile – small pants and shirts that are Dyl's, a funky-smelling sheet, probably from Lily's bed. She leaves Jude's clothes in their own pile, and cleans the kitchen, the bathroom – she's good at this! – and when the laundry is dry, she makes up Lily's bed fresh, with the sheets as smooth as she can, and the pillows plumped. While she works, Lily sleeps. Dyl helps by arranging every pair of shoes and boots and slippers in the house. This must be a favourite thing to do, Abi thinks. The toes of the pairs are perfectly lined up – just as he'd done with the boats – and in the narrow entry closet, he's lined them, pair to pair, exactly. The task keeps him busy for a long time.

More tea, and Abi's on her way.

Horace had said she can keep the bike for a while, so she rides it home. It's almost five and the sun is cooling, and it's wonderful to fly down the river road with the wind with the freedom of a bicycle. She slows as she nears Hood's. She doesn't want to bump into Jude coming out at the end of his day. She passes and sees the sign in the window. HELP WANTED. Another word has been added by hand. IMMEDIATELY. She pedals harder.

So that's what they were still looking for. What they'd always been looking for, she guesses. The position never had been filled. Another lie! On the beach, Jude had said that it would have been hard to work with her right next to him all day, and he'd made it sound like a compliment. But what was it really about? He didn't want anyone too close? He didn't want to be "tied up?" Was this what he'd meant about his little bit of freedom?

She's glad for the wings of the bike under her.

Regular People

She's glad, too, for the work week to begin again. Weekends are long.

"We're at Mr. S's first today," says Amanda as Abi climbs into the van. She hands Abi a thick slice of watermelon from the bowl that's between the seats of the van. "More breakfast?" she says.

The watermelon is good. The day is hot already. No fall warning chill today.

Mr. S has great bunches of strawflowers hanging upside down. "Drying nicely," Amanda says, approving. She finds a sticky note and writes *good work* on it and posts it next to the flowers.

There are more socks than usual left lying around. "You'd think he'd have none left in his drawer," says Abi.

"Or to put on his feet!" adds Amanda. "Good thing it's summer! He's probably living in sandals."

"Isn't he a lawyer?"

"He is, but something tells me that doesn't stop him from doing what he wants to."

"Wow!" Abi has just walked into his workroom.

Amanda peeks in. "He must have been trying to look something up."

There are books everywhere. Stacks on the desk, the two small tables, on every chair – he can't have sat down at all to do his "looking" – and even on the floor. One stack was so tall that it has slithered down, and the books look like downed dominos across the floor. Three of the bookshelves are empty. Amanda begins to pick them up and replace them.

So it goes at his house: lots of pickup before cleanup. "Regular cleaning people don't do this, you know," says Amanda. "People have to pick up everything before they come over."

"Like the Ralphs' house."

"That's right." Amanda nods.

"But we're not regular?" asks Abi with a grin.

"You want to be regular?" Amanda has a hand on her hip.

Abi thinks for a minute. "Don't think I've ever seen myself as 'regular,' nope."

"Besides," Amanda adds, and she pulls herself up tall, "we can charge a little more for our impeccable service."

Funny, this business side of Amanda. How she fits it in with the part of her that reads worn-out books on the beach, and snuggles her puppy, and jokes around with her brother and his friends. She seems so much a carefree teenager, yet at work, well, she's Amanda-at-Work.

Mr. Grinstead has left them a treat, as always. More of that wonderful dessert called "trifle." Abi's been hoping he'd make it again.

She's wondering if Colm is going to be waiting for her again this Wednesday. But he's not. And Dad's not home either. Now that's a little disorienting – Dad not there, TV off. She feels panicked for a moment, before she sees the note on the counter.

Found a boat! I'm taking your Da for a cruise!
Colm

She wonders how he ever convinced Dad to leave the house, and feels a wave of gratefulness toward Colm. She holds the note between her two palms as if in prayer. *Thank you.*

Another thank you when she opens the fridge to discover that Colm left her a juice container full of the best lemonade on the face of the earth. She pours a tumbler full, and slowly drinks it, sitting out back. The weather has been muggy now for three days and the wind off the river feels good. She does like this: this feeling of working hard, having the now accustomed weary muscles, and the feeling of absolutely deserving this glass of juice, this feeling of knowing there's no other place she should be than right here, feet in the water, listening to the river. All the times she's been angry with this old mud river, and right now, this moment, it's perfect. She closes her eyes.

And opens them as a boat engine roars by. Colm is at the helm, his arm in a high wave. Dad sits beside him and there is a smile on his face. A tired smile, but a smile.

A slow smile spreads over Abi's face, and she leaps to her feet, jumps up and down. The boat fights with the wind-driven whitecaps, roaring forward and then away, and Dad turns so he's still looking at her as she jumps and waves. The water washes over the dock in waves, both from her jumping and from the wake of the boat. Dad finally waves as they pass out of sight and she stands still, a wonderfully throbbing ache in her legs. What an odd thing, that: to see her father out there, away from her, yet feeling closer than he has in a long time.

She sits down on the wharf again, but doesn't close her eyes this time. She doesn't want to miss anything in the world around her.

It's almost dark when Colm brings Dad home, but at last the door does open.

"Here he is then, Aba!" says Colm, and his voice is full of grin.

Dad has a shadow of a grin on his face too, and Abi wraps her arms around him. It takes him a moment, but then he wraps his long arms around her.

Yes, there is a feeling that anything might happen.

A feeling like that can't last long, though, and Thursday another feeling catches up with her, a feeling that she recognizes as a sad and growing one. Wondering how Lily is. Abi remembers that sometimes Jude works late on Thursday, and she thinks that if his boss is that desperate for help, maybe he works late often. She takes the chance, and when Amanda drives her home she asks if they can stop by the yellow and orange house first.

No truck.

"Want me to come in, or wait awhile?" Amanda asks.

"That's all right. I'll get a bus or walk."

"It's a long walk," says Amanda.

"Really, I'll be fine."

"Next time, I should come in with Mortimer. Dyl would love to meet him."

"He would. Next time, then." Abi waves Amanda away.

There's a stillness to the house. The door is closed, curtains closed, though Abi tries to peek through. She knocks on the door, suddenly wishing that she had asked Amanda to stay. She has to knock a second time before she hears a sound. Then the curtain is pulled aside and she sees Dyl, and hears his footsteps come to the door. He lets her in without saying a word.

The couch is empty.

"Where's your grandmother?" she whispers.

He stands staring at her for a moment, then softly pads to the back of the house, to his grandmother's bedroom. Here, too, the curtains are closed, the room is in murky darkness. Lily's thin form is under the quilt. Abi is glad she can hear the slight rasp of her breathing, and she is horrified that this is her first thought.

She whispers to Dyl. "Let's let her sleep. I'll make you some supper." They go to the kitchen, where she finds the fridge door open and a jar of peanut butter on the floor in front of it, some broken crackers, a knife.

She closes the fridge door, and then realizes what it's all about: Dyl's been making his own food. He points to the floor, and says, ashamed, "Me splooshed shuice."

Her heart aches for his shame. She puts a hand on his thin shoulder, and when he doesn't pull away, she kneels and gives him a loose hug. "That's okay, Dyl," she says softly. She wants him to believe her words. "It's only juice on a floor. All two-year-olds sploosh juice. It's your job! It's my job to clean it up and your other job to help me... Have you been taking care of your grandma today?"

He nods, and she gets a washcloth and begins to clean the floor, hiding her face from Dyl so he can't see how angry she is. *It's all wrong, this. Very, very wrong.*

She finishes the cleaning, puts the crackers and peanut butter away, finds some vegetables to cut up, and some mayonnaise as dip. Makes a sandwich with a bit of ham, finds a kids' TV show, opens the front room curtains, and sets up a picnic for Dyl. So far all he's said to her is his words about the juice spill.

"There," she says when it's ready, and puppets are on the screen, singing a happy song. "I'm going to go talk with your grandma now, okay?"

He nods.

In the dark room, she sits next to the bed. She hates to wake Lily, so she waits. Her eyes adjust to the gloom, and she notices one small painting, framed, and in place on the wall over the dresser. It might be called an abstract, Abi thinks. Perhaps this is it: Jude's painting. If so, it's the only one as far as she's seen. She tiptoes to take a closer look. In the lower right hand corner there is a name, but the name is Lily, not Jude.

Abi returns to the seat, and realizes that the woman's eyes are open and she's been watching.

"You paint," Abi says.

"Long ago," is the answer.

"Does Jude?"

"When he was a child." She pauses. "He wanted to."

Her eyes close again and she rests, and Abi thinks. About what it is to want things, and to work towards them, or not to. What it is to dream. From the front room she can hear Dyl humming, and she realizes it's the first time she's heard this from him, and she can't think of a better sound.

Lily rouses again, and with the slightest smile, she says "Thank you." She reaches for Abi's hand, and together they are quiet. There are the television sounds, and beyond the house there are summer sounds of music, coming-home traffic on the main road a few blocks away. There is the faint smell of barbecue. At last, Lily speaks again. "You have a connecting heart, Abi," she says softly, leaving Abi wondering. And before she can say anything, Lily's eyes close again, and within seconds her breathing is even and she is again asleep. After a while Abi goes back out to the front room, which is now darkening with twilight, and she sits with Dyl – he lets her put an arm around him – and waits until she hears the sound of the truck out front. Then she gently pulls away from Dyl, and tries to hurry without seeming to.

"You stay right here," she tells Dyl, knowing he won't argue. She goes out, closes the door behind her, and meets Jude on the far side of his truck, away from the house. She doesn't want Dyl to hear what she has to say. Jude's face flushes as he sees her. "You again," he says.

Before he says more she starts. "*You* bring him to *me* when you need help. So don't tell me not to come here to help."

He cuts her off. "I won't be bringing him around any more."

"What are you going to do with him? You can't leave him with your mother anymore. Your mother..." She stops. "Your mother needs to be in the hospital."

Now Jude's face is red, angry red. "Don't you tell me what my family needs! What would you know about family needs anyway? Or anybody's needs. Do you think I want you hanging around here? Cleaning up after my mother and making my son cry for you when I get home? You think I want that? Do you think I need your help? I don't. And I don't want to see you again. Ever! Am I clear?"

What Abi did not want to happen is happening: Dyl is listening to every word, his eyes in their usual shape – round and scared. Abi looks at him, and tears come.

"Stop!" she says to Jude, in a tight low voice. "Just stop!"

"No – I'm not going to stop until I see you leave. See the last of you." He begins to walk with her down to the end of the driveway, a half-step behind her. She has the feeling that if she moves in any other direction, he'll pick her up and carry her all the way home. Her head feels fuzzy, the edges of her vision seem blackened, her feet are heavy, but not too heavy to pick up and keep moving. She wants to turn around, but Jude is on her heels. It isn't until she's halfway down the street that he finally turns away, and she's almost to the end of the street before she turns around. She's hoping for a glimpse of Dyl's face, hoping she can send him a promise in a look. But he's gone. Just as well, maybe.

There are no promises.

Tangle

"Are you all right?" asks Amanda.

The bottle of window cleaner has slipped right through Abi's hand. "Oh yeah, I'm fine," she say, but it doesn't sound convincing.

Amanda straightens from where she's working on the bathtub. "You can talk to me, you know, Abi."

Not about Jude, I can't.

"Thanks, Manda," she says aloud.

Amanda nods thoughtfully. "Hey, why don't you come to my place Saturday, spend the night. There's a party I'm going to. You too. It'll be fun."

"All right."

"It's at Geoff's house. He was at the beach the day we met – remember him?"

"I don't think so." *The only guy I was noticing that day was Jude.*

Jude might be there.

Amanda reads her mind. "I think Geoff and Jude had a falling out a while back."

Abi nods, and wonders if her relief shows as plainly as she thinks it does.

Saturday morning, Abi heads over to Horace's for tea. This could become a routine. She has her knitting to show to Ernestine, who promised to be there.

Just a couple of days earlier, Ernestine had phoned her, "just to chat" she said. "Now you're working, it's not leaving me much time to be a Big Sister."

"That's how it should be," said Abi. "It *is* leaving you a whole lot of time to spend with Horace," she pointed out.

The moment of silence on the other end of the phone, the telling pause, caused Abi to feel a stab of disappointment. *Come on, Ernie!* she thought.

"Yes, I suppose it does," she responded finally. But that was all she said. "Are you coming around for Saturday tea?"

"I'll be there. I'm just about finished the sleeves of the sweater. I need your help with the sewing together and the collar."

"Oh, good!" said Ernestine, thrilled to be needed in the way she knew best.

So now the bag of knitting is in the old newspaper basket on the front of the borrowed bicycle, and Abi's on her way. She pedals lazily in the heat — it's been a record-breaking week — and ponders her friends. Horace used to seem like such an "open book." Abi remembers a teacher using that phrase and, until now, it seemed to fit Horace. But he's not. He has fears and longings and they're trapped by his shyness. It's as if he's stumbling over the very words he needs, and he can't even see them at his feet. Abi suspects that, if he did, he wouldn't know what to do with them anyway.

And Ernestine. Mary Rhodes. *Who might have been Abi's own mother!* Now, there's a thought — except of course, it doesn't work that way. Abi — who would have a different name — would be quite different altogether. Or how does it work? How does anything work? Like Lily: it was supposed to be that, when you got sick, people took care of *you*, and not the other way around. But Jude...

Abi really does not want her thoughts to go there; she is relieved to see the red of Horace's home. She rises from the pedals and pushes harder as she nears. Horace is tending the track, and he waves as she swings into the driveway. It is hot enough to catch the heavy fragrance of dry pine needles.

"Mary said you'd be coming!" There's an odd pitch to his voice that Abi takes note of.

She jumps off the bike, leans it against the fence. "What's up?"

"Oooh, nothing much..." he says.

"I don't believe you!"

Instead of walking around the yard, he goes up the front porch stairs and through the front door.

"Wait just a minute!" says Abi. "Whoa!"

Standing by the door are two suitcases. One is old and leather, and the other is very new, and flowered. "What are *these* all about?"

Horace turns around and puts his hands on his hips. "What?" he says, but he's grinning.

Abi points to the old one. "That's yours," she says, and pretending ignorance: "Whose is *that*?"

"Oh, that's mine too!"

She raises her brows.

"That's mine." Ernestine steps up beside him from some-where down the hallway.

So I was wrong about them! Abi shakes her head, pretending she has to clear it. "Is there something anyone wants to tell me?"

Obviously, Ernestine isn't going to say a word.

Horace just looks out at his tracks, then he can't keep it in anymore. "Thought we'd go for a train ride."

"A real train?" As soon as the words are out of her mouth, Abi laughs at herself. What a silly thing to say – as if they'd pack suitcases and sit at the *Ladner Junction* in the front yard.

Horace laughs with her, but Ernestine emits only her funny hiccupy sound. Abi tries to catch and hold her eyes, but Ernestine's eyes slide away after a mere second. *Are they steadfast, or are they flat and dull?*

Come *on*.

"Where to?" Abi asks.

Horace makes a grand motion with his big paddle of a hand. "Over the Rockies – to Banff!"

Abi looks back to Ernestine. "Oh, wow," she breathes. "That's perfect!" Finally, Ernestine gives her a half smile, nervous still, but at least a small admission of *hey, this is good!* For now, it's enough. Abi wonders how many hours have been spent this week, with Horace trying to convince her.

Ernestine heads back into the house. "Let's make the tea and finish that sweater," she says. Last week, Ernestine cast on the two sleeves – actually she insisted Abi do the second while she watched.

This week, it's macaroon cookies. Uncle Bernard used to make them. Macaroon cookies is one of Abi's very few memories of her uncle. "I always called these 'marooned' cookies," says Abi, biting into the sweet coconut. Ernestine laughs too loudly.

After tea, Abi lays out the knitted pieces, and Ernestine shows her how to sew them together. There are not many seams, as the pieces have been knit mostly as one, and it doesn't take long.

"The collar will take longer, but it is the finishing touch, and it's important to take your time. Here," says Ernestine, "I'll show you how to pick up the stitches." Her face has none of the earlier tension. This is her world. Abi can see, just from how she handles the yarn and the needles, that this is close to her. This act of taking one thing — a ball of string — and turning it into something else. "A sweater warms the insides of the person as well as the outside," Ernestine says.

Abi is about to say that she'd like to make a sweater for Dad, but she stops herself. Ernestine doesn't let her off easy. "I've picked up a few stitches...see? From the outside. You do the rest." She hands it over, and watches closely as Abi picks them up, one by one. "That's right," she says.

Horace pours more tea, and watches, too. "Maybe I should start."

"Start what?" Ernestine looks up.

"Knitting."

"You?"

"Why not?"

It's hard to know what Ernestine is thinking, but it does take her a bit too long to repeat, "Why not!"

Then it's done, buttons sewn on, dark rich green to match the wool. Ernestine had them in her pocket, ready. "It's beautiful!" says Horace. Ernestine looks proud. Abi can't quite believe she's made this, and she hugs it to her.

The morning has passed. What's left of the tea is cold.

"We need to be at the train station at half past two," says Horace shyly.

"Oh, but I need to wash up here," says Ernestine, and with a lot of arm movements, and skirt swishings, she seems to make the job of gathering up the few mugs and plates look like twice what it is. Horace picks up the tray for her to set them on, and he seems somewhat mystified.

"It shouldn't take long, and I can do it — *we* can do it — I've been washing dishes for some time now," he says. He follows her as she bustles into the house, and there's a great clattering, even a crash, and the pouring of water sounds as if she's turned the tap on full. Horace staggers back to the doorway from inside, looks at Abi, and rolls his eyes. "She has her ways, Mary does," is all he says. "But I've called us a taxicab, and she'll have to put an end to it all then."

He begins to lock up the house, securing the windows, the back door under the porch. A cab pulls up the driveway. "Mary! It's here!" There's a sudden silence from the kitchen. Then another crash. A typical, though not so chirpy "Oh my!" that makes Abi want to laugh. Or cry.

Horace just says, mildly, "Don't worry about it..." Then, after a few seconds pass and they don't see Ernestine, he says less mildly, "And don't you *dare* touch a broom!" Finally she shows up, locking the front door behind her, checking it, and checking it again.

"That apron is still on you," Horace points out. "And the flowers clash with the roses on your suitcase." The grin on his face is wide, though. He picks up her suitcase and bounces down the stairs.

"Oh my," murmurs Ernestine under her breath and looking after him. "How did I get here?"

"I don't know," Abi says, and takes the apron from her because she's taken it off, but doesn't seem to know what to do with it. "But when you get *there*, ask someone to take a picture of you two for me, okay? I want to see the mountains." *And you, together.*

Ernestine gives her a look, and again, Abi's not sure how to read it. *A bit terrified*, she thinks, as she sees a last wave from the cab pulling into the street. Abi's left standing with a daisy-covered apron in her hand, at the end of the driveway. She waits until the yellow car is gone from sight and then she wanders through the yard to where she's left the little sweater and the bag of leftover wool and needles. Horace has put away the train cars and there is a deserted feel to the place.

She packs the apron with the sweater into the bag and puts it in the basket on the bicycle. Now, if she had any courage at all, she'd cycle over and see Lily and Dyl. But she can't. She can still see Jude's face, his dark eyes with a brightness to them – anger? – and it makes her shudder. No, she can't bring herself to do that. Not yet, anyway. So she climbs onto the bike and turns in the direction of River Road, and there she turns east. Once she leaves town, she settles into the rhythm of the bike and the road and, in spite of the humid heat, and the perspiration trickling between her breasts, she begins to enjoy the pedaling and her thoughts. *I can start work on a big sweater now. I know enough. One for Dad. Then one for me!* Pedal, pedal. The river churns on the far side of the road, moving away, making her speed seem faster.

She sees a familiar blue truck coming in the opposite lane, at top speed, hurtling through the curves. Jude doesn't even see her, and then he's past. Where can he be going like that? A couple of other drivers honk at him.

Abi doesn't even realize she's climbed off the bicycle and is staring after him until she moves to get back on and she's shaking so badly she can't. Something is terribly wrong.

She walks the bike a bit, pushing it in the gravel. *Dyl? No, it must be Lily. Should she follow? No. But maybe. Yes.* But she circles back to *no*, and pushes the bike on. She's close to her house now. She'll phone, that's what she'll do.

She drags the bicycle onto the porch, leaves it by the door, and goes to the phone. The local telephone books slips from her hands, and her fingers fumble the pages before she can get it right.

She's quivering, frightened for Lily, wave on wave of fear, frightened for herself because she doesn't want to hear Jude shout at her again. At least she won't have to see his eyes. But she can: they bore right into her head now. The phone to her ear, she turns away, faces the side window, the back window, but she still sees those angry, hateful eyes.

"Yeah?" That's his voice.

"Jude?" she says. "I saw you on River Road...what's happening?"

The phone almost slips from her hand, she's shaking so hard. Her eyes close, expecting his rage, but it doesn't come.

His voice is tired, and he speaks quickly. "I can't talk now, Abi. An ambulance is coming for my mother. She's going to the hospital."

There's a sound in the background: Dyl crying.

"Dyl?" Abi asks.

"He's with me. Look..." He pauses. "I'll let you know."

"Thank you," whispers Abi, and she holds onto the phone long after she hears the click of his hang-up. She replaces it slowly, and stands in the kitchen, not moving, waiting to hear something outside herself. There's no TV. She can hear the gentle rasp of her father's snore. Then she can hear the river. She goes over to the chair and kneels beside it, lays her head on the arm of the chair, near her father's hand. Tears flow silently from her eyes. The snores stop and she can feel big fingers tangle in her hair.

Paper Boat

"I'll pick you up at about eight," says Amanda.

"How about earlier," says Abi. "I'd like to go to the hospital. Lily was taken to hospital today."

"I'm sorry to hear that, even though it's where she needs to be. Yes, of course. When do you want me to pick you up?"

"Soon."

"I'll be there."

Abi wonders if Amanda has ever not kept to her word about something.

Jude never did call back, so there's even a chance he may still be at the hospital. Abi hopes not, but she has to take the chance. At least he didn't shout at her.

At the information desk, a nurse tells her which room Lily is in. The ward is hushed. Abi sees only one other visitor in another room, a woman who looks very directly at her, and does not smile. There's a smell here, and other smells trying to hide it.

A nurse is tending Lily when Abi comes into the room. "Are you family?" she asks.

"A friend."

"She's not doing too badly – she's not in too much pain, I mean." She's nodding, and she looks at Lily quite tenderly, Abi thinks.

"Have you been caring for her today?" asks Abi.

"Since she came in, yes, and I'm here for another six hours into the night."

"Thank you," says Abi. She does feel that she needs to thank this nurse who so obviously cares for her patient.

"Oh," says the nurse, surprised. She squeezes Abi's arm with a gentle touch. "I'll leave you with her for a bit, then. Push the buzzer if you need me. She comes to now and then."

Abi sits in the chair beside Lily's bed and looks at the older woman's hand resting on the blanket. *But she's not old. She shouldn't be dying.*

Abi knows she doesn't need to think about Amanda waiting. Amanda brought along a thick book and told Abi to take her time. So she does now, taking Lily's hand in her own.

She can't think of anything to say, even though she knows that there was a lot she wanted to before she got here. Now she just holds the pale hand. Much like two days earlier, but she knows that this time it's different.

Then Lily speaks. "It may be that you can't," she says. "I'll understand." It's just breathy words.

"Lily?" Abi speaks softly.

Lily's eyes don't open.

"Are you talking to me? Abi?"

There's only silence

The nurse is standing in the door. "Are you Abi?" she asks, and she sounds surprised.

Abi nods.

"She left me something for you. From what she said, I expected you to be older. Here," and the nurse hands Abi a piece of folded paper, then notices that her eyes are watering, and hands her a tissue. Abi puts the paper into a pocket and wipes her eyes, blows her nose. She hands Abi another and another, and goes on. "I was going to give it to the son to pass on to you, but here you are..." She looks at Lily. "I'm sure she's glad you're here."

Again Abi nods, and the nurse stops her companionable babbling and backs out of the room. Abi sees a pad of paper lying on the bedside table, and she tears off a sheet and fold by fold makes a boat. She tucks it into Lily's hand. Waits awhile before she whispers *goodbye*.

"I don't think I want to go," says Abi, back in the old Dodge van, with Amanda rattling the engine to life.

"No?" Amanda doesn't push it. "Do you want to come back to my place and hang out?"

"Not that either." She hopes that Amanda doesn't ask for an explanation. "I'd just like to go home." *Home.* The place by the river. For all her wanting to leave it, it's surprising how easily the word slips out.

"Okay." Amanda swings out onto the road, and soon they're by the river. "You'll phone me on my cell if you change your mind, right? Wherever you want to go?"

"Yeah." Abi can see that there are dirty whitecaps on the river. After a week of sultry, humid weather, a wind is rising. She opens her window right down, and the wind tears at her hair, blows it into her face.

"Did I tell you that Horace and Ernestine went downtown to the train station today? They're going through the Rockies."

"No!" The significance of this is not lost on Amanda – she's heard all about those two – and a grin comes over her face.

Abi tries to hold her hair back, and fails, lets it blow, its ends licking into her eyes, her cheeks.

"Why don't you close the window – halfway even."

"No." Abi wants to feel the wind. It gives her an excuse for the tears that are streaming out from her eyes.

All at once, there's a jag of lightning.

"Whoa...! Did you see that?" Amanda cranes her neck to look up through the windshield.

The roll of thunder answers. "Okay...not too close," she continues, but Abi notices that her hands tighten on the wheel.

Abi thinks how as a kid she'd count off "one Mississippi... two Mississippi...three Mississippi..."

"Sure you don't want to come? Somewhere with me?"

"Manda!" Abi laughs. "Are you afraid to be alone?" Before Amanda can answer, she adds, "Just teasing! And no. I feel like being at home." But inside, a feeling is growing. Nothing she can put a name to yet. The clouds are rolling as they rarely do in this part of the world, except maybe, yeah, the odd August. There's not a boat to be seen on the river. She knows what it'll sound like under the house tonight. Like they're a part of the river. There'll be creaking and moaning, and snapping sounds... Dad will turn the TV off and listen... He always listens to those sounds.

Another memory surfaces. The wind draws it up from the depths: there'd been a storm like this last August, not long before Mum left. She always hated them. Last one, she'd tried to convince Abi and Dad that they needed to sit the storm out on the front porch. "It's the only part of this damn house that'll be left after this round" – as if it was a fight – and then she'd gone out and sat there herself. Maybe that was when she'd concocted the whole idea of leaving. Her running-away plans. Abi has a new thought: what if Mum hadn't thought of it as running away? What if she thought of it as running *to*? What would she run to? *I'm going to teach you to be independent and strong*, she'd said so many times to Abi. Was that what Mum wanted? To be independent and strong? Did that mean having to be alone?

Abi hardly says goodbye to Amanda. She climbs out of the van quickly, and goes into the house with a half a wave. She's pushing at the door before she's turned the knob all the way, and for a second, just a second, the thought comes that the door's been locked. Then she turns and pushes and almost falls in.

Dad is standing near the back window, looking as if someone just kicked him in the seat of the pants. He has one hand resting on the back of a hip, and the other hand is scrabbling vaguely at his temple. "What is it?" he says. "What's all the racket about?"

"It's a storm, Dad," says Abi.

"A storm," he says. "Is it trying to tear our house apart again?"

"Something like that, yeah, Dad."

He scratches his head. "I wish it'd stop that," he says. "This is a good little place, ours." He reaches out to brush his fingers over the wall.

"Dad," Abi says – but she speaks gently – "Dad, it's a *house*."

He looks at her and there is confusion in his eyes. "I thought it could be a home for us."

Abi's not sure who exactly is "us."

The house goes dark, power out.

In the back corner of a cupboard is the emergency lantern. Abi gets it, lights it, sets it on the table. Dad standing there looking lost bothers her, and she motions to him to take a seat. He does, stares at the light for the longest moment, and then lays his head down on his arms.

"Dad," she says. No response. "DAD!" She pushes at his shoulder.

The house sways and she can feel the river suck at them, but no. It spits them back out before they're in. In the front of the cutlery drawer, there is a small flashlight. She takes that and, leaving Dad at the table, head-on-his-arms-old-man, she makes her way to the back door, struggles with the wind to open it, and steps out, follows the railings on the walkway wharf, glad for the extra nails in them now. Water sloshes over her feet, as she moves onto the hinged dock, and the whole thing sways. There it is, the greenhouse, rocking, one corner right out of the water for a moment, then the other. She holds tight and watches, a sort of prayer tumbling through her head.

She'd like to be in that greenhouse one more time, in the middle of a sunny afternoon, surrounded by tomato smell. Maybe that was all her mother wanted: that smell. Now, in the deep blue-black of the world around her, and the dark grey churn of the water, she can almost see the figure of Mum inside the frame of the thing, bending over those stupid tomatoes. *Those damned stupid tomatoes.* Abi grips the railing and moves hand over hand down to the end of the dock as the water foams and clutches at her. The greenhouse thrusts toward and away from the dock. There's a boom sound, then a wrench, then boom, a splash with every boom, then that sucking sound, liquid yawn with hidden teeth. Then a last sickening wrench, and the dock under Abi's feet moves so fast. She screams as her feet scramble, slide, and scramble back.

Just in case. Just in case. Mum had those extra chains on *just in case.* But it's gone now. The chains have broken free, a board has come loose from the dock where Abi stands, and there goes the greenhouse. Lightning makes the last bits of glass silver-white. A deadhead strikes the side, makes it bobble as it goes. Abi imagines she can hear the breaking of more glass – but she can't really have heard in all that fury. Thunder. Rain sluices over her, and she realizes that her arms are aching from hugging the railing. In the same moment she realizes the very dock she is standing on is attached to the wharf nearer the house with hinges as old as the greenhouse chains. And she should move. She arm-over-arms back up to the house, pulls the back door open, slips inside before the wind hammers it closed behind her, and she stands there, forehead against the window, breathing as if she's just been beaten. It's gone. In her there's an ache.

"Dad?"

Dad is still at the table, unmoved. Abi sits on the nearby chair. She can hear the wall clock still ticking with its battery. But the TV is silenced with the power out. The phone won't work either.

She leaves the table to search in the kitchen drawer. She'd thrown that card from Colm in it. Must still be there. There it is. She pushes it into her pocket. Colm will help Dad; she can't. There's something else she has to do. *Just in case.*

She pulls a long raincoat from the hook by the front door, over her wet clothes, and she takes up the bicycle by the front door.

There is almost no traffic on River Road, not in these conditions, with all the lights out, and the blinding rain, and she can ride the bike on the concrete. Cars are actually stopped, waiting for the worst to pass, as she makes her way along. The wind is behind her, though at times it buffets from her left, pushing her toward the water. *Just in case.* That is the rhythm she pedals to. *Just in case.* Seems like a long time before she reaches town, and she pedals on from where she'd turn off to Horace's. She pedals to the yellow and orange house. There's only one crack of light between the curtains of the front room, and there is no truck. *No – he's taken him with him. It's all okay. He won't be here.* But behind all those words that Abi tells herself, there's still the *just in case, just in case...*

She climbs off the bicycle, her knees stiff with damp, and goes to the curtain opening. *Just in case.* There on the couch is Dyl, huddled under a blanket, his knees up to his chest. He has a thick flashlight in his hands. He's been holding it long enough for the light to be waning, yellowing.

She raps gently on the window. She doesn't want to scare him. Though the sound is not loud, he hears it immediately, as if he's expecting her. He gathers up his blanket and goes to the door, where she meets him. As ever, he stands back when he first sees her, and she resists the urge to grab him and wrap her arms around his little body.

She kneels. "Where's your dad, Dyl?"

"Hopital," he says. He's frowning.

She finds a candle and matches with the light that is still in the flashlight. And she finds a cell phone left on the coffeetable and calls the hospital, asks if a Jude Arden is visiting Lily Arden.

The voice on the other end is a careful one. She won't give anything away when Abi says, no, she isn't family. But she does say that Jude left at dinnertime. So he hasn't been back to the hospital since before Abi was there. Abi doesn't ask about Lily: the woman's voice tells her, and she has to fight a sob as she hangs up.

"Did your dad make you something to eat?" she asks Dyl.

"Peanut butter," is all he says. So it could be that he's made his own food. She pours a glass of milk and finds a banana for him, and they sit at the table. Her mind shivers with questions, her body with cold. *What to do?* Dyl is shivering, too, with his blanket off.

"I have something for you," she says suddenly. *Of course.*

She goes to the bicycle just outside the door and grabs the plastic bag, brings it in and unwraps Ernestine's apron. "A sweater." She holds it up. It feels chilled, but not wet. She warms it in her hands.

Dyl stands close beside her and touches the green wool. She pulls it onto his arms, does up the buttons.

He puts his arms around her. *Bring on the Velcro,* she thinks. *Oh yeah, this is how it should be — none of this keeping to the corners. There's too much feeling scared. But now what is she going to do? Wait until Jude comes back...from wherever? Then he'll just yell at her and tell her to go away. And if she leaves...alone...she knows the answer to that...* Dyl's still holding onto her, and she to him. *Velcro-kid*. She holds him tighter, fiercely, then frees him, and sits back on her heels, wondering what to do.

She looks at the phone again. *Manda*. Abi dials her cell number.

"You'll have to speak louder!" Amanda shouts. In the background, there are party sounds. "My phone's gonna die. Are you okay?"

"I'm okay, but..."

In the background now, there is a flurry of greetings, laughter. "Oh my," Abi can hear Amanda saying, then there are snuffly sounds as if a hand is over the phone, and Amanda's voice is low and muffled. "I can't believe who just walked in – Abi, it's Jude."

Abi cuts her off. "He just got there? Is he planning on being there a while?"

"What's that? I can hardly hear...a while? Yeah, looks like. He's got a half sack he's putting in the cooler. Look, the phone is dying. Do you want me to come and pick you up?"

"No, I'll stay here for now."

"I can come and get you...anytime."

Her friend's kindness chokes Abi. "Thanks," she manages to get out, and then she hangs up.

"Dad?" Dyl is standing right behind her.

"Uh...no," says Abi, uncomfortable with even half-truths with him. "I was talking to my friend Amanda."

He nods, so solemnly, and she looks at him. She feels the greenhouse ache again, and recognizes another. The ache that she's carried for the past year, the ache that's been a part of her. The greenhouse ache is nothing more than that one coming loose – Abi looks at Dyl and it all swells inside her with the surging push of river water. *My mum isn't coming back. And your dad will – eventually – maybe too late – but then he'll go away again, won't he?*

Dyl's such a little person, he could fit scrunched in her bicycle basket, for God's sake. He's got to be missing his grandma so much. *It's just not right…it's just not right.* Abi makes her decision. She scoops him up, grabs the blanket from the couch, wraps it around him, and takes him outside. He does fit inside the basket. She puts her floppy rain hat on his head, and they go, the rusty bicycle slow at first.

Now if we could just fly up in the air and ride the face of the moon!

This night there is no moon.

The wind isn't so driving; the rain is steady, but is no longer biting into her face. But where to go. She turns to her house on the river, when she stops. *Not there.* She turns back. Amanda's is too far, though she could call. No, she can't involve them. She's crazy. *I'm crazy – what am I doing?* Running: that's the answer. She's running away. Some people run away successfully, with no one knowing where they're gone. *But they don't take a child with them, especially someone else's child.* Abi hadn't quite thought about it like that before. *Kidnapping.* Is it kidnapping when you're taking a child no one seems to want? At least, no one alive. *The ache is for Lily, too.* She doesn't want to think about Lily right now.

She's pedalling back toward town. If only Horace was around – to think that the one time he leaves town... Wait a minute. *His house is empty.* She takes a wide turn, and pedals faster, faster. It's different, pedalling with weight, and she has to hold onto the handlebars tightly because the front of the bike wants to turn.

Dyl hasn't said anything more. Maybe he doesn't ask too many questions. Maybe he's learned just to accept. Aren't two-year-olds supposed to question everything? Maybe he did the Velcro thing extra well because he didn't get to do the other.

She rides the bicycle down the driveway. Somehow – and it shouldn't be – the dark house is a shock. She hadn't realized that the warmth of Horace's home was Horace. She climbs off the bike and carefully wheels it in behind the house, glad for the tall hedges that guard the property. She wonders if he had time to tell his neighbours that he was going away. She's never done anything like this: this sneaking around, this...*scheming.* She lifts bundled Dyl out of the basket and carries him up to the back porch and settles him on the wicker loveseat there. "This is where my friend Horace lives," she tells him.

Earlier that day, she noticed Horace locking up a door in the basement. The door is set in a step, in a recess under the porch, and there are nine small panes of glass in it. It'll be easy enough to break the one closest to the door handle. Not easy, to find a rock in the dark, but she does. One edging the garden by the back wall. She wraps Ernestine's apron around it, makes it so that she can swing it and keep her hand away from the glass. She misses the first time – pulls back on it – and then the second, there's a shattering, and she can't reach right away for the inside knob because, just for a second, she sees the greenhouse. It's what she's always going to associate with breaking glass, isn't it? Then she reaches in and unlocks the door, opens it.

Now *this* is dark. She's never been in this part of the house, so she doesn't have the slightest idea where anything is. She can reach up and feel ceiling studs right over her head, so she knows it is one of those old-house basements, more like a cellar. If there are windows, they're small and they let in no light whatsoever. She feels around the doorway for a switch, but there is none. She wonders if the power is out in this part of town too. She gropes forward, her thoughts with the bundled Dyl up on the porch above her. *Please don't follow me.* She trips over something. A large brick? She moves her feet forward very slowly after that, feels ahead of her. Before she finds anything of a light, she reaches the bottom stair. *Yes.* Up, holding the narrow railing. Another doorknob, pull. It's locked! From the other side. She pulls hard. Harder, as if it's going to help. Kicks. Just on the other side of that door, inches away, is a kitchen with the most beautiful table in the world, is food, is a stove for hot chocolate. Just a few feet from all that, is a porch door, with Dyl curled up waiting for her.

She sits on the top step. *No.* She wants to cry, but she can't. *You've got to think, Abi.* How long has it been since she talked with Amanda? An hour? Jude is going to go home eventually, and he's going to find Dyl not home, and he's going to call...the police. What is she going to do? Run away forever? *What if she takes him and finds her mother?* The thought hardly crosses her mind and she's stomping on it, putting it out. *Is she crazy?* At this point, she could take him back, wait for Jude to be there for him, then just pedal home, go to bed...

"Abi?" There's a little voice from the doorway. Abi can see the lesser-black of the doorway, distinguished from the black-black of the basement. Dyl must be standing there. How'd he know where to find her?

"I'm here, Dyl. I'll be right down," she says softly. It's a bit easier, finding the doorway with his little shape in it.

"Horse gone away?" he asks.

He makes her laugh. "Yes, Dyl. Horse — Horace — has gone away. Let's go back and sit on the porch."

"Okay," he says agreeably.

Abi makes a mental note to teach him that he's supposed to say no, as well as ask a lot of questions. Then he comes to a complete stop in front of her and she almost topples over him.

"Bike?" he asks.

In her mind, the plan had been forming that they'd spend the night on the porch furniture and see how everything looked in the light of morning, but Dyl's question makes her reconsider.

"All right." And she finds herself wrapping him up again in the basket.

The rain has stopped at last, and they ride to a corner store. She is glad to see that the corner store has lights on, and farther down the block, more lights. She stops at the phone booth outside the store, leans the bike — Dyl still in the basket — against the brick wall, and digs for a quarter in her pocket. *Always keep a quarter in your pocket.* Yet another bit of wisdom in her mother's survival book. Abi phones Amanda's home, and Amanda answers.

"I've been worried. I phoned you at home, and there was no answer," she says.

"The phone was out. I'm at the corner of Trunk and Tenth."

"I'll be right there."

"I have the bike with me."

"It'll fit in the van."

Abi remembers thinking that you could – if you wanted – just drive off in that van, the house on wheels, and live forever somewhere, anywhere.

She hangs up the phone, and then adjusts Dyl's blanket. She pulls out Colm's card and reads it in the light from the store window. She dials. There's only an answering service, but she knows that as soon as he gets the message he'll take care of Dad.

She turns over the card to where he'd written *Mrs. Taylor foster-parent Wellburn Drive – house with lots of bicycles and tree house in front yard – close to corner of Birch Place.* There's a phone number too. But Abi had only the two quarters.

When Abi turns away from the phone, she finds that the store clerk is standing in the doorway, staring at her and Dyl. "Late and stormy to have a tyke up and out, no?"

Abi pushes Dyl and the bike towards the sidewalk. Horrible woman – it's none of her business. *But it would be like that, wouldn't it?* If she just ran and kept running? It would always be like that: looking over her shoulder, feeling defensive every time anyone spoke to her. And money. What would she do about that? No, you can't run away with a kid. She should phone Jude too, she's decides. But not until Dyl is safe.

It feels like an hour, but it's only about ten minutes and Amanda's van pulls up, and she jumps out to help Abi with the bike. Then she sees Dyl and stops short. "Thought that was a knapsack in your arms." She sounds breathless. "Does Jude..." she starts.

"No!" Abi says sharply. And she leaves the bike to her friend, and climbs into the front seat, with Dyl on her lap. He feels heavy. She pulls the blanket away enough to realize he's fallen asleep.

Amanda climbs into the driver's seat, but she doesn't start the van. "What do you want to do?"

"I *want* to have a little warm house where I can take care of Dyl – where he has a place in the world – a house that's not going to float away some day. And I want a big kitchen table, and on the table there's a bowl of fruit that's never empty, and I want to see kids' hands reaching into the bowl. And I want a big jug of flowers on the counter, and bright walls, and a fireplace for winter, and..." Her voice is getting all choked.

"Right now, Abi. What do you want right NOW?"

She sits and thinks.

"Do you know where Wellburn Drive is?"

Mother-Ears

Abi's starting to think that Amanda's not going to answer.

"What's on Wellburn Drive?"

"A neighbour of Colm's. A foster mother."

"You don't want to come to my house, and call the police?"

Abi shakes her head, and after another moment, Amanda starts up the engine.

"Colm must not know the exact house number. He just wrote that it's the one with a tree house in the front yard."

Amanda laughs. "Sounds like my kind of mother." They drive slowly, watching for the corner of Birch Place.

Even though the house is dark, they can still see the half-block-away streetlight on the pile of bicycles at the base of the giant elm in the front yard. The old Dodge rattle fades after Amanda pulls the key, and they sit at the curb. Abi sucks in her breath. She wonders how far away Colm lives – he'd said they were neighbours – and what are the chances of seeing Fiona tomorrow or the next day, and what might that mean.

Nothing, she decides. It's going to mean absolutely nothing. She sets her hand on the door handle of the van.

There's a basketball hoop in the driveway, and a plywood jump at the edge of the driveway.

"Someone with mother-ears heard us pull up," says Amanda, as a hall light flickers on and a shadowy figure crosses the frosted window beside the front door. The door opens and the figure comes into view. It is a woman, they can see now, heading across the yard, calling out "Who's there?" in a not-so-sure voice.

Abi pulls on the door handle and steps out with Dyl in her arms.

Amanda is already halfway across the yard with her hand out, and Abi can hear a few low words of greeting as she nears. "Colm gave me your address," she says.

The woman has a flashlight in her hand, and she doesn't point it at Abi until after she's shined it at herself. "I'm Mrs. Taylor. Please, come in." Then she shines the light somewhere near Abi's knees, so that she can see Abi and her bundle in a soft glow of light. "Come," she repeats, and with the light, leads the way to the house.

"Careful!" Amanda grabs Abi's elbow and steers her around the pile of footwear in the hall – sandals and sneaks, beach shoes and rubber garden shoes.

"This way." Mrs. Taylor leads into the kitchen.

"Mums?" There's a sleepy Stu Stevenson in the doorway.

"Hey," she says. "Put the kettle on, Stu-boy."

He does, seemingly still asleep, then he turns around, leans against the counter – the counter can't be seen for the pots and dishes on it, boxes of cereal and empty milk containers.

He looks at Abi and recognizes her. "You," is all he says, and scratches under his loose cut-off T-shirt. He has on bright plaid pajama bottoms.

"Hey," says Amanda.

He nods at her.

"I need to talk with these young women," says Mrs. Taylor. "I'll bring you down a cup of tea, though."

He nods, to say "okay" to her and "good night" to Abi and Amanda. Grabs a cookie out of a jar on the way out.

"Take two," says Mrs. Taylor. "So you don't wake up hungry again."

At the door he stops and turns back to Abi. "It's okay here, you know," he says, as if he knows her fears, knows why she's come.

"Thanks," she says, aware that these are probably the first words he's ever said to her other than that earlier "You." But she remembers the shy smiles he's always had for her in English class, and he seems like a friend. She wonders why she didn't see this before.

There's a deep window seat in the kitchen, and Mrs. Taylor motions to Abi to put Dyl there. Without him in her arms, though, Abi suddenly feels very alone. She pulls the blanket up and over Dyl, and then returns to her chair to find Mrs. Taylor's eyes on hers.

"You're in trouble," says the woman, and Amanda starts to explain, but Abi takes over. Mrs. Taylor doesn't say anything as she speaks; she only asks brief questions now and then to clarify something. At the end, she says she has to call her social worker.

"Social worker?" *Of course. I knew that. There has to be someone official.*

Amanda squeezes her hand. "It is going to be all right, Abi."

Mrs. Taylor looks hard at Abi. She says, "I don't know what you consider 'all right.' But we will do whatever needs to be done." She gets up and prepares tea, and Abi looks at her back — her robe is a deep blue — and wishes that she could give just a little more of a clue. Some motion, some word, that it *will* be all right. Even as she thinks this, she knows there is a whole lot of truth to what the woman just said, and she herself doesn't know exactly what 'all right' is.

The woman pours a big mug of tea and takes it downstairs – she's not forgotten her promise to Stu. What had she called him? Stu-boy? He'd called her "Mums." She doesn't seem a "Mums" sort. She does seem more like…well, as she'd put it herself: someone who does what needs to be done. But still – she did remember the tea.

When she comes back up the stairs, she pours three more mugs, lots of sugar and milk, and hands them around, and they sit, sipping in silence.

"I'll make up a bed, and find you a nightshirt," she says. "I'm sure Ms. Harvey will want to meet with us first thing in the morning. I'll be calling her now." Then she disappears with her mug, and Abi can hear a murmur of voices as she calls.

Amanda tries to cover a yawn.

"You go," says Abi.

"Sure?"

Not at all. But go. Abi nods.

Amanda kisses the top of her head. "Call me right away."

Abi knows she means "right after the social worker." She wonders if the police will be involved. "Can you call Jude when you get home and tell him Dyl is safe? And I'll tell him more tomorrow."

Amanda says yes, and gives her a good night hug, and then is gone.

Abi goes over to the window seat and snuggles next to Dyl, feels herself drifting off to sleep. It's raining again, a summer-night rain, raining it all out so it can be sunny again for the day. She's glad she thought to phone Colm; she can go to sleep now.

Mrs. Taylor finishes her phone call, and finds Abi and Dyl like that. She goes to get a pillow and another blanket, and tucks Abi in too.

When Abi opens her eyes in the dawn, it's the silence that awakens her. What is it?

There's no river – that's what it is.

Hadn't there been a storm?

Now there's only gentle breathing: Dyl.

Abi raises her head and looks around. They're in a kitchen. It looks different from the night before, though, Abi thinks as it comes back to her. Last night the woman – Mrs. Taylor? – had had to clear spaces on the table just for the mugs of tea. Now the counters are clear – when *did* she do that? – and the table has a pot of flowers on it.

There's a fragrance to the room: coffee. There's a coffee machine on the counter. Looks like some kind of a timer on it. It smells so good.

She is pulling herself up to a sitting position when Mrs. Taylor comes into the room, swaddled in her robe, pushing the skin of her face into place after a too-short night of restless sleep. She smiles, though, when she sees that Abi is awake, a quick smile.

"Coffee?" she asks.

"Please," says Abi in a whisper, though Dyl shows no sign of waking. Abi wonders if he usually sleeps like this.

"Does he always sleep like that?" Mrs. Taylor asks.

"I don't know. I hope so."

She looks into Mrs. Taylor's face. There are some good things there: a light warmth, a curious interest. But there's something more Abi would like to see, and she can't. Doesn't mean it's not there; maybe the woman hides it.

"Ms. Harvey will be coming in an hour. She's the social worker. I spoke with her last night."

Abi has another memory, this one of murmuring voices that went on and on as she fell asleep. Mrs. Taylor must have cleaned the kitchen after that. Which meant that she, Abi, must have been sleeping much as Dyl is now.

Mrs. Taylor points out the two piles of sweatpants and shirts and towels at the foot of the windowseat. "Clean duds for you and the little one. You can go have a shower if you like. I'll watch him."

Abi finishes her coffee and takes the "duds" with her. Mrs. Taylor seems prepared for every possible emergency. The bathroom is stocked with plain soap and three types of tooth-paste. The toothbrush holder on the wall has five brushes in it, and there are four brand new, still wrapped in crinkly cel-lophane. There's a towel holder, and each arm has a towel on it. Before Abi closes the door, she sees a schedule written out on a Wipe-it! board. The special felt pen hangs on a string beside it. She sees that she's taking Stu's shower time, but he's not complaining. Maybe he's glad to sleep in.

The shower feels good – not like sitting in the rust-tub – and she stands, head bowed, letting the hot water pour over her shoulders, loosen her muscles, until she thinks of Dyl. Then she gets out, pulls on a towel, then the sweats. On the counter there is a small dish of ponytail holders. Most of them look brand new and she wraps one around a ponytail. So that must mean there's a girl here, too. Mrs. Taylor's hair is short – "tidy" comes to mind.

She has breakfast waiting. A bagel with cream cheese, and sliced canteloupe.

"Usually everyone makes their own breakfast."

Abi nods. She's probably supposed to take note of that. Dyl wakes up then, and she's glad she cut her shower short, because he looks around with his usual anxious look and then, when he sees her, he smiles. Before breakfast, she runs a warm bath for him, and helps him with the fleecy pants and T-shirt.

They share a blueberry bagel, and Mrs. Taylor sets mugs of warm milk on the table.

Ms. Harvey wears a dark green suit. Her shoes look brand new and stiff. It is exactly nine o'clock when she arrives, and she wastes no time. She sits at the table, and looks through her papers.

Stu has taken Dyl into the backyard to play on the swings. Again Abi has the sense of being alone that she had when she laid Dyl on the window seat the night before.

Ms. Harvey has a folder and papers and pen. The room doesn't feel like the same kitchen anymore. Ms. Harvey doesn't look at Abi. Well, she does, but her eyes slide past Abi's ear, then she looks back at her papers.

"You can stay here temporarily," she says. "Until we find a placement. We've worked it out, and Rebecca and I have discussed it."

Abi assumes "Rebecca" is Mrs. Taylor, but she wonders who the "we" is.

Ms. Harvey checks her papers, flips through. Check. Flip. Check. Flip. Then she continues. "The boy will go to a home in Richmond...temporarily."

It takes Abi a moment to realize that she's talking about Dyl.

"No!" she says. "Dyl stays with me!"

Ms. Harvey finally looks at Abi, but there are no words in her eyes.

"You don't understand," Abi says. "His dad doesn't want Dyl. Not really. He left him alone in the house. All by himself. That's how I found him. And Dyl's grandmother, who's taken care of him...she died yesterday."

"Yes, his grandmother," Ms. Harvey says thoughtfully.

"His mother left him. Went away." Abi fights down her tears. She can't cry right now, she just can't.

Ms. Harvey writes on one of those pieces of paper.

"You don't understand," Abi repeats. "His dad just *left* him."

Again those wordless eyes look briefly at Abi. "Actually, his father has nothing to do with this," she says.

Abi can only stare at her.

"Lily Arden – his grandmother – was his legal guardian."

Abi is perplexed. Jude is Dyl's father.

Ms. Harvey goes on. "A little more than one year ago, Lily Arden legally adopted her grandson. Now she is deceased. That makes him a ward of the Province."

Legally. Deceased. Ward. Province. Abi takes in the words.

"But he needs me," is all she can say.

Now there are words in Ms. Harvey's eyes. The words say, "This is my JOB!"

Mrs. Taylor speaks up with a soft voice. "Why don't they both stay here for now, Sal?"

"You have three." Ms. Harvey still sounds as if she's saying *this is my job.*

"But Ron will be gone in less than a week," Mrs. Taylor points out.

More flipping and checking. Ms. Harvey likes her papers. Abi can imagine her as a little kid, sleeping with a sheaf of papers, instead of with a teddy bear like a regular kid. Abi would smile, except the twist in her insides won't let her. She finds herself grimacing, and when Ms. Harvey does look up from her papers, she's surprised. She stares at Abi.

"All right," she says. "While we work this out, then. For now."

Abi gets up from the table so quickly that her coffee spills and she has to clean up before she can go find Dyl in the yard. She's still swiping at the table when Ms. Harvey leaves.

Mrs. Taylor hands her a cloth to dry it, and then she hauls a basket of clean laundry up from where she left it on the floor, and begins to fold.

"It's not much to hold on to, is it," she says. "Those words *for now.* Still. It is something."

She joins socks, tucks in a collar.

"What does Dyl mean to you?" she asks then.

Abi is happy to hear her use Dyl's name; Ms. Harvey

hadn't once. Abi reaches into the pile to help with a T-shirt. "He needs me," she says. "He needs someone not to run away from him."

Mrs. Taylor listens. "You need him, too, I think," she says. Abi nods.

"You're quite determined? That you should stay with him? He with you?"

Another nod.

Mrs. Taylor sighs. "Taking care of a child is hard."

"Yes, I know."

"Well," Mrs. Taylor says, reminding Abi a bit of Ernestine. "We have *for now*, don't we?" She begins to fold Abi's jeans, already washed from the night before. Something is in the pocket, and she reaches for it. "Missed this," she says, and hands it to Abi. Abi has a sudden remembrance of the nurse handing this slip of paper to her.

She unfolds it. The paper is worn at the creases, and the ink has run slightly, but the message is clear.

My dearest Abi —

I'm hoping you'll consider taking care of Dyl. He loves you and I know you love him too.

She can hear Lily's voice through the words on the paper.

But you are young and this may not be the best for you, so
please know that there are other options. My lawyer has my
will and can discuss it with you. Thank you Abi, you have
brought a light to my last days here –

Lily Arden

Mrs. Taylor doesn't speak as Abi looks up and hands her the paper.

"This might change the *for now*," she says after she reads it.

"Yes, I think it might," says Abi.

The sound of Dyl laughing floats in the open doorway.

Mrs. Taylor nods toward the back door. "Go," she says.

Abi steps into the backyard. Grass that was probably brown yesterday is green today after the rainstorm. Leaves rustle in a wind overhead, and she looks up, then farther up, in time to see a short broken string of Canada geese overhead, practicing with a few young for the flight south. There's more laughter, and she sees Stu pushing Dyl on the swing. She's amazed because the rope of the swing is flat out and Dyl is flying. And he's not afraid. She stops herself from calling out to Stu to slow him down. It's beautiful, him swinging like that, and laughing.

This is my, my, my beautiful Sunday...

Acknowledgements

I'm grateful for the support of the British Columbia Arts Council.

And thanks to Gayle Friesen and Christy Dunsmore for the hours and evenings spent with each other's work – we are blessed.

All dictionary quotes are from *The New Oxford Dictionary of English,* ed. Pearsall, Judy, Clarendon Press, Oxford, 1998. (With sole exception of definition for the letter "f" and word "farce:" *The Houghton Mifflin Canadian Dictionary of the English Language,* ed. Morris, William, Houghton Mifflin Canada Limited, Markham, Ontario, 1982.)

Beautiful Sunday

Words and Music by Daniel Boone and Rod McQueen

(c) 1972 STIRLING M^CQUEEN MUSIC LTD.

About the Author

Alison Acheson has published two previous juvenile fiction novels, *The Half-Pipe Kidd* and *Thunder Ice*, which was a finalist for the Geoffrey Bilson Award, and the Manitoba and Red Cedar (BC) young readers choice awards. She has also published a collection of adult short fiction, *Learning To Live Indoors,* and has had work published in several anthologies – *Carnal Nation, Write Turns* and *When I Was a Child.* Work for children has appeared in "Ladybug" magazine and the Scholastic Early Literacy program.

Alison Acheson is an instructor in the Creative Writing program at the University of British Columbia, having obtained MFA (Creative Writing) and BA (History) degrees from that University. Born in Tsawwassen, British Columbia, she continues to live in the lower mainland. To find out more about Alison Acheson visit her web site at: *www.alisonacheson.com.*

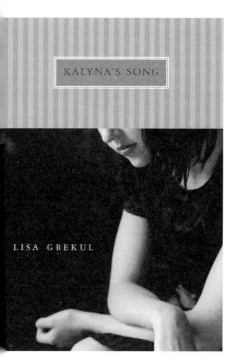